Story Summary

In 1866 on the empty Kansas prairie, two children shared a few desperate moments that changed their lives. For years afterward, each nursed a secret dream—that the other had grown into a special person—brave, good, kind.

When Norah Hawkins and Caleb Sutton cross paths again, dreams die. She is a bitter, suicidal widow. He is a gunman with little conscience and few scruples. Alternately angry, repelled, and attracted, the two form an uneasy partnership to hold land she owns and he covets against a marauding neighbor. Their bargain never included love, or did it?

Beautiful

B98

09/21

n

14/4/2023

Tynnwyd o'r stoc
Withdrawn

nell

This book is a work of fiction. Names, characters, and incidents are the product of the author's imagination. Any resemblance to actual events or persons is strictly coincidental. Some of the places mentioned do exist; however, descriptions may have been altered to better suit the story.

Copyright © 2012 by Ellen O'Connell
www.oconnellauthor.com

ISBN-13: 978-1480134331
ISBN-10: 1480134333

Beautiful
Bad Man

Prologue

Spring 1866
Hubbell, Kansas

Norah stopped stirring and dropped the spoon in the beans, watching open-mouthed as Jim Shanks and Isaiah Flood dragged a boy to the center of the wagon circle. No one that small and scrawny ought to be able to put up such a fight or provoke that kind of cursing and shouting from grown men.

"Ow, the little devil bit me."

"Watch your language around the women, damn it."

"You watch your language. He's probably got hydrophoby and killed me."

Norah glanced across the fire at her mother, who continued to tend to supper as if such an extraordinary thing happened every evening.

"What do you think is happening? Where could that boy come from?"

"He'll be from the town we passed by, and from the look of him, he came to steal. Your father and the other men will take care of him."

The population of the miserable collection of shacks and tents called Hubbell, Kansas, resembled nothing so much as a den of thieves and worse, all right. Norah couldn't imagine families there, or children.

She squinted through the gathering dusk. The men had subdued the boy at last by trussing him up like a Christmas goose. Mr. Flood had a sleeve rolled up, examining his bite wound, but Mr. Shanks still held the boy. As Norah watched, Mr. Shanks shook the small form like a rag for no reason she could see.

"I'm going to talk to Papa."

"Norah." Her mother lifted her gaze from the food, her face serious. "Don't embarrass your father with forward behavior. Tell him supper's ready so he has a reason to leave the other men if that's what he wants. He'll at least send the boys here, and I'll find the girls."

Her sisters were hiding on the far side of the wagon, determined to keep their distance from the stink of a fire fueled by dried buffalo dung, but Norah didn't tattle on them. She joined her father and brothers on the outskirts of the cluster of men surrounding Mr. Shanks and the boy.

"I'm telling you we caught him sneaking around the wagons. No reason to sneak except thieving," Shanks said.

"Yeah, and how many of us could afford another horse right now?" Flood asked. "You think he was after a hundredweight of flour? He was after any cash he could find and then the horses."

"If we're settling in this part of the country, we need to make sure the people around here know we won't put up with thieves," said another voice.

"I say we hang him." As he spoke, Flood accepted a bottle of whiskey from one of the other men and poured it across the wound on his arm. Then he took several swallows. "For the pain," he said, laughing and passing the bottle to the man on his right.

"For the pain," said one man after another before taking a swallow or two and passing the whiskey.

Norah didn't know most of these people well. They had only grouped together after leaving the train at Wamego and purchasing wagons and supplies for the journey to their new land. The sales agents described the soil here as so fertile even clerks like Papa could make a living farming it. Of course those same agents described the town of Hubbell as a growing center of commerce where settlers could buy anything they needed and sell anything they produced.

Shanks shook the boy again. "You got anything to say for yourself, horse thief?"

The boy spit and kicked, catching Shanks on the knee, and the man yanked the boy around and tripped him. With his arms tied behind his back, the boy fell hard. Norah saw something fall out of one of the many rips in his ragged shirt.

Ignoring her mother's instructions, Norah darted forward, grabbed the biscuit and held it up. "He wasn't trying to steal a horse. See, Mr. Shanks? See, Mr. Flood? He was after food. Look how skinny he is."

"Norah." Papa pulled her back to his side. He smelled strongly of whiskey, but she knew he hadn't had more than a swallow or two to show the other men he was one of them. That's all Papa ever drank.

"Hang him. I say we hang the little thief. Soon as we find a tree that is." Flood spoke slowly, but not slowly enough to disguise the slur in his words.

Was he mad? The Flood boys were constant troublemakers. Their father ought to be willing to turn a blind eye to anything any boy got up to short of murder. Sounds of agreement rippled through the crowd, but Papa always did the right thing.

"Talk some sense into them, Papa," Norah whispered. "He's just a skinny, hungry little boy looking for food, and hurting him isn't right. Tell them we'll give him some of our food. Tell them to let him go."

"You go to your mother and stay out of this. He's older than he looks, and the devil's in his eyes. Go on. Get now."

Unable to believe his words, Norah tried again. "Please, Papa. They'll listen to you. I know they will. It's in the Bible to be merciful and not to cast the first stone. Don't let them hurt him because they've been drinking."

"Don't argue with me, girl. Get back to the wagon and stay there."

The other men watched Norah's pleas with varying expressions. Her own brothers sniggered and elbowed each other. Flood's bleary-eyed stare made Norah's stomach clench even with Papa standing right there.

Shanks said, "That girl should be a boy. Make you proud he would."

Shanks' words all but guaranteed Papa would never listen, but Norah couldn't make herself stop. "Please...."

Papa left disciplining girls to Mama and saved his belt for the boys, but now he shook Norah as hard as Shanks had shaken the boy.

"No more," he snapped and shoved her toward the wagon.

As she walked by the fire with her head bowed, Norah didn't even look at her mother. Mama never argued with Papa in any way, and she wasn't going to become a different person tonight.

Norah hurried to the far side of the wagon and leaned against the rough wood, unwilling to climb inside and try to find a place to sit amid the piles of supplies and the few possessions they had been able to bring from home.

Home. A lump rose in her throat at the thought of that orderly, safe place where Papa never smelled like whiskey, never went along with something he knew was wrong, and never shook her like dogs did rats.

The lump turned into a knot of anger. She didn't want to cry. She wanted to stop whatever those stupid, drunk men were going to do, even if in the end they only dragged that pitiful boy back to Hubbell. That excuse for a town probably didn't have any kind of law officer anyway.

Cook fires burning near each wagon and the thin light of the new moon showed the shadows of Shanks and the other men as they dragged their prisoner to one of the wagons across the way and threw him inside.

Whatever the men did to keep the boy there caused another flurry of cursing and shouting. She hoped the boy bit every one of the men, including Papa and both her brothers.

Things quieted after that. Most of the men returned to their own supper fires, but a few still stood together talking. One of them tipped his head back in a distinctive way. *Still drinking too.*

Norah turned her head and closed her eyes, unwilling to identify her father or brothers among the shadowy figures. Those men would have to live with whatever they did tonight for the rest of their lives. *And she'd have to live with whatever she didn't do.*

Before she had time to reconsider, Norah climbed into the wagon, rummaged in boxes and sacks, and threw food in her apron as it came to hand—hard biscuits, dried fruit, jerked meat.

When she had as much as the apron would hold, she tied it into a bundle and fumbled around in the toolbox for the knife kept there. It wasn't as sharp as what Mama had by the fire, but it would have to do.

Sliding back to the ground by inches like the thief she'd just become, she took off around the outside of the wagons at a run. She slowed beside what she thought was the right wagon, but how could she be sure? If she chose wrong and someone was inside or heard, he might raise an alarm.

Nearby, men argued about how to hang someone without a tree. When one voice spoke out, wanting to take the boy back to Hubbell and hand him over to whatever law was there, hisses of disapproval drowned him out.

Norah ran her hand over the canvas wagon cover, scratching lightly. Nothing. At the next wagon, her touch provoked a frantic scramble inside. Staying as close to the wagon as possible, trying to blend her form with the bulk of it, she slid slowly to the back gate.

The argument continued, even Flood's slurred words carrying clearly, but the men were invisible in the night. She had to trust if she couldn't see them, they couldn't see her.

Afraid to climb inside with the wild boy unless she could calm him, she whispered, "Can you hear me? I'm the girl who argued about you before. I have a knife and some food, and I'll cut you free if you'll let me."

"Yesss."

Barely audible, that single word resonated with fear; the interior of the wagon reeked of dirty boy and desperation. Norah almost fell over him as she stepped inside. He had worked himself to a sitting position against a stack of crates, and her reaching hand hit his shoulder. When he stiffened, she almost jerked away, knowing he could reach her hand to bite.

Trying to quell her own fear, Norah kept her hand on him.

"They aren't evil men, but they are drunk, and I'm afraid for you."

His bones felt as light as a bird's. Skin over bones, that's all there was to him, yet warmth radiated from his shoulder to her palm. His small size gave testament to how wrong Papa and the others were. Whatever they thought they saw in his eyes couldn't make him older than eleven, maybe twelve.

Even in the dark of the wagon interior, she could still see pale blond hair falling into dark eyes gleaming with a feral light. She let go of his shoulder and brushed his hair back across his forehead before squirming to where she could reach his wrists and saw at the rope.

"As soon as I get you loose, run. There's food in that bundle. Take it and run and keep running."

Blood, slick on the knife handle, told her she'd cut him. He made no sound.

"I'm sorry." Afraid time would run out, Norah didn't slow down but kept sawing with all her strength.

At last. The rope parted. He didn't leap and run but closed one bony hand over her wrist with surprising strength and pulled the knife away with the other. Before she could react, he was gone. So was the food.

After a moment, Norah climbed down and sat against one of the wagon wheels, waiting. Pretending she hadn't been the one to free him would be the same as a lie. Now that it was done, the unknown consequences of what she'd done loomed large in her mind. What would drunk men who wanted to hang a boy of eleven or twelve do to a girl a few years older who thwarted them? What would Papa do?

No matter. Whatever happened next, she wasn't sorry. Remembering the sound of that one word, the unnatural, fragile bones, and the scent of desperation, she shivered in the warm night. She hoped that boy used the chance she'd given him wisely and lived to be a man. A good man.

Summer 1871
Fort Worth, Texas

CAL SLUMPED ON the wagon seat, using the lazy posture to hide the stew of resentment boiling in his guts.

Jake Kepler, self-described champion buffalo hunter, had tied his saddle horse in front of the hide yard and disappeared into the shack of an office sometime ago. His skinners, the ones who counted, had left their wagons and followed him.

Glancing at the wagon shadow, now shrinking as noon approached, Cal tried to estimate how long the others had been gone. They'd be back after a couple of drinks with the hide man—and way too much jawing.

Tying the horses of the other two wagons to hitch racks had been good enough, but Kepler had ordered Cal to stay put and hold his restless team while hordes of flies buzzed and bit. High on the wagon seat, close to the load of stinking buffalo hides, Cal knew exactly how the horses felt.

After five years, he also knew how the rest of the day would go and the next weeks and months. Last year he'd made the mistake of trying to quit Kepler as if this was a job, and the hunter had stomped him good. Remembering, Cal rubbed the knot where one of his broken ribs had healed imperfectly. Lesson learned.

Kepler, Billy, and Hank finally emerged from the shack, all but on fire from the whiskey and the knowledge of how much the thousands of hides in the wagons would bring. Rumor had it hides were bringing three dollars each this year, fortunes for Kepler and the skinners, even if the hunter would take the lion's share.

Kepler pointed at Cal the way he always did, with the same Sharps .50-90 rifle he used on buffalo.

"You take the wagon into the yard and help unload, then do the other two. By the time you're done, I'll be back."

Cal nodded and let his tortured team move through the gates.

Kepler and the skinners returned, all cleaned up and bar-bered, before Cal and the yard men finished unloading the last wagon. Billy and Hank sat in the shade and waited for the final count. Kepler paced, complaining about the wait.

The skinners disappeared as soon as they had their money, but Kepler stopped Cal as he drove the last wagon out of the yard.

"Here you go, boy. Take care of the horses and then get cleaned up and get drunk. Have a woman."

He handed over a small sheaf of bills Cal didn't bother counting. He knew what was there—a hundred dollars.

In spite of his determination not to say anything this time, bitter words spilled out. "Tell me honest for once, Jake, how long do I have to work for free before we're even?"

The big man threw an arm around Cal's shoulders, and Cal stiffened, hating the touch. Except for the Girl a long time ago, no one who touched him ever meant well, and Kepler's painful grip made sure Cal recognized a threat.

"There's men work for a whole year for a hundred dollars, you ungrateful pup, and that first year you hardly worked. A little cooking and carrying ain't work. The year after that all you did was eat and grow. You only been skinning worth a damn lately. Next year. Next year you get a share."

The story had been the same, or some version of the same, for three years. Which was about how long it had been since Cal had ruined a hide with a rip or hole. One way or another, there wasn't going to be a next year.

His time with Kepler had taught Cal what he should have learned long before. Every living thing was either predator or prey, and even when prey managed to survive, it lived a miserable life, starving and freezing, running and hiding. A predator would be long gone before Kepler finished gambling, drinking, and whoring.

The buffalo hunter had beaten through any gratitude Cal felt early on, and twenty was long past the age of a pup. Not only was he leaving this town as a wolf, he was going to have his fair share of hide money with him when he went.

CAL TRIED THE door to a room in the best hotel in Fort Worth an hour before dawn. The doorknob turned. Nervous anticipation quickened his heart rate. He'd been right to stay patient and keep checking night after night, waiting for Kepler to stagger to his room too drunk to lock the door.

Cal stepped into the room and shut the door as quietly as he'd opened it, then waited for his eyes to adjust to the trace of moonlight filtering through the windows. Kepler's snores resonated so loudly, stealth hardly seemed necessary, but Cal slid to the side of the bed like a shadow. He eased the blanket back just far enough to see part of the money belt Kepler never took off unless it was empty.

Cal had just slid the blade of his knife under the belt when Kepler jerked awake with a snort and yanked a pistol from under the pillow.

"Why you little...."

Cal shoved the knife down and in, twisting and tearing. The pistol fell from a flailing hand, and Kepler clawed at the knife before falling back lifeless.

Pulling the blade out, Cal wiped the blood off on the bed clothes then finished cutting the belt free. On his way out of the room he saw the long shadow of the buffalo gun leaning in the corner behind the door.

The thought of learning to shoot a gun he'd been forbidden to touch held a certain attraction. He took the Sharps too. After all, maybe he'd be good with it.

1

November 1880
Hubbell, Kansas

As THE NEWEST hire, Cal rode a short distance behind the other men Webster Van Cleve claimed he needed to protect his ranch. What Van Cleve actually wanted was different of course, and running settlers off their land wasn't Cal's usual line of work. He figured to watch and learn.

Strange to have spent years in this area and recognize so little. When it came to the land, he'd never seen much except his uncle's place, but he'd been to town a few times, and Hubbell no longer bore any resemblance to the excuse for a town he remembered.

The old town probably disappeared within a year of the coming of the railroad. He'd seen it in other towns. The new buildings were twice the size and ten times more numerous than what they replaced. Two saloons had whores working upstairs.

His horse followed the others through a swift-running creek. Water splashed on his wool trousers and soaked through. The icy burn was one more reminder of the early onset of what old timers predicted would be a long, hard winter.

Another sod house appeared in the distance. From the day Cal hired on, Asa Preston had led the way to one homestead after another where they all sat on their horses and stared at hard-faced farmers and their sons, who stared back over the sights of their rifles. Preston made threats, the rest of them did a little damage, and they rode away, a half-dozen gunmen frustrated by a handful of sodbusters.

At first Cal thought this would be more of the same tedious routine, but no farmer stood ready to defend this house. The overcast sky and lifeless brown fields all around added to the deserted, hopeless air of the place. Preston reined in close to the front door, and Cal maneuvered next to Ike Kerr. The little bald man was the only halfway friendly one among the gunmen. He was also a talker.

"We're too late to drive anyone out of here," Cal said. "They're gone."

"All that's here is a widow woman. Her husband had a bad accident a while back." Ike's grin made Cal wonder how the husband died but not enough to ask.

Preston jumped down from his horse, yanked the door of the soddy open, and disappeared inside.

"Looks like she's gone," Cal said.

Ike shook his head. "We been out here and warned her twice, but she's not the kind who listens. She had her chance, and this time's lucky. For us, not her. She ain't even got a gun, and she won't put up much fight."

Cal swore under his breath. If some stupid, pigheaded woman hadn't hightailed it to safety before it came to this, he'd have to watch and hear what they did to her. If he rode off, he'd never be able to trust any of these men at his back. He weighed his options, not liking any of them.

Preston strode out of the house, anger and frustration on his face. He remounted and started barking orders.

"She's somewhere around. You, look in that shed." He pointed at the only other structure in sight, another soddy with only three and a half walls. "The rest of us will cover the whole damn place."

Before Preston stopped speaking, a woman walked around the corner of the house, dragging a burlap sack.

She didn't look stupid or stubborn but worn out, as if the life had already been squeezed out of her. The heavy brown coat hanging to her knees must have belonged to the dead husband. The scarf on her head and the part of her dress visible were the kind of gray that had started out some different color long ago.

From where he sat, Cal couldn't see her clearly. Her face was only a pale oval marked by large shadows like bruises where eyes should be. He suspected getting closer would only show eyes as washed out as her dress.

Keeping a tight hold on his horse, Preston spurred until the animal danced then forced it to skitter around the woman, bumping her one way and the other. She stayed on her feet but didn't try to get inside the house or run.

Preston backed the horse off only to leer down at her. "I figure you haven't gone to town yet because you need a ride, and since we're such nice fellows, we're going to give you a ride. We're going to give you lots of rides."

The woman's tired expression didn't change, and she didn't raise her voice. It floated to Cal on the cold air, slid over him, wrapped around him, and quickened his heart and breath.

"You are an evil man, Mr. Preston. You are all evil men. I know you murdered my husband, but I'm not afraid. I don't care any more, and I'm not going to run and scream and make it more fun for you. I'm not running."

"Evil men." "I'm afraid." "Run, running." After all these years Cal still sometimes dreamed of the night he'd escaped from hell, and this used up, worn out woman's voice was an echo of the Girl in the wagon.

Nothing he'd seen or heard that night hinted those settlers were going to take land near Hubbell. Odds were they'd kept going west for days, even weeks.

Interfering with Preston's plans could get a man killed. Cal had no intention of doing anything that risky. She couldn't be the Girl. This nothing of a woman could not be the Girl.

Preston gigged his horse again until it spun and knocked her down. She sat against the wall of the house where she'd fallen. Except for drawing in her legs, she made no effort to protect herself from the hooves.

"No-rah Haw-kins." Preston chanted the name over and over in a singsong falsetto.

Cal never thought of the Girl by name because he'd never been sure what he'd heard her father say that night—Laura, Dora, half a dozen names had that sound. Like Norah.

She couldn't be the Girl, but what if she was? Damn it, damn it all to hell.

Shifting reins to his left hand, Cal urged his horse forward, pulled his Colt, and thumbed back the hammer. "Leave her be."

Preston had started to get off his horse. When he heard the words and saw the gun, he settled back down in the saddle. "I heard Cal Sutton was a man to ride the river with. I guess I heard wrong."

At times like this the world changed for Cal. Time slowed. The landscape and everything in it became brighter, edges more distinct. The smallest sound reverberated like thunder in his head, yet he could hear the blood flowing in his veins.

Without taking his eyes off Preston, Cal saw the woman climb to her feet. He knew each time a man shifted in his saddle or a horse twitched an ear. Even so, a gunfight could only end one way, and bucking the ramrod too hard in front of his men would end in shooting.

"You heard right, but this woman's a friend of mine. I didn't recognize her until you said her name because it's been a while."

Preston's pale eyes glittered with malice even as he bared tobacco-stained teeth in a poor imitation of a smile. "So the rest of us should ride off and leave you to get reacquainted with your *friend*, is that what you're saying?"

"I'm asking you for a favor, Asa. Leave this woman be. I'll explain to Van Cleve, and I'll buy you all a drink next time we're in town."

Two men were sure to die if shooting started, Cal—and Asa Preston. Cal watched Preston make the calculation and decide to fight another day.

"You'll never make this right with Van Cleve. But you're still going to buy me several drinks. And a woman."

Cal lowered the gun to acknowledge the deal but didn't change where the barrel pointed.

Preston shouted face-saving orders, wheeled his horse, and started back the way they'd come at a gallop. One by one the rest of the men turned their mounts and followed.

Without taking his eyes off the retreating gunmen or holstering his gun, Cal dismounted. His horse, unhappy at being left behind, tried to pull away, then settled at the sound of a few soothing words and the feel of Cal's unyielding hold.

The last of the gunmen to turn, the one who had shown the most sneering reluctance, was Yost, a young man with more swagger than sense. If he lived long enough for the spots on his face to clear up and his beard to come in as more than fuzz, he might learn better. Cal watched Yost haul back on his horse and yank it around and knew fuzz was all there'd ever be.

Yost jerked his pistol out and rode back shrieking like an Indian, his legs drumming against his horse with every stride. Some men might gamble that wild shots from the back of a galloping horse would never find a target. Cal wasn't one of them.

His bullet hit Yost in the center of the chest. The body slumped and slid. Blood blossomed against the light gray wool coat. A boot caught in one stirrup for a few strides as the body fell, sending the panicked horse racing back toward its companions.

Cal yielded to the pull of his own horse a little and spoke softly again to quiet it, never taking his eyes off the men in the distance. They had all pulled up and turned now. Preston's voice sounded, words indistinct, but tone unmistakably furious.

One of the men caught Yost's horse and led it back. He heaved the body across the saddle without ceremony, tied it in place, and rode away without a word or a glance.

As Preston and his men disappeared in the distance, Cal's world returned to normal. Muscles clenched too hard too long ached. His belly went hollow as tension ran out. Cold air crawled under his coat and bit through his sweat-soaked shirt.

He turned to take a better look at the woman, ready to ask the questions that would tell him if she was the Girl.

"You killed that man with no more feeling than stomping a bug," she said. "What's wrong with you? What's wrong with all of you?"

This close Cal could see he'd been right. Her eyes were washed-out gray. So was her skin. The dark hair hanging around her face was as dull as the rest of her.

"Whatever you want from me, you're not getting it," she said.

He couldn't imagine this woman ever having anything anyone would want. He'd made a mistake and risked his neck for nothing. His silent regard finally provoked an expression—hostility.

"If you expect thanks, you're not getting any," she said bitterly.

Cal swung back on his horse and looked down at her. "The only thing I ever expect is trouble."

Touching spurs to his horse, he started after Preston and the others.

2

CAL RODE BACK to the V Bar C deep in a brown study. Preston's men were unlikely to avenge Yost with a bullet. The other gunmen were as much lone wolves as Cal himself; none called any other friend.

One or two of them might use today's difficulty to try to put a new man in his place, though. Preston would take pleasure in waiting to hand Cal his walking papers until after a bloody, even crippling, brawl.

No matter. Cal rode with a Winchester repeating rifle in the scabbard on his saddle these days, but the Sharps in its custom-made elkskin case lay under his bunk at the ranch. Even if the job with Van Cleve was over, no one was going to stop Cal from retrieving his favorite gun.

The bitter winter night closed in by the time he unsaddled and turned his horse into a corral near the barn. He'd traveled back from the Hawkins farm at an easy pace that hadn't raised a sweat on his horse and knew it put him far behind Preston. Reaching over the corral rails, Cal touched the neck of the closest animal. Sure enough, ice crystals had formed on a sweat-soaked shaggy coat.

Shaking his head, he approached the bunkhouse from the side and let himself into the attached cook shed.

"You're too late," Cookie groused. "I fed everybody else, and I ain't serving special for you."

Cal grabbed a chunk of bread from one of the plates still on the table and smeared a thick layer of butter over it. The old man muttered and cursed but in the end found a leathery piece of beef and enough beans to fill a plate. Cal washed the meal down with coffee that could pass for tar except for the grease floating on the surface. He refilled the tin cup and carried it through to the bunkhouse proper.

Conversation died around the crowded room as he walked in. Preston, his men, and the regular cowhands all gave Cal the same knowing look.

"You've been a while," Preston said, blowing more cigar smoke into the cloud that hung over the room. "You must have had a lot to talk about with that old friend."

Cal ignored the insinuation along with the grins and sly laughter spreading through the gunmen and cowhands alike. "Thanks for cutting me some slack there, Asa. I meant what I said about explaining to the boss."

"I already *explained.* He wants to see you. Now."

Nodding, Cal moved across the room, dropped his hat and coat on his bed, and took another sip of coffee. "I'll go as soon as I finish this."

Beason, a hulk of a man more impressed with his own size than he should be, crowded into the small space between Cal's bunk and the next. "You killed Yost over the sodbuster's whore, and now you think you're going to make the boss wait?"

Cal already had the bottom of the metal coffee cup cradled in his palm. He drove the cup straight into Beason's face, the rim breaking nose and teeth. Blood spurted, and Beason collapsed, making sounds no grown man ever wanted to make.

Pivoting so his back was to the wall, Cal asked no one in particular, "Anyone else have anything to say about my friend

Mrs. Hawkins?" No one did. "Then someone needs to clean up this mess by my bed before I get back."

ACCORDING TO THE hands who had been with Van Cleve since he'd first appeared in Hubbell and started buying up everything for sale and a lot that wasn't, the lumber for the house and barns had come from Van Cleve's mill up north. He had anything else he needed or wanted shipped by rail from the East.

Cal had seen houses as large as Van Cleve's before but never been inside one. The big white house gleamed in the night. A wide veranda extended across the entire front. Balconies jutted from second-story rooms.

Lanterns burning on either side of the tall double doors of the entrance illuminated a heavy brass knocker sculpted into a bull's head. Ignoring the knocker, Cal gave the door a couple of whacks with his fist and waited.

The woman who answered the door looked the way a rich man's wife should, as different from the Hawkins woman as humanly possible. Blonde hair piled high gleamed in the light of the hall. Assessing cool green eyes made him aware of worn clothes permeated with the smell of horse, two-day beard stubble, and the fact he couldn't remember his last bath.

"Cal Sutton, ma'am. Mr. Preston says your husband wants to see me."

"He's in his study. This way please."

She turned away without offering to take his hat or coat or indicating a place for them, so he carried one, unbuttoned the other, and followed. The skirts of her deep green dress rustled and swayed more than they needed to as she walked.

Cal watched for a few steps then ignored her in favor of taking in the details of the house—the polished wood floor underfoot, the patterned paper and framed paintings on the walls, and the furniture he could see in rooms they passed. Houses fascinated him, probably because he had been in so few.

A study turned out to be a room stinking of cigar smoke just like the bunkhouse, but all similarity ended there. Heavy drapes covered the windows, shelves of books filled one wall, and a big map of the ranch and surrounding properties hung on another.

Van Cleve sat behind a desk as shiny as the floor, except the desk was bare and the floor had a thick carpet over it. Everything was of the first water, but disappointing in some elusive way. A fire burned under a marble mantel. The room was too warm yet not warm at all.

"Have a seat."

Tossing his hat on the indicated leather-covered chair, Cal pushed back his open coat and propped a hip on a nearby table.

Van Cleve shook his head. "No need for that." As if to emphasize his words, he turned his back and poured generous measures of amber liquid from a cut-glass decanter into matching glasses.

Cal took the offered glass in his left hand, and Van Cleve laughed out loud. "Careful, are you? I like a careful man."

An experimental sip of the whiskey went down like smooth fire. Not many places stocked whiskey like this, and those that did hid it under the bar.

Instead of returning behind his desk, Van Cleve propped his own hip on a corner, grinning as if that made them two of a kind.

Cal studied the dandified little man. Van Cleve shone from the oiled dark hair on his head to the spit-polished boots on small feet that barely touched the floor. Good thing he could afford everything made custom because he'd have to take boys' clothing off shelves in a store.

Imagining Van Cleve on a buffalo hunt or chasing settlers off their land in person was impossible. Shooting a man between the eyes or in the heart? No. A bullet in the back? Sure.

"I guess you know Preston wants to run you off the ranch and not wait till morning. Can you give me any reason I shouldn't let him do just that?"

"You lost one man today, and you've got another in the bunkhouse that won't be much good for a while. You probably don't want to lose anyone else tonight."

Van Cleve lost his smile but didn't ask about the second man. "You're right," he said. "I don't want to lose you."

Cal had been referring to losing Preston, which was what would happen if the ramrod tried to run Cal anywhere, but he let Van Cleve keep his illusions.

The rancher made a show of offering Cal a cigar out of a fancy box, choosing one for himself after Cal declined. "The problem is if you only hired on to protect kin, I'm better off without you, aren't I? And if you know the Hawkins woman, you must be from around here, which tells me you're related to the Suttons up north. Was old Henry Sutton your father?"

"Uncle."

"So I'm right. You came here to protect the Suttons and today you decided to throw the Hawkins woman in with the family."

If Van Cleve believed that, he'd have given Preston leave to do what he wanted. The rancher was probing, not accusing.

"I came here because parting Uncle Henry from that land would be such a pleasure I'd pay you for the privilege. Finding out he died before I hired on almost put me off my feed."

After one startled look, Van Cleve's grin returned. "What are your feelings for the rest of them?"

"I don't have any." That was a lie, but Cal didn't want to examine his feelings about Jason Sutton or any other kin. He wasn't admitting his mistake about the Hawkins woman either. A predator who admitted mistakes became prey.

"How long ago did you leave?"

"Fifteen years come spring."

Van Cleve whistled. "Never been back?"

"No."

The rancher squirmed off the desk corner, which had to have been biting into his small but well padded behind, went back to the decanter, and refilled his glass. When he looked up again, he changed the subject.

"Preston sang a different tune when you first showed up here, you know. Said he was pleased as punch to have a man of your caliber in his crew. He told me what you did in Colorado."

"I got lucky."

"Three men coming at you from three directions, and you were the only one who walked away. You call that luck?"

"I do." Bad luck was what Cal called it. One of many men hired in a fight over a town not worth fighting over, he'd been the first targeted for killing by the other side. Surviving had only brought a lot of unwanted attention.

If men like Preston knew the story, so did hotheads like Yost and Beason, which explained a lot and gave Cal a strong urge to leave here, head for Montana, and change his name.

"It didn't sound like luck to me." The rancher leaned forward, black eyes bright. "Preston's too stupid to realize he shouldn't have told me what happened today. Admitting he backed down when he had half a dozen men behind him says he's got a yellow streak, and you don't."

"I asked him for a favor, and he gave it. It wasn't worth dying over. Yost was stupid. Asa's not."

Van Cleve snorted disbelief and drained his glass.

"You want his job?"

"No. I'm not sure I want the job I've got. When I hired on, I told you I wouldn't do anything that could get me thrown in prison or hung."

"Nobody would end up in prison over having a little fun with a woman like that." Van Cleve held up one pink, manicured hand. "Don't take it wrong. Since she's a friend of yours, we'll go around her for a while, but you know as well as I do after Preston dumped her in town she'd never admit what happened."

"She wouldn't have to. Men get drunk and boast, or they get religion and repent."

Van Cleve waved off any such concern. "The county sheriff works for me. He's not arresting any of my men over a drunken boast—or anything some sodbuster's woman says either. But we need to be clear—I never told Preston to hurt a woman. He's supposed to convince those people to sell me their land. If he gets carried away and does something criminal, it's on him, not me. You've heard straight from me how it is, and you can tell anyone who asks."

Van Cleve filled his glass a third time, took a swallow, and lifted his brows, questioning. He wasn't asking if Cal wanted more whiskey.

Cal met the rancher's eyes, considering. So Preston would take the fall if things got bloody enough to attract attention from outside law. And staying on the payroll meant agreeing to be a witness to Van Cleve's righteous intentions. After enough time to indicate he had thought it over, Cal lifted his glass in acknowledgment, nodded, and tossed down the last of his drink.

Making a devil's bargain didn't bother him particularly. Neither would breaking it. He put his glass down and eased to his feet.

"Thanks for the drink, Mr. Van Cleve, and I appreciate the—understanding."

"I'll show you out." But Van Cleve drifted to the map on the wall, not the door, running his hand over it the way some men would a woman.

"It's hard to think of you as a boy, sweet on Gifford's daughter. At least your uncle knew how to farm, but those clerks and shopkeepers should have stayed back East."

Cal moved closer and looked at the map over the shorter man's shoulder. He saw the parcel with Gifford crossed out and Hawkins written underneath. The parcels Van Cleve already had acquired sported large x's through them.

"These aren't homesteads, you know," Van Cleve said, almost dreamily. "Gifford and his friends bought that land along the creek from a land company. No measly hundred and sixty acres for them, and they still went deeper in debt every year. The ones with half a brain knew I was doing them a favor buying them out."

Van Cleve's voice droned on, but Cal had stopped listening. Two of the parcels near the Hawkins land bore names he remembered with icy clarity. Flood. Shanks. The big x's over the names made no difference. A roaring started inside his head. His mouth went dry.

"So Mrs. Hawkins and her husband inherited her father's land," he said.

The interruption not only stopped Van Cleve's fantasies of empire, but put a suspicious frown on his face. A friend of the woman should know things like that.

Cursing his own mistake, Cal covered as best he could. "I knew her before her father took land. They were living out of wagons near town."

"Oh." Van Cleve's expression smoothed out. "No, as far as I know the father's still alive. Slippery devil, Gifford. When he realized I wanted the place, he sold it to Hawkins, picked up the rest of the family, and headed west."

Van Cleve left his map and headed for the front door at last. "Sounds to me like you don't know her that well, but if you want to do her a favor, talk to her. If she doesn't sell, Preston is going to do something you and I wouldn't approve of. You can't protect her forever."

The door barely had shut behind him when Cal heard a half-expected voice from the lee of the porch.

"He didn't sack you, did he?" said Asa Preston.

"No. He offered me your job."

"I don't believe you."

"Your choice."

"I've seen a man killed with that cup trick, you know."

Not unless whoever did it used a broken bottle instead of a tin cup. "Is he dying?"

"Maybe not, but he needs more doctoring than Cookie can do, and you're the one who almost pushed his nose into his brain, so you can haul him to Hubbell tomorrow after you bury Yost."

Preston was pushing to reestablish his authority. Cal suppressed the urge to push back harder. Giving the rest of the men a couple of days to cool off wouldn't be a bad idea.

"Let me use a team and wagon, and I'll haul them both to Hubbell. The undertaker there can do Yost proper."

"You do that, and you pay."

"Sure, that's fair." Cal knew his easy agreement would aggravate Preston, but he was unprepared for how much.

"I killed Henry Sutton," Preston said in the tone a man used to insult and provoke. "I grabbed him one night on his way to the privy and threw him down his own well."

"Was it cold?"

"What?"

"Was it cold the night you did it?"

Preston seemed flummoxed by Cal's unexpected reaction and the question. "Not like tonight," he said finally. "It was late spring. Cold enough, I guess.

"Good. I hope he lasted long enough for the cold to get to the center of his bones until he could feel everything that made him alive dying an inch at a time."

Cal turned and strode toward the bunkhouse, not caring that a man with a grudge was behind him. His hatred for Henry Sutton seldom slipped out of the dark place inside where it lived. Ashamed that it had gotten away from him tonight, he shoved the feeling and the memories back down deep and forced his thoughts to the equally disturbing names on the map.

Much as he didn't want it to be true, the Hawkins woman had to be the Girl. When he dreamed of what happened all those years ago among the wagons, he dreamed it the way it had happened. Sometimes when he was wide awake, though, he dreamed of the kind of woman the Girl must have grown to be.

He didn't picture her as an elegant, icy beauty like Van Cleve's wife. The Girl would be pretty as nature made her without needing to be cinched in under a dress made by someone else. Her eyes would shine with a quiet strength, and if she saw him again, she would know him.

He lay on his bunk fully dressed, knowing he'd be lucky if sleep came by morning, and angry that he couldn't stop his churning mind. How could the Girl, who had the courage to defy her father and a crowd of belligerent drunks, have grown into a gray woman all used up and bleached out?

Why was he even thinking about it? She was none of his business. Whether she liked it or not, today he had repaid any debt he owed her.

He'd take Yost's body and Beason to town tomorrow, bring the wagon back, and maybe he'd move on. He didn't want to see any kin, and Van Cleve could find someone else to "talk" to the Hawkins woman. Maybe Preston's kind of talk would jolt her out of that spineless resignation.

3

NORAH HUDDLED IN bed under every quilt and blanket in the house, all her clothes, and the saving grace, a buffalo robe.

Without the robe, she'd have frozen in the night. Which meant she should burn the thing today. It would probably last longer and smell better than any cow chips she'd have the strength to gather.

The problem with that, of course, was where to draw the line. If she could just decide where to draw the line.

All she wanted was to see Joey again, hold him, hear him laugh, and for that to happen, her death couldn't be her own fault. If God ruled that she had caused her own death by not trying hard enough.... Well, that wasn't going to happen, so the buffalo robe would have to stay.

The pale light of early morning strengthened until a bright square of sunlight appeared across from the east window of the soddy. She turned away, unwilling to watch the beginning of one more day. Soon she'd drag herself up, go out, and gather enough cow chips to cook another of the few squash left in the root cellar, fry the last of the corn meal into a mush.

For a while yesterday, it seemed as if Preston and his men would make it unnecessary to decide where to draw the line. Even if he and his men hadn't killed her, after what they were going to do, no one would blame her for crawling off and drifting away.

Then that interfering, evil man had ridden out of the mob. They were hired killers, all of them. They had killed Joe. The interfering one had shot the reckless young one without batting an eye or changing expression, yet he had to have qualms about attacking a woman.

No man who looked down at her with so much contempt did what he did because of her in particular. She shivered, not because the cold penetrated her mountain of blankets but because of the memory of the cold eyes in his cruel face. The curt dismissal in the words he'd thrown at her repeated over and over in her mind.

She'd taken comfort in being beyond feeling, yet he'd made her feel small and no count. What right did he have? The others could have killed him for what he did. He should have minded his own business. If only he had minded his own business.

Pounding on the door exploded through the house.

Norah jerked upright under the pile of bedding, heart in throat. Van Cleve's men wouldn't knock. It must be a neighbor, and how was she going to convince a nosy neighbor to leave her alone when they would be able to tell she'd still been in bed this late with the house cold as a grave? As rude as she'd been to Mabel Carbury the last time the poor woman had shown up, it couldn't be her.

Frantic, expecting more pounding or even hollering, Norah dug her way out of the bed. She peeled off several layers of Joe's wool stockings so her feet would fit into her icy shoes and tried to smooth her hair into place as she stumbled across the room.

Yanking the door open, ready to be as rude as necessary, she stared at the empty space where a helpful neighbor should be standing, then at the bloody thing hanging from the edge of the roof.

Van Cleve's men *were* back! Who else would hang something like that from the roof, and if they thought they could scare her into leaving....

She scanned in every direction. There. She spotted a wagon in the distance, across the creek already and appearing to grow smaller and smaller as it retreated across the dull yellow winter prairie.

Up close, the thing hanging from the edge of the roof didn't resemble the body of some hapless animal. Well, yes, it did. It was part of an animal, a prime piece of what had been a cow.

Worse yet, a pile of boxes sat below it, boxes Norah knew without looking contained food. She kicked at one, hot with resentment. No neighbor ever had beef to give away. Only Van Cleve could give away beef, and she knew his evil, interfering, hired killer had brought these things.

She knew it, and she knew in a day or two he'd be back. He'd claim she owed some enormous sum for the food, or he'd pretend surprise at finding beef on the place and threaten to have her jailed for rustling.

He'd use the threats to try to frighten her into signing the property away. When she didn't frighten, he'd hurt her. As if she cared. A brittle little laugh escaped, her breath puffing white in the cold air.

She went back inside, slamming the door with anger-driven strength. That food could all sit out there and rot, or the coyotes could carry it off. Her chest heaved as she leaned against the inside of the door, struggling to repair her shell of indifference.

The dull, gray place inside eluded her, and she had to face a truth every fiber of her being rebelled against. When it came to food sitting available in her front yard, the line she worried about was drawn so dark no one could mistake where it lay.

Time passed. Her small flare of temper receded, and resignation returned. She carried the food inside, picked up her sack, and went to gather cow chips for the stove.

The next morning Norah rose early and heard the jingle of harness and creak of approaching wheels bearing a heavy load. She made it outside as the wagon disappeared around the side of the house and hurried after it.

The driver pulled the horses up, set the brake, and jumped down. The sight of firewood piled high in the wagon bed distracted Norah. She could barely remember the scent of wood smoke. Like beef for the table, settlers on the treeless prairie did without wood for their fires.

She forced her attention back to the man—sure enough, the interfering one. Too tall and broad in the shoulders for comfort. Evil-looking, with empty dark eyes. Several days' beard growth emphasized the predatory, hawkish look, as did that noticeable crook in the bridge of his nose. As if she cared. He didn't scare her. Couldn't.

"Take that away. I don't want food from you, and I don't want wood."

He gave her the same contemptuous look as two days before. "Don't you have a coat that fits?"

"You're trespassing. Go away and leave me alone."

He ignored her, gathered an armload of wood and carried it past her. Frustrated, she followed him into the house and watched him drop the firewood beside the stove with a clatter.

"What's the matter with you? Are you deaf? I don't want that wood. Go away."

"I wish I could. The trouble is I owe you, and we're both stuck dealing with it."

That made no sense. He couldn't owe her anything. The only way he could owe her was if....

A wave of dizziness had her groping for the edge of the table for support.

"You killed Joe," she whispered.

"No, Mrs. Hawkins, I did not. Here. Sit down before you fall down." He pulled out the closest chair, but she darted around the table and dropped to the one on the opposite side.

The quick movement brought back the light-headed feeling, but he didn't need to know that. She set her jaw and glared at him, letting the hate show.

"I'm going to unload that wood and stack it," he said, ignoring her attitude. "Why don't you take a crack at doing something useful, like cooking some of that food you don't want. Then we'll talk."

Norah listened as pieces of wood bounced first off the frozen ground and then off each other. What right did a killer have to talk to her like that, to look at her with such contempt? So she was tired and discouraged and had decided life wasn't worth living. How she felt and how she lived her life or didn't live it was none of his business.

If she didn't cook, would he do it himself and try to force her to eat? If he hadn't killed Joe, or at least helped others do it, how could he owe her anything? He had to be lying, but why would he bother?

She rose to her feet and stood a moment, relieved when the dizziness didn't return. She needed to visit the privy, and after that maybe she'd fetch water and make coffee. That might satisfy him, and it would take her mind off the regular thuds coming from outside.

Once the coffee was ready to boil, Norah's hands kept working as if they had a mind of their own. Biscuits, a man-sized steak, gravy, fried potatoes. After all, the more food he ate, the sooner it would all be gone.

At first she tried to cover the sound of him working outside any way she could, cutting meat and potatoes with vicious whacks of the knife, banging pots and pans, rattling cutlery.

The house warmed, not only as the temperature rose but with the familiar scents of cooking food. Gradually Norah relaxed, accepting the symmetry of the man working outside as she worked inside.

She gave up trying to guess what debt he could believe he owed her. "We'll talk," he'd said. He would explain, and she would set him straight.

The sounds outside stopped. She filled a plate, refusing to turn as he walked in without knocking. Her plan to feed him and ignore him went awry immediately. He dropped another armful of wood beside the stove, and she all but dropped the coffee pot she had just picked up.

"Don't you have a wood box?"

"Of course not. We never had wood."

"Huh." He draped his coat over the back of a chair, left his hat on the table, and moved to the washstand near the door, washing his hands with the last of the water she'd hauled in earlier as if he did it every day.

Seeing him there, in the place where Joe had performed the same ritual hundreds, no thousands, of times, Norah realized how much bigger Joe had been. They were both well above average height, but Joe's head had reached an inch or so closer to the top of the door, and their bodies—the difference was like that between a draft horse and a race horse.

He stood there, drying his hands, taking in everything in the single big room that was her house. His mouth no longer curled with contempt, and the expression on the hawk's face was curious, as if he'd never seen such a place before. She waited for a belittling remark about houses made of dirt or people who lived in them.

"This is nice. You fixed this house up nice. I like those blue curtains."

The compliment disconcerted her. She wasn't used to compliments. Even faint ones. Was that one? Before she decided, he returned to more familiar behavior.

"If you're going to set one plate on the table like that, you could have put it outside in the dirt. That way you could pretend you're just feeding a dog."

Crazy. Now she had an explanation for it all. He was mad. Talking to him would be useless, and she couldn't think of anything to say anyway.

Crazy or not, he found another cup, plate, and utensils fast enough.

"Sit."

Norah sat and watched him push a share of everything she'd piled on the one plate for him onto the empty plate. He finished by cutting a piece off the steak and slapped that on the plate too.

"Eat," he ordered.

"Or what?"

"Or nothing. Eat it. You can commit slow suicide by starving yourself to death some other day."

Her breath caught in her throat. "I'm not.... Don't you say.... Don't you dare say.... I am not...."

"Good. Eat that and prove it, and then you can drink this." He poured coffee, sat across from her, and began to eat.

After a few mouthfuls, he said, "You're a good cook, Mrs. Hawkins. You ought to have the sense to enjoy your own cooking."

Another compliment. He made her want to take her knife to him. Instead she picked up her fork and began eating. After all, she had eaten a little yesterday. Just enough to prove.... She banished the thought.

She pushed her plate away after eating no more than half of what he'd put on it.

"I hope that's good enough for you, because I can't eat any more. Would you please tell me what you think you owe me? I'm sure whatever it is, we're even now."

The corners of his mouth pulled straight back, but his lips turned toward each other, keeping the smile inside and controlled. "I owe you for saving my life a long time ago."

"I never saved anyone's li...." Her voice tapered off.

"Yeah, you did. That night in the wagon."

Norah stared at the tall, lean killer across from her, unable to believe it. Not wanting to believe it. His hair was blond, but a dark blond, nothing like the boy in the night.

"No. You're trying to say you were the wild boy. No. He was too small to be you. His hair was almost white."

"Boys grow. Their hair gets darker. I probably started growing that night from the food I stole and what you gave me, and I didn't stop for years."

"He died. Everyone said I killed him by letting him go. He died alone out on the prairie."

"I would have died without what you gave me, but a buffalo hunter found me a couple of days after the food ran out. He never had any trouble believing he saved my life, and he sure figured my life was what I owed him."

"I didn't really save him," Norah whispered. "They wouldn't have hung him. It was just talk."

"They were drunk enough to do it, and it didn't matter. They wouldn't have let me go, and if they sent me back where I came from, I'd have finished starving to death soon enough."

"Where did you—he—come from?"

She could not accept that the man sitting across the table from her was the Boy. She would not accept it.

"Henry Sutton's place. I'm Cal Sutton—Caleb."

Norah's mind churned, trying to find a way to deal with what she didn't want to believe. To deal with *him*.

"If the Suttons are your kin, how can you work for Mr. Van Cleve?"

"Easy. You saw me fifteen years ago. Do you think there's a lot of family feeling there?"

"You ran away. You were out on the prairie alone for days. Weeks even. You.... He...."

"I got away the morning of the night you saw me."

"No."

He slammed his empty coffee cup on the table, and Norah flinched. "Your choice. Don't believe me. I met a fine fellow one day who told me about a girl who saved his life one night. So now you tell me, how did that girl grow into a self-pitying heap of a woman so useless she would sit out here alone starving and freezing instead of saving herself?"

His contemptuous look was back. She wanted to slap it off his face.

"What do you think I could do? You murdered my husband and stole everything he had with him. I have no money, no horse, no gun. Nothing."

"I told you I didn't kill your husband. I came back here last month because I heard some rancher was running sodbusters off their land near Hubbell, Kansas. I figured if someone was going to part Uncle Henry from that land it should be me. Killing him knowing Van Cleve could keep it quiet would have been even better, but he was already dead."

He said it as if he were joking, but Norah saw the truth of his words.

"You really are evil," she whispered.

"The devil's spawn, but you didn't answer my question. How did the Girl with all the courage become a woman with none?"

"Don't you judge me! What do you think I could do?"

"You have decent family. Go to them."

"My family left here when Mr. Van Cleve first started running people out. Last I heard they were in Colorado and thinking of going to Texas."

"So go to town. Find work."

"Of course, go to town. I could walk. If a wagon can make it in a day, I could make it on foot in two days, maybe three, and let's see, what could I do once I got there? Work in one of the saloons? They probably don't want widows my age any more than anyone else, and if I'm going to hell, it won't be for whoring."

"You didn't have any problem with what Preston and his men were going to do. What's the difference?"

For months she had been suppressing anger, denying it. At his words, something broke inside, and it all poured out in a shrieking flood.

"The difference is they were going to do it to me. I wasn't selling myself and my soul. That's the difference, whether it happens to me or I do it!" She wanted to smash that look off his face. She wanted to draw blood.

His expression didn't change. "So it's like sitting out here starving yourself and pretending you're not committing slow suicide. Getting raped by a half a dozen men because you're being stupid and cowardly would be fine, but whoring to save yourself would doom you to hellfire. You don't want to believe I was the Boy because you don't want to remember being the Girl."

Norah jumped to her feet, planted her fists on the table to keep from hitting him and leaned toward him on stiff arms.

"You can't be the Boy because you aren't worth saving. Nothing was ever the same after that night, and I didn't do it for the likes of you. You say you owed me. Fine! You paid. We're even. Get out of here. Get out!"

He rose and moved toward the door. She prayed he'd leave without saying more, but of course he didn't.

"Let me tell you something about those whores you think are all hell bound, Mrs. Hawkins. Any one of them I ever knew who wanted to die would have the courage to use a gun or a knife or even rat poison if she had to. Whatever their sins, they have more grit and gumption than you do."

The door slammed so hard behind him, she looked up, expecting to see it fall from the hinges. No more than a minute passed before she heard the wagon leaving, but she stayed there, swaying slightly on braced arms.

That night in the wagon train had been a turning point in her life. No matter what she'd just said, she had never believed the Boy died alone on the prairie because of what she did. She knew he had lived.

Over the years she had pictured him many times. In her mind he had been everything from a farmer to a rancher, a banker, a doctor.

She had pictured him rich and poor and in every kind of situation, but the one thing she had been sure of was that he had grown into a good man. A decent man. The Boy could not have become a hired killer. He could not have grown into—that.

She grabbed her plate, still half-filled with congealing food, and threw it at the door. It broke in half and the mess fell to the floor. She threw her coffee cup with even more force, then swept the table clear with a crash and fell into her chair, burying her head in her arms.

The anger didn't subside but grew, tearing at her until she shook with it. She wished for the release of tears and knew it wouldn't come. Tears would never come again.

4

TRYING TO FORGET Caleb Sutton's ugly words or tamp down their effect proved futile.

Through the next days, Norah fought the storm of emotions destroying her indifference the only way she knew how. She worked to exhaustion hauling water and laundering every scrap of cloth she could lay her hands on.

She pulled the peach-colored muslin strips off the dirt walls and took down the blue gingham curtains. Joe had hated moving back to the soddy and grumbled over the cost of her efforts to make the house seem like a home.

Of course if she'd known back then how much they already owed the stores in Hubbell she never would have bought any of it, but he hadn't shared that, just complained.

Only other women and Sutton had ever noticed her efforts, much less uttered a compliment. For a moment she considered burning the cloth, but why give an evil, worthless man— who could not be the Boy—that power?

She scrubbed until her knuckles bled, ironed until her arm ached, rehung the muslin and curtains, and moved on to sweeping, scrubbing, and polishing.

She fed the stove firewood so generously she half-expected it to dance across the dirt floor and fed herself every bit as well. She *was* a good cook, and that was something else that only other women had ever remarked on. Oh, the devil take him.

The supplies Sutton had brought included five gallons of coal oil, and she used it recklessly, holding off the early darkness for long hours, darning stockings and mending clothes Joe would never need again. Maybe someday she could get to town with them. Maybe someone else could use them.

Catching herself making plans for the future, however tentative and vague, Norah accepted defeat. She was alive and probably going to stay that way for some time. Wallowing in misery had only left her vulnerable to contempt from a man lower than a bug's belly. Blaming him and nursing anger could only disguise the truth for so long.

He still couldn't be the Boy. He'd all but admitted to meeting the good man who had been the Boy somewhere and stealing the story. *Then how did he recognize me? I never told him my name. Maybe the real Boy heard my name and told him.*

She'd never see him again anyway except as one of the crowd of Van Cleve's killers, so it didn't matter, but if he was the Boy, he had repaid her for saving his life by saving hers.

Of course the Boy had been willing to be saved, more than willing, eager, and she'd wanted to be left alone, but it was done now. She needed to start thinking about tomorrow. All the tomorrows.

On the first tomorrow, Norah wrapped up several layers deep from head to toe. In her mind she heard him again. "Don't you have a coat that fits?"

Today, she answered cleverly, "Of course, I have six others, all custom made, but I chose this one today." In fact, all she had was a much-mended old thing that even new hadn't kept her half as warm as Joe's coat.

She hiked past one deserted farmstead after another, all Van Cleve's now. The burned out hulks of wood frame houses on two of the places attested to one of the ways Van Cleve convinced people to sell.

Norah knew all about sudden fire in the night. The blackened remains of the house Joe had loved so much sat on her property.

In the past she'd never paid attention to how far the Carburys lived from her. Today she calculated the distance by the quarter-sections of land she crossed, half a mile for each one. The Carburys were five miles away as crows flew.

Each of those empty quarter-sections represented neighbors who had wilted under Van Cleve's onslaught, sold their land to him, and moved on. Most had been friends she and Joe had helped and been helped by, gathered with at christenings, funerals, weddings, barn raisings, and picnics.

So few were left now, no one from the wagon train except her. The families holding out were almost all like Carburys, with enough menfolk to defend against Van Cleve's killers. Occasionally the Carburys divided forces, half staying on guard at home and half making a trip to town for supplies—or to Norah's house to urge her to accept the help she sorely needed and had stubbornly refused.

Norah walked without fear, long past worrying about Preston and Van Cleve's other men catching her in the open. They could just as easily come to the house again. Had she made Sutton as angry as he'd made her? If so, had he revoked whatever protection he'd granted her? She hoped so. She wanted nothing from him. Nothing.

Relieved in a way she didn't want to admit to see Carburys' comfortable house still standing and smoke rising from the stovepipe, Norah quickened her pace toward their door. One of the sons stepped out of the barn with a rifle cradled in his arms. He watched her for a moment, waved, and moved back out of sight again.

"Norah!" Mabel Carbury's hug felt like everything safe in the world, and Norah hugged back fiercely.

"Oh, my girl," Mabel said, pushing Norah away by the shoulders, "you look so much better than last time I saw you. I should have visited again. I should have...."

"Don't say that," Norah begged. "Please don't say that and make me feel worse. I was inexcusably rude. You did everything you could. You were kind, and I was beyond awful."

"You were grieving. Too many losses too fast. A person can die of a broken heart, you know. I've seen it, and I thought it was happening to you and there was nothing I could do. I should have tried harder. I should have...."

Norah hugged her again. "You were wonderful, and you still are. Please say you forgive me, and let's not talk about it any more."

"I don't forgive you because there's no need. Now come in and warm up. Archie and the boys will be in for dinner soon, and you'll eat with us, and we'll share the latest news, and it will be like old times."

Mabel's voice quivered on the last words. Norah had a small lump in her own throat.

"Maybe everyone would like to have a slice of this after dinner," she said, handing over the cloth-wrapped package she'd brought with her and hanging Joe's coat on a peg by the door.

Mabel stood in her parlor with its whitewashed walls and wide board floors holding the package as if she didn't know what to do with it. Finally she unwrapped a corner to expose the golden crust of the raisin-studded loaf of oatmeal bread inside.

"We worried about you starving. How could you make this? What happened while we were both being stubborn and foolish?"

"Later, when your men come in and I can tell you all at once, I actually have a story to share," Norah said, realizing she did. She had an extraordinary tale and only had to decide how much to tell.

"I knew I heard someone talking to Ma down here."

Becky, the Carburys' only daughter and their wild child, skipped down the last of the stairs and hugged Norah as hard as her mother had.

Tall and blonde, with strong features that combined into an arresting whole, Becky was the image of what Mabel must have been before the years had laced her hair with gray and taken her figure from willowy to matronly. Seeing them side by side again, Norah wondered as she always did whether Mabel's calm blue eyes had once danced with as much curiosity and mischief as her daughter's.

"I'm so glad to see you," Becky said. "Two of my own brothers are going to stay here and guard the house instead of coming to my wedding, but you'll come, won't you? Say you will."

"Wedding? Last time I talked to you, you and Mr. Butler had quarreled, and you were never going to forgive him."

"But I did forgive him, and we're getting married the day after tomorrow. Say you'll come, Norah. Please, please."

"I, I'd love to come," Norah stammered, "but you know I can't. I can't stay overnight in town, and if I went, I'd have to."

"You can too come, and you can squeeze in with us at the Butlers' house overnight," Mabel said. "Archie and the boys are staying in the hotel, but Becky and I won't have to set a foot in that place, and neither will you."

The two of them had an answer to every one of Norah's objections. She didn't exactly agree with their plan, but she began to feel swept away by the inevitability of it.

The three women worked in the kitchen together, getting dinner on the table, while chatting about the wedding. Mabel and Becky both shed a few tears over how their lives would change when Becky moved to town with her new husband, who had proposed the day after he landed a job managing Hubbell's railroad station.

The Carbury men filed into the house for dinner and greeted Norah without surprise. Unlike Becky, who was in all ways a younger version of her mother, the four Carbury sons all showed their father's influence in their dark hair, gray eyes, and thickly-muscled, sturdy bodies. None of them stood more than average height, but Norah had never seen another man challenge Archie or his oldest boys.

Maybe Ben, the only one of the boys younger than Becky, would become like his brothers by the time he got his full growth, but so far he seemed more like his loquacious, enthusiastic sister. He often made Norah laugh.

The conversation stayed focused on the wedding and Becky's new life until Mabel remembered the oatmeal bread. "You promised us a story," she said.

Norah had decided on the whole story except for a few details about the visit from Preston and his men and how nasty her conversation with Sutton had turned at the end.

At first Mabel and Becky interrupted with exclamations and questions, but before long the whole Carbury clan sat silent around the table, listening.

"So that's why I could bake oatmeal bread," Norah finished. "At least for a few more weeks, I'm eating as well as Mr. Van Cleve. In fact I suspect I'm eating his food and burning his wood."

Her audience came out of its collective trance and began reaching for coffee cups, finishing the last of their slices of oatmeal bread.

"I can't believe it," Mabel said finally. "One of Van Cleve's men, I mean. They don't look like the kind who feel obligations the way ordinary folks do, much less try to repay."

"Well, this one does," Norah said. "Of course he didn't give a hoot how I felt about it. He decided what he wanted to do and did it."

Less curious and more prosaic than his womenfolk, Archie said, "So you have provisions and you're safe from Van Cleve for a while. How are you going to get by when what he gave you runs out? You don't want his kind hanging around. Once we get you to town, you stay there. Sell out to Van Cleve and you can live on that long enough to find yourself a good man."

Archie Carbury didn't usually hand out unsolicited advice, and Norah wished he hadn't bothered this time. For one thing, there was no chance at all of Caleb Sutton hanging around. He'd probably turn in the other direction and put spurs to his horse if he saw her again.

For another—"Joe hasn't even been gone three months. I'm not looking to remarry so soon, maybe ever."

"You should be," Archie said, getting to his feet with a grunt. "If Becky here can find someone to put up with her, so can you. You're still a young woman."

With that he led the parade of his sons back to work.

After washing dishes and putting the kitchen to rights, silent except for a few words about the chores, the three women sat at the table with cups of coffee and shared the last of the oatmeal bread.

"There's nothing for me in town," Norah said. "I don't want to sell to the man who killed Joe, I don't want to live in town, and I don't want another husband."

Mabel patted her hand. "I understand, but what can you do? Archie's right, you know."

Archie's rightness was one of the pillars of Mabel's existence, and Norah had to admit Archie was no fool.

Becky's face lit up with excitement, and she set her cup down so hard Norah looked to see if it or the saucer had broken. Oblivious to Norah's concern or her mother's tsk of disapproval, Becky said, "I know. I know what you can do."

Her face fell as fast as it had lit up. "Oh, except you wouldn't want to. No one would, I guess."

"What could I do that I wouldn't want to do?" Norah asked.

"Ethan told me Mrs. Tindell is looking for a housekeeper again. They're taking bets in town how long a new one will last."

Mabel gathered their plates and cups and slid them in the wash pan. "That's why no one would want to do it. She's been through half a dozen girls that I know of and not one of them was good enough for her. She works them to death and complains day and night they don't do anything right. You know at least some of those girls were good workers. If you don't want to marry again so soon, we can find you something else."

"Like what," Norah said. "A job working in Mr. Tindell's saloon instead of his house? He never—bothered the girls who worked at the house, did he?"

"Heavens, no. He's as afraid of that mean old woman as anyone else. She's the problem, not him or the sons."

"Did you ever wonder if part of the problem is that he owns the saloon?" Norah said. "Sometimes I think that people resent the way she acts so, so superior when he makes his money from whiskey and gambling and...."

"And women," Becky filled in gleefully, earning another disapproving glance from her mother.

"Sure that's why people think she's got no right to act so la di da," Mabel said, "but that doesn't make her any less of a witch."

"I wonder how much she pays. If I could stand it for a few months, it would be spring, and I'd have some cash money. I don't want to sell to the man who murdered Joe to get our land."

The three of them spent the rest of the day and the evening discussing nothing but Becky's upcoming wedding and Norah's possibilities. The next morning Archie and his oldest son drove Norah home in their wagon and helped her pack up everything in the soddy.

She rode to Hubbell wedged in the wagon between Mabel and Becky only after every one of the Carburys promised that if she wanted to come home after the wedding, they would bring her home.

If Caleb Sutton knew how to laugh, he'd probably laugh at having turned her life upside down so thoroughly.

She wondered how long it would be before she knew whether she should curse him or thank him, not that she'd ever have a chance to do either.

As soon as the railroad had arrived, Hubbell had started to grow, but the Tindell house was still unique in the town. Norah gave it a good looking over from the street before approaching.

Three stories high, dripping with ornate trim, the house was a tribute to ostentation. Norah's concern was with the size of the thing, which she knew she'd be expected to keep spotless. Housekeeper was simply Mrs. Tindell's idea of a more impressive term for maid.

Becky's new husband had already reported that so far as anyone in town knew, Mrs. Tindell hadn't replaced her last unfortunate girl. Betting on the new employee's staying power, whoever she turned out to be, continued unabated.

Norah learned that the job included room and board and a small salary, but no one could tell her what kind of room or how much salary.

The house sat back from the road on a large lot surrounded by an iron fence with spiked pickets to keep riffraff out. Probably she should go around to the back, but she wasn't hired help yet.

Squaring her shoulders, she marched through the front gate. The brass horse head knocker on the carved front door winked at her. Examining it closely, Norah could see that polish would fix the eyes so they matched, but she wasn't going to be the one to point that out.

A girl in a gray dress covered by a large white apron answered the door. Norah backed up a step and almost fell off the porch.

"Oh, I'm sorry. I came about the housekeeper's job. I didn't know the position was taken."

The girl reached out and fastened a hand like a steel trap on Norah's arm, pulling her inside.

"It's not taken," she said with an Irish lilt. "Mr. Tindell all but threatened my da to get me to work here a few hours a day, and if you've come to save me, I'll pray for you every day for the rest of me life, I will."

Norah swallowed hard. "It's that bad then? Does she pay, though?"

"She's the devil draped in silk, she is, but she pays what she promises."

Steps sounded on the polished wood floor behind them, and the girl dropped her voice to a whisper.

"You wait here. I'll tell her about you, and she'll have me escorting you to the parlor like she's a queen and can't walk out here."

The girl disappeared, and Norah stared around the hall at the ornate furniture and papered walls. Housekeeping here would certainly be different than in a dirt-floored soddy that measured sixteen feet by twenty and was home to a thriving insect population and the occasional snake in summer and generations of mice all year round.

After a wait that proved she was in the riffraff category, Norah followed the Irish girl to the dragon's lair. Seated at an elegant desk in front of the room's tall windows, Mrs. Tindell appeared more frail than frightening.

A second, more careful appraisal hinted at a spine of steel keeping her slender form so rigidly straight. Light brown hair framed delicate features, but none of the lines in her face came from smiling, and the gray eyes held no warmth.

Norah stopped a few feet in front of the desk. She was not invited to sit.

"Mary tells me you've come about the housekeeper's position," Mrs. Tindell said in an unexpectedly deep voice. "She forgot to get your name of course."

Of course.

Norah reminded herself that she owned more than three hundred acres of good farmland and could go back to it tomorrow if she wanted.

"I'm Norah Gifford Hawkins, ma'am. My husband was killed three months ago, and yes, I've come to see about the housekeeper's position."

Norah answered a string of increasingly personal questions politely, then asked one of her own the first time Mrs. Tindell paused long enough.

"Before we go further, I'd like to know the terms of employment with you, Mrs. Tindell."

The woman looked offended. "The terms are of no concern to you unless I decide to employ you."

Norah nodded. "I understand. I'm sure you have other more qualified applicants."

She turned as if to leave, amazed at her own nerve, but she'd had enough of questions that were none of this woman's business.

"Wait."

Norah stopped and looked back over her shoulder.

"Room and board and ten dollars a month. Sunday and Wednesday afternoons free after serving luncheon to the family."

Ten dollars! No wonder the woman worked people like slaves. For that Norah would even polish the wink out of the brass horse's eye.

She turned around and gave an imitation of Caleb Sutton's smile. When she rejoined the Carburys and Butlers, she'd celebrate. Until then nothing mattered except getting the best terms possible.

"That sounds reasonable," she said, "depending, of course, on what is expected."

Becky had married for better or worse. By day's end, Norah was employed and feeling the same way about it.

5

EVERY DAY HE spent with Preston and his men increased Cal's desire to quit. He didn't like Preston, didn't like Van Cleve, and didn't like the work. Packing up, saddling up, and catching a train west sounded better every day.

Trouble was every time he decided tomorrow would be the day, the image of Preston dancing his horse over Norah Hawkins rose in his mind. Finding out the Girl had turned into a woman like that had been a bitter disappointment, but leaving her to Preston's tender mercies didn't sit right.

The fact he had that feeling in the first place and couldn't make it go away in the second place annoyed him no end.

Van Cleve solved the problem by summoning Cal to his study again. This time Cal took the indicated chair, but he still accepted the glass of whiskey with his left hand. The rancher's approach was no longer affable. He stayed behind his desk and got straight to the point.

"Preston tells me you've been visiting the Hawkins woman. He says you used one of my wagons and took her a load of my wood."

Cal sipped at the whiskey, enjoying the warmth it spread in his veins. "He must be a spy of the first water. I did that all right."

"So. Am I going to get my money's worth? Will she sell?"

"No. She knows you had her husband killed. Maybe somebody could hurt her bad enough to make her sign a paper, but I'm not even sure of that."

Van Cleve slammed his glass down so hard whiskey spilled over the polished surface of the desk. "I didn't kill her husband. I told you. I don't give those kind of orders."

Cal took another swallow, letting silence speak for him.

Van Cleve leaned forward, wagging an index finger. "I don't care if you knew her back when, no more helping her hold out by giving her ranch property. When you draw pay from me, you ride for the brand. From now on Preston deals with the woman, and you stay away from her. What's more, I'm taking the cost of the wood out of your pay."

One last swallow emptied his glass. Cal turned it in his hand a moment as if giving the matter serious thought. "That sounds fair," he said finally. "Maybe I'm wrong and Preston can convince her."

No one waited for him outside this time. Howling wind drove icy flakes of snow against his face like flying needles. As soon as the weather cleared, he'd discuss Norah Hawkins and the price of wood with Van Cleve in more detail.

THE WIND RAGED, driving sleet and snow before it on and off for days. Cal walked out of the bunkhouse on the first clear morning and looked over the landscape with a critical eye. Bright sun had already melted away shallow snow cover in open areas scoured by the wind. Another day or two like this, and even the deepest drifts would be gone.

After filling his belly with V Bar C breakfast, Cal left the rest of the crew discussing the day's work over a last cup of coffee, packed what little he had brought with him in his bedroll and saddlebags, and caught up his horse.

He rode far enough down the ranch road to be out of sight of anyone watching, then swung around behind the house and left his horse in heavy brush. As he'd expected on a big house like Van Cleve's, there was a back door. Locked. A little broken glass took care of that.

A small brown woman wearing a white cap and apron over a black dress was serving Van Cleve, his wife, a girl maybe five and boy a couple years older breakfast in a sunny room not far from the back door. Cal had heard about the children, but they were kept away from Preston's men so well, he'd never seen them before.

"I need to talk to your husband, ma'am," Cal said, nodding to Mrs. Van Cleve. "Why don't you and your friend there take those children for a walk."

Mrs. Van Cleve showed signs of being the fainting kind, but the maid was made of sterner stuff. The little woman had both her employer's wife and the children gone from the room in less than a minute. Whatever Van Cleve paid her, he ought to double it.

As soon as the door closed behind the women, Van Cleve jumped to his feet.

"Who do you think you are coming in here like this? Get the hell out of here right now, and I won't have Preston shoot you as you leave."

Cal smiled at the little man as he headed for him. Van Cleve held up his hands. "I'm not heeled. You can't shoot an unarmed man."

"So that hideout gun in your coat doesn't count? I'm glad to hear it. I'm not shooting you. I'm explaining something to you."

Cal snaked a hand inside Van Cleve's jacket, relieved him of the hidden pistol, and threw it through the nearest window. The sound of breaking glass and rush of cold air gave him considerable satisfaction.

"I not only gave Norah Hawkins a load of firewood. I gave her maybe a tenth of the food and supplies Preston and his men stole from her husband when they killed him. I figure you owe her. Now since you want me to pay, I'll pay. You keep the wages I've got coming, and we're even, but I want a receipt, so let's go get one."

Hoisting Van Cleve high enough only his toes reached the ground, Cal pushed him down the hall to his study. The choking noises the man made couldn't have anything to do with an arm hard around his neck, so Cal ignored the sounds while he yanked open one drawer after another until he found pen, paper, and ink.

"Now, you sit here and write out that I paid for one wagon load of firewood and one wagon load of provisions and delivered it to Norah Hawkins, and you authorized it all. Date it last month."

"You can't make me write that."

"Sure I can." Cal grabbed an ear and twisted. When Van Cleve's yell changed to a scream, Cal let go and put the pen in the man's hand. Van Cleve wrote.

Once he had the paper tucked in a pocket, Cal shoved the gun under Van Cleve's nose.

"I don't care if you steal every piece of land from here to the Mississippi or how you do it, but if you ever go near Norah Hawkins again or let Preston or anyone like him go near her, I'll kill you. You stay away from her and stay off her land."

He started to turn toward the door and paused. "And if you're smart, you'll stay away from the spare pistol that's in the top drawer of your desk there."

As he left, he could hear men charging into the house through the front. The women had run to Preston for help of course. Cal smiled as he slipped out the back.

THE CLOSER HE got to the Hawkins place, the more Cal regretted letting his temper loose with Van Cleve. The fact the arrogant runt thought he could dictate what woman Cal could or could not see had been considerable provocation, but in truth Cal didn't want to see that ungrateful, bad-tempered shrew again. His desire to check on her irritated him, and he definitely didn't want to stay in the area to ensure her safety.

She'd called his debt to her paid and set him free. Why didn't he feel free of the memory and the obligation?

If he left, would dreams of the Girl be gone forever? Would they be replaced by ones of the Hawkins woman screaming at him or of Preston knocking her around? Would she join his ghosts? He had enough ghosts already.

The house came into sight. No smoke rose from the stovepipe. He reined up in the yard and sat taking in the desolate, deserted yard. If she'd finished killing herself....

He gave the door two hard knocks and walked in, tense muscles relaxing when he didn't smell death and a quick glance revealed no body.

There wasn't much else to see either. She was gone. And so was every single useful thing in the place except the stove and furniture. No blankets on the bed. No dishes, no pots and pans, no coffee pot. No food.

Not much wood was left either. She couldn't have used so much. Whoever had helped her haul everything away had taken as much of the wood as he had room for.

Cal looked around and decided to hole up here for the night and start for town in the morning. He had a little jerked beef and some crackers in his saddlebags.

The blue curtains still hung at the windows, and he fingered one, marveling at the small, regular stitches along the edge. Even now, with almost everything stripped out of the house, it still felt more like a home than any place he'd been, and the curtains had something to do with the feeling.

She hadn't sold to Van Cleve, so where had she gone, and what was she doing there? The thought of her actually whoring in one of Hubbell's saloons made his stomach clench and a hot wave of sickness shoot up through his chest to the back of his throat. No, whatever she was up to, that wouldn't be it. She equated whoring with throwing her soul right onto the devil's pitchfork at the center of the fires of hell.

He touched the curtains again, crossed the room to the rocking chair, and gave the back a little push. Shaking his head in a vain attempt to throw out unwanted thoughts and feelings, he went back out to take care of his horse and get the saddlebags.

Cal made it to Hubbell late the next day, hungry, cranky, and after a look at the town's only hotel, not looking forward to a night there.

Hubbell's one restaurant was a palace compared to the hotel. Better yet, a pair of elderly gossips at the next table saved him having to ask around for Norah Hawkins.

"Most of the folks who bet she wouldn't last a month already lost their money. I bet February fourteenth myself, and I'm thinking maybe that's too soon."

"Well, what did you expect? A widow like that, used to doing for her own place. Of course she knows how to keep a house up. Even so, I heard she hasn't been so much as a step out of the yard since the day she started."

"Maybe so, but Old Lady Tindell can still find something to complain about. I heard her after church, telling another old biddy the new girl isn't respectful enough."

"Well, *he* told me she cooks better than anybody they ever had. Maybe if his missus lets her go, she'll come work here. These biscuits would make doorstops."

The biscuits weren't that bad, but they weren't like Mrs. Hawkins' either. The old men left. Cal paid for his breakfast and asked casually, "Do you know where I can find the Tindell place?"

"Sure. Everybody knows Tindell. He owns the Queen of Hearts right up the street."

That wasn't exactly what Cal meant, but he didn't ask more. Someone at the saloon would tell him what he wanted to know without him asking. Better not let some persnickety old lady know Cal Sutton was asking after her new maid.

6

NORAH WRUNG OUT the last of the week's laundry, carried it to the line, and began hanging it. This late in the day it would barely begin drying before freezing, but it could thaw and finish tomorrow.

"Doesn't the Tindell woman know there's a laundry in town?"

Caleb Sutton. The contempt was gone from his expression, but his dark eyes were as cold as ever, his face set in the same harsh lines.

"She doesn't trust them to do it right."

"And she'd have to pay them on top of what she pays you."

"I'm not sure that's a consideration. Whatever else she is, she's not stingy."

He was no more than six feet away, leaning against a winter-barren tree, and he put her in mind of a cougar ready to spring. She couldn't make herself look right at him. She focused on the tree.

"I owe you an apology. I'm sorry I shrieked at you the way I did. You were right in what you said and making me that angry was—was good for me."

"We cleared the air. We were bound to disappoint each other after all these years."

"Maybe so." *No we weren't. You could have been a decent man. Even a halfway decent man.*

She pulled another sheet out of the basket, gave it a shake, and lifted it to the line. "I can't stand around and talk, you know. I have to keep working, but I'm glad you stopped by so I could apologize."

"They say in town you haven't been off this place since the day you took the job. Aren't you supposed to have some time off?"

She put the last clothespin in the sheet and shook out another. "I attend church every Sunday. What would I do with free afternoons? Until I finish my first month and get paid, I can't buy anything, and I don't know anyone in town to visit."

That last was a fib. Becky and her husband lived in town, and now that they'd had some time for their honeymoon, Norah would love to visit them. Since she could barely keep up with the work by going full speed from first light until she nodded off at night over ironing, mending, or polishing, she didn't dare try.

"How about taking some time today? You can have supper with me at the restaurant. The food's not as good as yours, but you won't have to cook it or clean up after."

Norah dropped one end of the sheet she was hanging. "I can't. My free afternoons are Sunday and Wednesday."

"You should have credit for the times you stayed and worked. Tell the old lady you want some free time tonight. Want me to talk to her?"

"No!"

He had what he probably thought was an innocent look on his face. Someone should tell him his face wasn't capable of innocence. "I will ask her," Norah said.

"Don't ask her. Tell her. I'll meet you here about five."

"No! Not five."

By six she could have the Tindells' supper ready. Dinner. She had to remember that unlike everyone she knew who ate breakfast, dinner, and supper, the Tindells ate breakfast, luncheon, and dinner. Speaking of supper gave a person away as less than in Mrs. Tindell's world.

Her mind back on the real problem, Norah decided she could tell Mrs. Tindell she would serve *dinner* and do the cleaning up when she got back. That might work.

"Six. I can be ready by six."

He tipped his hat and left. She watched until he disappeared from sight.

He didn't even walk the way a man should. He walked like someone who wouldn't leave footprints. And wasn't that silly. She knew what he was and so her mind invented fanciful things.

She would go to the restaurant with him, and he would disappear again, and she'd have another story to tell when she could visit Becky.

Mrs. Tindell's suspicious questions made it clear she didn't believe for a minute that Norah had an old friend in town only for the day. Norah held her breath, surprised to realize how much she wanted to forget about never-ending chores, walk out into the fresh air of the night, and eat food she hadn't cooked in an actual restaurant, even if it meant doing it in Caleb Sutton's company.

"All right," Mrs. Tindell said finally. "You may go so long as you clean the kitchen when you return, and of course you understand, Wednesday will no longer be a free afternoon."

Norah thanked her employer and fled, afraid true feelings would slip from behind clenched teeth and ruin everything.

Ten dollars a month, ten dollars a month, ten dollars a month.

The rest of the afternoon passed in a blur. She worked by rote, her mind on getting away. Her best—or more accurately least worst—dress hung in her room, clean and ironed, waiting for a visit to Becky that never happened.

How could she find time to wash and redo her hair? Should she wear her own shabby coat or stick with Joe's?

Having to pick a few lumps out of the gravy flustered her more. She forgot to put bread and butter on the table and knocked over the sugar.

"Oh, for pity's sake, Norah, go," Mrs. Tindell said. "You're worse than useless tonight. Go."

She went.

Her coat wasn't that warm. Norah walked into the frosty night and shivered, wondering how long she should wait before accepting he hadn't meant it. He probably just wanted to see how much aggravation he could cause by threatening to talk to Mrs. Tindell.

"Shouldn't you be a few minutes late, just to teach me a lesson?"

Her heart jumped as his shadow separated from those of the night. "What lesson would that teach you?"

"Damned if I know."

"Something to do with your language I expect."

"That must be it."

They walked side by side without touching, yet Norah buzzed with awareness of him, his height, the breadth of his shoulders, the way he moved.

The dark streets held no menace. The occasional drunken shout from a saloon was of no consequence.

Tonight the worst danger in town was at her side, on her side, and she was safe. How long had it been since she'd felt like this, female, protected, almost floating with it? She couldn't remember.

Moist, warm air enveloped her as she stepped through the restaurant door. In the dim lamplight she saw bare wooden walls and less than a dozen plain wood tables, no more than half of them occupied.

Every head in the room lifted, every eye took in first her old, much-mended coat, and when she had given that up, her equally old and mended dress. The floaty feeling dissolved, and she moved toward the closest table.

"Away from the door is better," Caleb said. His hand, warm on her arm through the dress sleeve, guided her toward the only empty table far from the door and close to the stove.

To her relief, he didn't hold a chair for her or do any of those other foolish things Mrs. Tindell expected of her husband. By the time Norah seated herself, the other diners were at least pretending they'd lost interest in the Widow Hawkins and Van Cleve's gunman.

"Your eyes are blue."

He sounded surprised, and Norah stopped looking everywhere but at Caleb Sutton. The shadowy light in the room made it easier. "You sound surprised. A lot of people have blue eyes."

"I am surprised. That day in your yard they were gray. I didn't think eyes could change like that."

"They didn't change. It was an overcast day, and I.... You didn't get a good look is all."

He made a sound of disbelief. "Your eyes aren't all that's different. You're still too skinny, but you look good. I always knew the Girl would be pretty."

She opened her mouth to reply but couldn't think of a thing to say. Was he making fun? She decided to pretend he hadn't said it, but the floaty feeling came back, just a little.

"Do you know I've never eaten in a restaurant before? I don't know what to do."

"All you have to do is eat. You've never been any place to eat? Not even back where you came from?"

"Baltimore. Papa did, and he took Mama sometimes, but my sisters and I never went."

"In cities they have restaurants ten times this big with white cloths on the tables and chandeliers overhead, but this isn't bad for Hubbell."

"It's nice. Kind of cozy really, and oh, does that mean we can choose?" Norah tipped her head toward the large slate board hanging on the wall beside the door to the kitchen. Chicken, beef, pork were written there, one below the other.

"Usually. Sometimes they forget to erase if they run out of something. Remember, Tommy back there is some behind you as a cook."

"There were lumps in my gravy tonight."

"There are lumps in his every night."

She laughed, glad to be free and away from the Tindells, amused by the covert glances at Caleb from two young women across the room. Curiosity provoked those glances. And envy. Scary or not, he was handsome in a dangerous way. Light from the nearest lamp picked out gold glints in his hair and in the two-day beard growth covering the lean cheeks and jaw.

The gun belt over gray wool trousers emphasized his lean hips, and the blue flannel shirt did the same to his shoulders. Or maybe the clothes had nothing to do with it. Other men in the small restaurant sported suits, white shirts, and collars with ties. Compared to Caleb Sutton they all looked tame and—ordinary.

Tonight she didn't care if he was one of Webster Van Cleve's hired killers and should probably be in prison. She was out in the night. He'd said she was pretty and a good cook, and once long ago he had been the Boy.

Tommy's cooking was as advertised. One side of her pork chop was black, and both the mashed potatoes and the gravy over them were lumpy.

Norah hardly noticed. Unlike Joe, who always ate with single-minded devotion to his food, Caleb showed a sociable streak.

"Did the old bat give you a hard time about coming out tonight?"

"She's not that bad. She was—nosy."

"She's afraid you're meeting some beau and might be on your way to remarrying, and she'd lose you."

Norah paused, fork in midair. She decided to ignore the beau part. "She'd rather have notice so she could go straight from me to someone new, but she wouldn't mind losing me.

She's used to unsatisfactory help and having to find replacements."

"You're not unsatisfactory. Tindell's telling everyone in his saloon they should place their bets months further on. He likes your cooking, and she admits you're the best worker they ever had."

"I don't believe it. She never said anything like that."

"Of course not. You might want more money."

"She's paying me ten dollars a month."

His brows went up slightly. "That is pretty good. Have they got you eating their leftovers?"

"You shouldn't believe the worst of everyone. I cook enough for all of us, and I set mine aside before I serve. I'm eating like royalty."

"Better than this then."

"Better food, but eating alone in the kitchen... I *like* this, Caleb. Thank you for bringing me here."

"No one's called me Caleb for a long time. Just Cal."

"Oh, I shouldn't call you either. Mr. Sutton. I'm sorry."

"Given names are fine with me. After all we have history."

Still flustered, Norah said, "I shouldn't.... If you don't like Caleb I won't.... Did your uncle call you that?"

"No, he never called me by my name that I can remember. The one who called me Caleb...." He gave her an assessing look before reaching for his coffee. "Go ahead and use Caleb. It's good."

Scars stood out on his hands, straight white lines, thin and thick, short and long. The fact she hadn't noticed before proved how much he had upset her the day they argued in the house.

"I didn't make those scars, did I?"

She almost bit her tongue, embarrassed to have asked anything that personal and rude. What was the matter with her tonight? Before she could withdraw the question and apologize, he answered.

"Only one." He traced one thin line that ran from the base of a thumb and disappeared under his shirt sleeve. "I'd still owe you if you made them all."

"You really don't owe me anything. You never did, but if you felt you needed to do something, you did more than enough."

He ignored her, still fingering the scars. "The rest are from skinning knives. After I got away from your wagons, I skinned for the buffalo hunter who found me for a few years. When I started, the other skinners thought it was funny to jerk the hide so the knife slipped."

"But that's dangerous."

"It was all dangerous."

"What did you mean when you said that buffalo hunter thought you owed him forever for saving you?"

"He thought he had a slave for life, and for five years, he did."

"And then you left him?"

"And then I killed him."

She gasped and dropped the fork.

"Why the surprise?" he asked. "You know what I am. Not worth saving, right?"

One corner of his mouth curled in a cynical half-smile, and his dark eyes chilled her to the bone. Once she had thought brown eyes always warm. No more. Why would he tell her a thing like that? To scare her, that's why. Her first instinct, to jump out of the chair and run, died.

"If you've changed your mind and don't want company for supper, say so. Otherwise stop trying to spoil my first time in a restaurant."

The half-smile widened into a real one, even if it was in that controlled, inward way.

They ate in silence for a few moments before he said, "Talking about slaves, you can't mean to be that old lady's slave forever. What are you going to do?"

"Not kill her."

He ignored both her tone and the words. "Now that you've cleaned out your place, are you going to sell?"

"How do you know I cleaned it out?"

"I stopped by to see how you were doing yesterday. I figured you had to be in town and came looking."

"Well, I'm not selling. The Carburys helped me pack and store things in their barn. I'm going to work here as long as I can, and then I'll have cash money and can go home."

"Go home and do what? Sit and starve again?"

The harsh growl of his voice had people at other tables turning to stare, then looking away quickly. Norah didn't want to quarrel with him in public. In fact she didn't want to quarrel with him at all. Not tonight. Tonight was going to be a good memory in spite of him.

"I'm not sure yet. I'll think of something. I always wanted goats, but Joe wouldn't hear of it."

"Goats."

At least that took the snarl out of him. "Goats. On our way out here all those years ago, we met a farmer who kept goats. He told us how they're much easier to keep than cows. They give a lot of milk for their size, and since you don't keep just one, they don't all freshen and go dry at the same time, so you always have milk. You can sell goats' milk. And cheese.

"Cheese."

"Yes," she said firmly. "Or if not that, something else. If I can keep earning long enough and save, I can find a way. Mr. Van Cleve's last offer for the farm was a hundred dollars, you know. I can earn that in ten months."

"Van Cleve and Preston will be after you again if you go back. So long as you're in town, you're safe, but I can't keep them away from you much longer. I've been thinking of moving on."

Good. With luck he'd stop thinking about it and do it. One night like this to leave everyday cares behind and eat in a restaurant was a treat, and she wanted to erase the memory of that terrible shrieking time, but she didn't want him in her life.

"Where will you go?"

"West. It's a big land."

"I'm glad you're going to quit working for Mr. Van Cleve. I can't understand a man like that. Why is he so greedy? He has so much land. Even when he first started pushing people out years ago, he already had so much."

"Some men are just made that way. If he owned everything from here to the Mississippi, he'd start coveting everything to the ocean."

"And you, Caleb Sutton? Are you just made a certain way? Couldn't you live some other way?"

"I don't want to live another way. Look around you. Everyone you see is either predator or prey, wolf or rabbit. Wolf is better."

Norah feigned interest in the last of her meal. She didn't want to see the world in such stark terms. She didn't want to hear any more ugly things from Caleb Sutton.

They avoided touchy subjects after that and walked back to Tindells' in silence. Safely inside with the door locked behind her, Norah leaned her head against the door and listened as his footsteps crunched on the gravel walk and faded away.

7

A NIGHT IN the hotel left Cal scratching at red welts and determined never to set foot in the place again. Yet hopping the
first train out of Hubbell was no longer possible.

Last night Norah Hawkins had been the kind of woman
he'd always pictured the Girl growing to be.

The first sight of her hanging laundry in Tindells' yard had
been a pleasant surprise. The dark hair made such a thick
knot at the back of her neck he had to wonder how long that
hair would be down. Her face was still too thin, but her eyes
no longer looked like bruises. She was pretty, even if that big
white apron and the colorless shawl that didn't seem to be
keeping her warm made her into some sexless servant.

In the restaurant, though—in the restaurant the first sight
of her without the pathetic excuse for a coat had taken his
breath away. The thin fabric of her old dress outlined her
unmentionables underneath and the real shape of her, and
her real shape was just fine.

She was as she should be, female in an honest way, the
curves of her breast, waist, and rear inviting hands. His first
instinct had been to wrap her right up in the coat again. Then
he'd realized the lamplight wasn't strong enough for anyone

farther away than he was to see what he saw and settled in to enjoy the sight.

She also acted the way the Girl should act, not having a female conniption fit when he told her about Jake Kepler. If a good temper tantrum had jerked her out of that spineless, suicidal behavior he'd first seen, he'd be happy to keep her angry for....

Catching where his thoughts were headed, he stopped them in their tracks. Whatever else he owed her, not thinking about her like that had to be high on the list.

If she lived a quiet life with that husband on their farm, her claim they were even would wash, but as long as she was a target for Van Cleve, she couldn't set him free, and he could see no way to free himself.

So he needed a place to stay, a place close enough to keep an eye on Norah, and her house was sitting empty and would do fine. After all, something about the place appealed, and he was staying around Hubbell because of her. He'd 'fess up and pay her rent when he left, which would add to her cash supply.

Of course staying in the soddy presented its own problems. He could get enough supplies out there on a packhorse, but he'd have to buy one. Two horses in winter needed feed. Not only was there none on the place, there wasn't so much as a foot of fencing to keep them from wandering off what grass Hawkins had left unplowed and onto V Bar C land.

By the time he purchased a packhorse and everything he needed and started for the Hawkins farm, Cal had an idea about feed. Pushing both horses at a steady pace, he kept a sharp eye on the countryside for any sign of Preston or other Van Cleve men.

A bullet could ruin all his plans, and he really wanted to see how those blue curtains looked by lamplight.

NORAH WALKED TO church on Sundays at the same time as the Tindell family but joined Becky and her husband Ethan in a back pew for the service. Somehow hugs and inquiries about health always filled the minutes before church, and Norah had to hurry off afterward to get the Tindells' dinner, ah, *luncheon* on the table.

The Sunday after her evening out with Caleb Sutton, Norah stole a few extra minutes to talk to Becky. "Do you know anyone in town who's been here a long time and who could tell me about Henry Sutton and his family?"

"Oh, you mean about your gunslinger's family?" Becky all but jumped up and down, her blonde curls bouncing around her eager face. "You've seen him again, haven't you? You never said what he looks like. Is he handsome?"

Becky was a sweetheart, but sometimes her youth made her hard to deal with. "I don't have enough time to...."

"You have enough time to visit some old codger you don't know yet and listen to him ramble on, but you can't visit me? You can't even tell me a little about the man you want to know about? Do you want my help or not?"

"I'm sorry," Norah said, the barb about not visiting Becky hitting home. "Yes, I've seen him. No, he's not handsome. He's scary, if you must know." Dampening Becky's enthusiasm seemed more important than literal truth.

"Oooh. Scary how? Is he big? Bigger than Joe?"

Asking Becky for help had been a mistake. Next week Norah would ask the preacher. "He's at least an inch shorter than Joe, maybe two."

"For heaven's sake, that means he's still at least six feet tall. Joe was a monster."

"Joe was not a monster!"

"Well, a bear then, or a buffalo."

In spite of her exasperation, Norah had to smile. She'd often thought of Joe as a bear.

"Caleb Sutton is more of a wolf and every bit as dangerous. He said he might leave town soon, but in case he doesn't and he comes by again, I think it would be prudent to find out as much about him as I can."

"Prudent." Becky made a face as if the word tasted bad and stopped teasing. "Do you mean—is he bothering you?"

"No, not any more. I mean not that he ever did, but it felt that way at first. Please, do you know anyone I could ask about him?"

Ethan wrapped an arm around his bride and said, "She's being a brat. My grandfather claims he put up the first tent to start the town. Roy Butler. He lives...."

Becky put a hand over his mouth and favored Norah with a defiant smile. "You can just stop by our house, and I'll show you where Grampa Roy lives."

"I can't be there until two."

"Two! You're supposed to have the afternoon off. After. Noon. It's afternoon right now, and you should just...."

Ethan pulled Becky away, a smile on his face. "We'll see you at two, Mrs. Hawkins."

Norah didn't make it to the young couple's rented house near the railroad station until almost two thirty, her tongue sore from biting it over all the last minute Tindell demands. Her bad mood lifted when she found Becky and Ethan had brought Grampa Roy Butler to their house and primed him for a chat.

"Ethan wouldn't even let me ask him about your gunslinger yet," Becky grumbled. "What could it hurt if I warmed him up for you?"

Ethan's grandfather had snowy white hair and a stout body he had trouble lifting from his chair when Norah walked into the parlor, but she saw a keen interest in her and her concerns in his bright blue eyes. She hoped he'd known the Suttons well enough to turn that gaze on them.

Becky insisted on showing Norah every detail of the house. Norah controlled her envy over the separate rooms and wood floors and even over Becky's new sewing machine, but the soapstone sink in the kitchen with the water right over it turned her green. The house was cozy with some things she recognized from the Carbury house and others that were new.

She caught herself taking comfort from the memory of Caleb Sutton telling her he liked the way she had fixed the soddy. He had, in fact, paid her more compliments in the hour or two they'd spent together than her husband had in eight years of marriage, and he'd done it in spite of the fact the one time he'd been in the house all they'd done was insult each other.

Compliments or not, he was evil, or at least very bad. The whole reason for her visit was to determine how bad, and she couldn't let a few casually tossed out compliments affect her common sense.

When Becky finally ended the house tour, Norah settled in a chair across the fire from Grampa Butler and leaned toward him. "I appreciate your coming to tell me a little about town history, Mr. Butler."

"I don't think a young woman like you is interested in town history. With you ladies, it's always a man. Who is it you're investigating this week?"

Norah couldn't help but laugh. "Caleb Sutton. He's Henry Sutton's nephew."

"Caleb. Caleb. I never heard of a Sutton with that name. Henry had three sons, Jason, Eli, and hmm. Malachi? No. Matthew? No. Something like that. It'll come to me."

A stab of disappointment went through Norah, but the old man continued.

"Nephew. I do remember a nephew, but I never heard a name. Only saw him a couple of times. Skinny little boy, a towhead. Never heard a word out of him. Sat where he was put and stared off into the distance."

Norah swallowed hard. "That's the one. So you don't know anything about him? What about the uncle? I met him a few times back when people used to get together, and he seemed ordinary enough."

"Henry Sutton was a Bible thumper, and not the good kind. You know there's good and righteous men like Reverend Densmore, there's those of us who do our best, and then there's self-righteous hypocrites. Henry was the worst kind of hypocrite. He was a mean man and used scripture to justify his meanness."

Grampa stared into the fire and stroked his chin. "Thinking back on it, I remember more. The reason I never heard the boy's name is Henry never used it. Called him the devil's spawn, bad seed, like that. He was sure dealing with the boy was earning him his ticket to heaven."

"So that's what...." Norah heard her voice wobble and started again. "Caleb told me that. He said he was the devil's spawn, but I thought he meant because he's working for Mr. Van Cleve."

"I hate to hear Henry was right about the boy, but I guess even one like him was right some of the time."

"He wasn't right!" Norah avoided Becky's knowing look and lowered her voice. "He's not a good man. He's working for Mr. Van Cleve, and that's the kind of work he does, but he's not the devil's spawn either. What could a little boy do to deserve being treated that way by his own family?"

"First thing he did was get born. Henry had a lot to say about his sister too, the boy's mother." The old man exchanged a look with Ethan. "I shouldn't be talking about this to you ladies."

Becky went to him, kissed him on the cheek, and said, "Now, Grampa, we're both *married* ladies, and I think we already know what you're going to say. Tell him it's all right, Ethan."

Ethan rolled amused eyes at his wife, but from the look he gave her, Norah knew Becky would be able to wheedle most anything from him. *I hope it lasts for her.*

Grampa also saw the way of things and continued with his story.

"It happened before they came out here, of course. They were from Pennsylvania or someplace like that, farmers, but they didn't own the land, and Henry had ambition. He saved. Considered himself thrifty, but the truth is he was a miser of the worst kind. Anyway, he came out here as soon as he learned he could get government land for a dollar and twenty-five cents an acre. No Homestead Act back then, you know. He bought under the Preemption Act."

Norah nodded. Her own family had discussed the ways to acquire government land for hours on end back in Baltimore. She knew them all.

"So Henry's sister got herself in the family way without a family," the old man said. "At least without the husband part of a family."

"And the baby was Caleb."

"Must have been. Like I said, he never used that name. Henry still got himself worked into a lather about it all those years later when I knew him, and he'd rage on about it at the drop of a hat. What bothered him most was she never re-pented and she never named the man. So he cast her out."

"Cast her out?" Norah said doubtfully, unable to believe he meant those words literally.

"Made her leave that farm that had belonged to both their parents, sent her out into the world without a dime or a change of clothes."

Becky made a sound as if someone had hurt her. "My folks would never do that. They'd be so hurt and angry, but they'd never do that." Ethan reached over and took her hand.

Norah wished she had someone to hold her hand too. "He kept her baby and made her leave?"

"Oh, no, he shoved her out into the world with the babe in the womb as they say."

"Did she die birthing him? Is that how Henry got Caleb?"

"No, he didn't get the boy until years later. The sister did what she had to and kept body and soul together and raised the boy." The old man eyed Ethan again, checking to see if he should stop, but Ethan said nothing.

"A prostitute," Norah said, remembering what she'd said about whores to Caleb and how that was when he'd turned nasty.

"She died when the boy was about ten, and I guess the other—people—in that place were going to keep him, but something happened."

Everyone looked at Grampa, waiting, and he drew out the pause, enjoying the attention.

"Henry didn't know exactly what happened. He claimed the boy almost killed a couple of those women, said one day the owner of the place showed up with the boy, said what happened, pushed him out of the buggy, and left. I didn't believe him then, and I still don't. It was at least a year after that I saw the boy, and he was barely big enough to kill a frog then."

Norah leaned back in her chair, closed her eyes, and thought of the Boy in the wagon and the way he'd fought the grown men who captured him. She did believe the story. Caleb could have almost killed two women at ten, especially if he had a weapon.

"It's a strange thing," the old man said thoughtfully. "To hear Henry tell it, on the one hand the boy was born bad. Sins of the father and all that. On the other, he was determined to drive the devil out of him. He was hard on his own sons. They were always quieter than healthy boys should be. The youngest one, Micah, that was his name, he left home young, and so far as I ever heard no one saw hide nor hair of him again. I never heard what happened to the nephew."

"He ran away," Norah whispered. "He ran away, and a girl helped him keep running."

8

CAL KNEW HE was getting way too fond of something that didn't belong to him, but he found a peace he'd never known in Norah's house and on her land.

He slept without nightmares, the ghosts weren't too troublesome, and he walked the land studying what had been done in the past and planning what he'd do the same and what he'd do different.

A few forays onto the V Bar C kept his hand in and provided material to partition the soddy shed for storage and for shelter for the horses if a blizzard hit.

Inventorying every abandoned homestead for miles in all directions, he found two places with enough unburned hay to be worth salvaging and hauled it home by travois.

Home. That was the problem. It felt like that but wasn't.

Another trip to Hubbell assured him Norah Hawkins was safe. Her first month at Tindells' had passed, and a lot of disappointed bettors in the saloon were trying again with dates far into the spring and even into early summer.

Cal thought of Norah collecting her ten dollars and pictured her in a new dress with color. Yellow as sunshine. Blue as the sky. Anything but gray.

Toward the end of December, he decided to see for himself.

Wednesday afternoon. He'd checked and made sure of the day. Cal waited until Norah stepped out of the back door with a rug over her arm. She shook it, threw it over the clothesline, and pulled out a carpet beater.

The bright dress he'd imagined was nowhere in sight. Her old coat hung open and under that was the big white apron that hid everything female.

Her dress was gray, not gray from a washed out color, but *gray*. Between that and the little white hat on her head a twist of anger started in his belly. That hat looked just like the thing that had been on the head of the woman serving food in Van Cleve's house.

"Didn't you use any of your ten dollars to buy a decent dress?"

She started at the sound of his voice, and he expected hostile words right back. Instead he got a smile that on another woman would mean she was glad to see him.

"I thought you said you were going to move on."

"I changed my mind, and you changed the subject. All your other dresses are gray, but they don't look like they started that way. Why get a new dress and get it gray?"

"Mrs. Tindell likes her housekeeper to wear gray." She gave the rug a good whop.

"If she likes it, did she buy it?"

"She bought the material." Another whop.

"Did you buy something with some color for yourself?"

She stopped beating the rug but didn't look at him. "No, I.... The dresses I have are all I need. I'm saving my money."

A very good liar himself, Cal recognized a bad liar when he saw one.

"She did pay you, didn't she?"

"Of course she paid me. I have the whole ten dollars."

Whop.

"You hit that thing again when we're talking, and I'll take it away and break it."

She lowered the beater and stood facing him, slightly slumped, smaller than he remembered. He wanted to grab her by the shoulders and shake the defeat right out of her.

"You don't understand. I have to keep working."

"You need to tell that old woman to back off."

"I did ask her if we could send at least the linens to the laundry. She lectured me for half an hour on how she doesn't want to sleep on sheets a Chinaman touched."

Norah walked to the porch steps and sat down as if now that she had stopped moving, holding herself up was too much effort.

"You know how you told me I was doing so well? I think the more I do, the more she decides I can do, but at least I'm working for my second ten dollars now."

"How many goats will that buy?"

"Don't make fun. I don't know. I don't even know where to buy goats."

"I'm not making fun. If you can eat them and drink their milk, they'd be useful, and anything you can sell for cash is a good idea, but you don't want livestock until Van Cleve gives up. If it's alive, someone can kill it."

She bobbed her head a little, a faraway look on her face, then snapped her attention back and lifted the beater in her hand. "I have to get back to work."

"It's Wednesday. It's afternoon. You get in there and tell that old bat you're leaving and not going to be back till late. Bring your ten dollars. We'll walk through town, and you can buy something pretty, and I'll take you for your second restaurant meal."

She bit her bottom lip and a little color flushed across her pale face. "Caleb, I can't. I want to, but I can't."

"You get in there and tell her, or I'm going to find her and wrap my hands around her neck so tight she'll wish I was a Chinaman."

Norah scrambled to her feet. "An hour, I need an hour."

As she disappeared through the door, he yelled, "Put on your own dress, and get rid of that damn hat."

When she met him at the back gate less than an hour later, her hair no longer straggled around her face, which shone with recent scrubbing. She didn't really look better in one of her own old dresses, her colorless scarf, and shabby coat, but at least she looked like Norah Hawkins again. The eager way she'd accompanied him last time was gone, though. She all but dragged her feet as they approached the main street of town.

Finally she stopped altogether. "I can't do this. I can't go to the stores."

"So she never paid you."

"Yes, she paid me. Here, look."

She dug around in her pocket, brought out a handkerchief bundled around a small object, and untied it to reveal a ten dollar gold piece.

Cal took it from her, gave it a heft and a suspicious look but had to admit it was the real thing.

"You can't be such a miser you won't spend any of that for things you need."

Color rose across her cheeks. He looked around, saw a bench in front of the boot maker's shop, and pushed her down.

"We know some pretty bad things about each other," he said. "How can you be too embarrassed to admit why you can't spend any of that?"

She darted a glance at him, then bowed her head again. "Joe and I got that land from my father, you know."

"I heard. Van Cleve's still angry your father didn't sell to him."

"Papa wasn't much of a farmer. Dreaming about it back East was one thing. Being out here.... He was glad to sell out and leave, but he didn't want Mr. Van Cleve to have it, and Joe couldn't pay him even as much as Mr. Van Cleve offered. He was offering a dollar an acre in those days."

"So your father gave it to your husband."

"No, Joe paid enough cash money so Papa could move on, and he assumed Papa's debt. Papa owed everyone in town. Everyone agreed to that. Joe was a good farmer, and he did pay down the accounts, but no one would give him credit. He had to pay cash and pay on Papa's accounts every time."

Understanding came to Cal. "You're saying they expect you to pay those accounts now?"

She nodded. "Not all at once, but to buy anything, I have to pay something." She looked up, her face tight with distress. "I know I owe it. I want to pay it, but it would be like paying double for anything. I only have ten dollars, and it's the first money I ever had other than a penny for candy from Papa when I was little."

He pulled her back to her feet. "I'll buy you a dress so long as it isn't gray."

"You can't do that. People are already talking about us."

"You can pay me back."

"No one will know that. My friend Becky will buy me anything I want. I just need to make time to see her."

"You have time right now. I'll walk you there, you get her to help, and I'll meet you later."

He had to find a way to set her on a better path. With her earnings, what he'd pay for rent, and what Van Cleve would pay for the land, she could get by for a year or more, long enough to find a decent man and marry again, or work that suited where someone appreciated her.

He decided to ponder on it some more in the barber's chair. If she could buy a new dress, he could sit through a shave and haircut.

BECKY'S SURPRISE AT finding Norah on her doorstep changed to delight at the prospect of tricking Mr. Lawson and buying Norah something pretty. The two of them pored over Becky's copies of *Harper's Bazaar* until they agreed on a pattern.

"Promise you won't get anything extravagant," Norah begged as they hurried to Lawson's.

"Of course I won't. Don't you trust me? I'll get something you'll love. I'm so pale I have to wear pastels or I disappear, but with your dark hair, you could wear red. Red with black trim would be perfect."

Norah had always envied Becky's pale blonde hair and coloring that allowed her to wear pastels and creamy yellows. Becky glowed with youth and a happy newlywed's optimism. Would Caleb Sutton consider Becky pretty, or even beautiful?

Catching the drift of her thoughts, Norah jerked them back to the matter at hand. "No! Becky, please. Something with a little color, but not so bold. Blue? I'm sure there will be some practical material in blue, and I can make trim. There's some of the gray material Mrs. Tindell bought for my dress left. I know she'll let me use that, and some white from the aprons."

"Pft." Becky dismissed thrifty concerns like that with a wave of her hand. "All right. If I can find a blue with a little style, I'll get that, but you're getting real trim that suits if I have to buy it for you myself."

"Oh, no, you don't. I have the money, and I'm buying my own. You can't know how good it feels to know I earned it."

"You earned twice that much."

Sometimes it felt like that, but ten dollars a month plus room and board was generous, and they both knew it.

Norah waited out of sight of Lawson's windows, fidgeting with nerves. Becky skipped out of the store with a paper-wrapped package clutched under her arm and wouldn't release it until they were in her parlor. Norah opened the package with trepidation and stared at yards of fine wool in a deep rose shade and a piece of cream-colored lace.

"See? See. Maybe not red but almost as good. You'll look wonderful."

Norah touched the cloth gently, half afraid it would change under her touch. "It's beautiful. Thank you."

Becky threw out her arms and danced around the parlor. "You can stay for supper, and we'll get started making it up."

Hating to disappoint the girl, Norah shook her head. "I'm sorry, Becky. I wish I could, but I already promised...."

"Do not tell me you have to go back and make supper for that mean old witch and her family. Do not."

"No, I promised Caleb Sutton I'd have supper with him at Tommy's."

"Oh, he's courting."

"He's not courting. He's—overseeing."

"What does that mean?"

"No matter what I tell him, he still feels an obligation, and he's trying to make me do what he thinks is sensible. Sell the farm, find a different position, like that."

Becky's excited expression changed to disapproval. "He's not looking out for you. He's working for Mr. Van Cleve. He probably gets a bonus if he gets you to sell. Stay here and eat with us. The sooner you get shut of him the better."

Norah knew Becky was right, but even so—supper with newlyweds, watching the way they looked at each other, or supper in the restaurant with Caleb Sutton, who said she was pretty, even if he was buttering her up so he could get a bonus. After all, she wasn't going to sell the farm, no matter who advised it.

"I'm sorry, Becky, but I promised. Next week. Next week we can spend time. There. Now I've promised you."

AFTER CONSIDERABLE INTERNAL debate, Norah decided to leave the package with the rose wool material in her room. If Caleb Sutton wanted to see what Becky had purchased, he could just come back once the dress was made up.

Descending the backstairs to the kitchen, she heard the sound of voices and laughter from the parlor and stopped to listen. Mrs. Tindell had dragooned her sons into hanging Christmas decorations.

After a morning spent bringing boxes from the attic, opening each one and setting the decorations out, dusting and washing when necessary, Norah's melancholy had returned, only to be banished by Caleb Sutton's appearance. The sounds of the young men teasing each other and their mother didn't bother her this evening.

I have Christmas presents of my own. I spent time with my friend laughing and teasing too. I have material for the most beautiful dress I've ever had, and I still have an evening to spend with a man who says I'm pretty. Even if he is lying, he's handsome in a scary way, and it's because of him I have the other things.

His voice came out of the winter night exactly as she expected. "Did your friend get you something not gray?"

"She did. It's beautiful."

"So where is it?" Close now, his head dipped as he stared down at the hem of her old dress.

"In my room. I have to make it up."

"And you're not going to even tell me the color."

"No, I'm not."

"That'll teach me."

"No, it won't, but I don't care. Are you sure you don't want to meet the Butlers? They're young, but they're good people."

"You don't want me around good people."

"What does that say about me?"

"You lose your way now and then."

That was so close to what Norah thought about her own behavior it silenced her the rest of the way to Tommy's. At least before he opened the restaurant door, she remembered to say what she had rehearsed as she got ready to meet him.

"I know you're going to tell me how I should sell to Mr. Van Cleve, but I'm not going to listen. You can try to scare me or scandalize me, but it's not going to work. I'm going to have a lovely time, and I'm going to coax you or trick you into telling me about the places you've been and things you've seen that

I never have and never will—things that have nothing to do with killing anyone."

"And what are you going to tell me?"

"I'll tell you about Baltimore, what I remember, and neither one of us will say a cross word or be angry with the other."

"That'll be a trick all right."

Embarrassed again at her own shabby clothing, Norah didn't really look at Caleb until she removed her scarf and coat and he hung them on the pegs by the door alongside his own. When she did, her heart skipped a beat.

Clean-shaven, dark blond hair freshly shorn, if the sight of Caleb Sutton had provoked sly glances from other women the last time they'd been here, those women would be falling off their chairs tonight.

Forgetting all about her old dress, she sailed to the empty table closest to the stove, absolutely certain she was the envy of every female in the room.

HE HAD COME to town resolved to tell her he was using her house and to pay her a fair rent. He'd come to take her out, determined to convince her to sell the land and stop being stubborn.

Watching her now, knowing either subject would spoil the evening for her, Cal decided to wait until next time and knew there would be a next time.

Hard to believe a woman's eyes could shine like that over eating mediocre food in a small restaurant, and the half-smile playing over her mouth started him thinking thoughts that should be reserved for a different kind of man.

A woman that pretty in an old rag would light up the room in a new dress with some color, although so long as no one else noticed, he enjoyed the private view of the limp cloth clinging to every female curve again.

There had to be a way to help her, and if he wasn't going to urge her to sell the farm tonight....

"Have you thought of collecting all the Tindell bet money yourself? Collect your next ten dollars, get your friend to bet the next day for you, quit, and even if you split it, it must be hundreds, or would that be the kind of cheat only evil men like me think up?"

"It would be cheating," she said primly. Then she laughed. "But we did talk about it. The problem is so many people have bet on those days, we wouldn't win much. Becky's husband checked for us. Every day has four or five names down, and some have as many as ten."

"Blue."

It only took her a moment. "Not blue."

He answered her questions about places he'd been and listened with half an ear to her memories of Baltimore.

"Yellow."

"Never yellow. I look sallow."

Whatever that meant. "Green."

"Not green."

He walked her to Tindells' back door, not sorry he'd listened to her. Why not give her an evening without harsh words. Next time he'd see the new dress and pay her the rent, convince her to sell.

A lamp burned in Tindells' kitchen, spreading just enough light through the window to see the pale oval of her face. He expected her to thank him the way she had before and disappear through the door. Instead she stayed close.

"You know that Christmas is only a few days away, don't you?"

He'd never thought about it. Christmas was just another day in his world.

"Thank you for today and this evening. This afternoon and tonight were my Christmas presents, and I know it's greedy, but I have one more thing to ask."

He tensed, expecting her to ask him to stay away. He didn't want to and wasn't going to.

"Would you hold me? Just for a minute?"

Surprise left him speechless and frozen.

"I'm sorry. I promised myself not to do that. It's forward and wrong, and I'm so sorry." She fumbled her key in the lock.

Still without a word, he turned her back around, slid his hands around her waist, and pulled her into his arms. She melted into him, head on his shoulder, her hands slipping round, holding him as he held her.

"I'm sorry, but it feels so good to be held," she whispered.

"Stop apologizing. You're not exactly hurting me. With a little more meat on your bones, you'd feel pretty good."

That was as big a lie as he'd told for a while. She felt more than good already, like something a smarter man would keep hold of, like something a man who had lived a different kind of life could keep hold of.

Her appearance had fooled him. She felt fragile, of no more substance than his ghosts. Was that how he had felt to her all those years ago as she kept her hand on his shoulder? Summer then, though, the warmth of her hand comforting through the flimsy rag of his shirt, not like now with the bulk of winter coats between them.

She straightened and stepped away, turned the key, and disappeared.

"Thank you, Caleb. Merry Christmas."

Merry Christmas, Norah.

9

WHEN MRS. TINDELL summoned her to the parlor on the last
Monday in January, Norah almost groaned out loud.

The parlor was the preferred locale for announcements of
new duties or faults found. Whether the next lecture would
be about the dangers of letting foreigners touch the linens or
a speck of dust found in some obscure corner of the house,
it would waste time and make her feel more than ever like a
faceless drudge.

Mrs. Tindell came straight to the point. "In spite of your
best efforts to keep your activities secret, yesterday after
church I had to endure the humiliation of Mrs. Grennich telling me what you've been doing with all this free time you've
taken. You know full well I won't have an employee of mine
associated with ruffians of the sort Mr. Van Cleve employs.
Did you think you could keep sneaking out with him, ruining
yourself and me with you?"

The accusation surprised Norah so much she took half a
step back. Mrs. Tindell made it sound as if Norah had been
caught meeting Caleb at the hotel.

"I didn't sneak anywhere. I spend most of my free time with
my friend Mrs. Butler. Mr. Sutton only comes to town every
two or three weeks, and when he does, we walk through town

in broad daylight and visit shops, and he takes me to supper at Tommy's restaurant where at least a dozen people see us."

"And where he whistles at you and remarks on your clothing."

Norah couldn't suppress a smile at the memory. Caleb's reaction to the sight of the rose dress had been extravagant and made her feel like a queen. Of course before the evening was over he'd called her stupid and stubborn and said the look on her face would better suit a mule.

Smiling was a mistake. Mrs. Tindell's expression hardened further. "You lied to me when you said an old friend was only in town for the day and you needed extra time. You led me to believe the friend was female."

Extra time! "I know I did not say my friend was female. If you assumed, I'm sorry. Caleb Sutton is an old friend, and he was only in town that day. I met him when my family first came to Hubbell almost fifteen years ago."

Ignoring that, Mrs. Tindell said, "If you wish to continue your employment here, you won't see him again."

Anger blossomed hot and red behind Norah's eyes. Yes, indeed, an old bat. "My free time is my own, and there's been much less of it than you promised. You can't dictate my private life."

"I can, and I am. My position in this community is important to me."

"Your husband owns a saloon!"

"Innkeeping is a respectable profession with a long history behind it."

Norah opened her mouth to enlighten the woman about those respectable establishments, then snapped it shut. Mrs. Tindell knew full well what her husband did. That was her problem.

"I'll be gone before the next thirty minutes pass," Norah said. "I'm sure you can have the last of my wages ready by then."

"Your salary is by the month. Today is two days short of the end of your month."

"I don't believe you're that stingy, Mrs. Tindell. Everyone else in town does, but I don't. I'll pack my things and come back here to see you."

Upstairs in the small third-floor room that had been hers, Norah threw the gray dress on the narrow bed, along with the silly white cap and baggy apron she disliked almost as much as Caleb did.

After changing into one of her own dresses, she repinned her hair and threw immediate necessities into the box she'd brought them in. She'd have to send someone for her trunk.

Mrs. Tindell still sat behind her desk, spine rigid and not touching the back of her chair. When Norah approached, the woman slid a single ten dollar gold piece across the shiny surface.

"If it is as you say, I'd like to think you are right and the rest of the town wrong. Are you firm in your decision? You've been a satisfactory employee in other ways."

"Yes, I am. My private life is my own."

"Is he worth it?"

Norah laughed out loud. "No. He's even worse than you think, but he's—he's someone who matters in my life." She searched for the right words to explain her feelings to herself as much as Mrs. Tindell. "I won't cast him out."

To her surprise, the older woman nodded. "You left the gray dress in your room, didn't you? I'll put it in with your other things. I hope you don't regret what you're doing. Good bye, Norah."

Norah left through the front door, her box of belongings clutched to her chest, her own coat on her back, and Joe's over her arm.

The brass horse on the door no longer winked at her. She hoped he recovered from her polishing soon and no one else ever robbed him of his personality.

When she reached Becky's, Becky would fuss and sympathize and help her plan what to do next. In fact she'd get to visit with Becky as much as either of them wanted in the next few days, not just an hour or so after church.

Except Becky and Ethan hadn't been at church yesterday. Her steps slowed as memory of her last visit with Becky rose.

She had only half-listened to Becky's happy babble about how her brothers were coming to town to escort her to the farm for a week because Ethan was going somewhere on railroad business.

As the reality of her situation struck home, Norah sank down on a bench in front of the bakery, glad to put the box down. How could she have forgotten?

She could have agreed with Mrs. Tindell for a few days and made her grand gesture when she had a safe place to stay. Folding her arms over her stomach, she bent forward, holding the ache inside.

She wanted to go home. Maybe she'd have to come back here and find out if Tommy wanted a better cook for his restaurant or if there was other work for someone like her, but right now she wanted to go home and visit Joey and sleep in her own bed and cook on her own stove and wash and mend her own clothes and linens.

A gust of wind blew right through her coat, and she exchanged it for Joe's. The hotel probably wouldn't even let a woman on her own stay there, but Mabel Carbury's description of the place kept Norah from trying to find out. She couldn't ask slight acquaintances like Ethan's family for charity. She couldn't.

The boarding house on the other side of town was respectable. Maybe she could rent a room there until someone who lived near her came to town. If nothing else, Becky's brothers would bring her back in a week, and they'd take Norah home.

The coins in her pocket already felt lighter, as if they could blow away on the wind. She picked up her box and trudged on.

CAL BANGED THE last nail into the grain bin he'd built for Norah Hawkins' soddy shed, straightened, looked at the thing, and threw the hammer across the yard.

After ripping the burned out buildings on the rise to the west apart, salvaging every piece of wood untouched by flames or only partially consumed, he'd sorted the pile into firewood and building wood and kept busy on projects like the bin.

The problem was why. Why was he fixing and building on someone else's land, land by all rights he shouldn't even be standing on? He fetched the hammer from where it had landed, put it away, and headed for the winter-barren fields.

Coming back to Hubbell had been a spur of the moment thing, born of boredom with working as a peacekeeper in a Wichita saloon and vague thoughts of revenge on Henry Sutton. He'd never expected to feel drawn to the land, to begin thinking about settling down, living by the cycles of the earth and growing things.

He'd have never believed he could be comfortable in any sod house, but this one with the muslin wall coverings that made it glow by lamplight and the curtains that showed someone cared enough to fix the place up was a place without nightmares. The ghosts came, but not so often, and they seemed less and less substantial. When he first moved in, he put the one book he could carry in his saddlebags on the crate by the bed, and since then he'd bought two others and kept them all.

More and more he thought about Norah in town, working half to death to earn ten dollars a month, and saw his own desire for the land and the house as the solution to both their problems. He could pay her the true worth of the place, and she could buy something smaller, close to town.

She could have her goats and enough to live on until she found a decent man. For all he knew goats could provide a living for a woman.

The last time he'd been in town he'd planned to confess to living here and come to an arrangement about rent. To start with she was so pleased about her new dress and looked so pretty, he'd put off serious talk. Then she'd gotten muley the minute he tried to talk to her about the place at all, so things had turned testy for a while. She'd been in no mood to ask him to hold her that night for sure.

He'd been keeping track of the days, knew it was Tuesday. If he started for town now, he could get there with an hour or so of light left. No more dancing around it, he needed to talk to her long and hard.

She'd fuss and call him names, but in the end.... In the end he wasn't sure what she'd do, but if he wanted to work this land, he needed to own it long before planting season.

Snow flurries swirled around him the last miles to the town, bringing an early night to the prairie and damp cold that settled in his bones. He left the horses at Ogden's stables and headed for the Royal Flush, wondering if the barkeeper would take a bribe again to let him spend the night in that storeroom upstairs. The man had been incredulous at the thought anyone could sleep through the noise from downstairs and the whores' rooms around, but sleeping in a brothel never bothered Cal so long as he could lock the door.

Shouts and whoops from the saloon reached him before he could even see the building. He'd heard quieter Fourth of July celebrations. Pushing through the crowd inside, he saw rows of stacked coins on the bar, the bartender and two of the whores counting more from the huge jar that had held the Tindell bets. A man put two-bits in the jar and wrote his name next to a day on the crude calendars tacked to the walls.

Cal bit back a curse. Tindell's Queen of Hearts must be empty tonight.

"Who won?" he said, figuring someone close enough to hear him would be eager to answer.

Sure enough. "Them fellers up at the front table there. Eight of them, can you believe it?"

Of course he could believe it. There'd been a dozen names on some of the days.

"They passed a hundred and fifty dollars in the count already."

"So Mrs. Tindell got tired of her after all."

"Nobody knows for sure. Yesterday Tindell wouldn't admit she's gone. He spent the night at the Queen, and we figured he and the missus had words. He liked that gal, you know."

"So what happened to Mrs. Hawkins?"

His informant shrugged a beefy shoulder. "I don't know. Went home to kin, I guess."

No, she didn't. Cal pushed his way back out to the street. She'd go to that friend of hers. He'd walked her there the day he'd made her shop and could find it again.

The little house sat quiet and dark as the night fell around it. He knocked on the door. No answer. Knocked again.

"If someone doesn't answer a knock like that, they're not home!" A small, white-haired woman stood on the porch of the next house holding a broom as if she considered that protection.

"They have to be home."

"Well, they're not. She's visiting her family, and he's off on the railroad."

Cal said a word that had the woman and her broom off that porch and back in her house instantly.

Norah couldn't be in the hotel. She'd better not be in that damn hotel, but she'd better be someplace safe.

She wasn't in the hotel, but a nervous desk clerk pointed him at the boarding house on the east end of town.

The woman at the boarding house wasn't as brave as the one with the broom. She spoke to him through a crack in the door. He considered telling her how a shoulder against the wood would break her nose and black her eyes, considered showing her, but that was just temper. No Mrs. Hawkins at the boarding house.

He tried Tindell's saloon. The man wasn't there. No one who was knew where Mrs. Hawkins had gone. He gave serious thought to forcing his way into the Tindell house. Scaring the old lady held a certain appeal. Getting arrested didn't.

If Norah had found a ride out to the farm, he should have passed her on the road today. Frustrated and angry, worried and not wanting to admit it, Cal returned to the Royal Flush to wait until the bartender finished counting quarters and could concentrate on a bribe.

10

THE WIND STRENGTHENED to gale force overnight, covering water troughs with ice inches thick and sending thoughts of spring into hiding. Streaky gray clouds hid the sun and spit small, dry snowflakes that bounced off Norah's face and Joe's coat as she walked from the boarding house to the center of town the next morning.

She sat in front of Lawson's store, hunched against the cold, and stared steadily at the empty street, waiting. As time passed, at least a dozen figures appeared and disappeared, darting from one warm building to another, but no wagon driven by someone who would give her a ride home came down the street. No wagons at all.

One more figure appeared, leaving the saloon of all places at this unlikely hour. She recognized Caleb from the way he pulled his hat down against the wind, the way he moved—and the way he started across the street when he saw her.

Maybe he had planned to see her this afternoon. Today was Wednesday, she realized with some surprise, but she didn't want to see him, didn't want to admit failure to him.

"What are you doing sitting here like that?"

"I'm waiting to see someone who lives out near me who can give me a ride home, and I want to be alone."

He ignored what she wanted of course. She refused to look at him when he dropped down to sit on the walk beside her, his long legs stretching straight out into the street. "I heard what happened when I got to town last night. I looked for you, but I couldn't find you."

"I forgot Becky is staying with her folks this week. I forgot and had to stay at the boarding house. It's very nice, but they made me.... They don't let rooms for just a night."

"I asked there. Some woman named Pollard said no Mrs. Hawkins."

"Oh. She's the proprietor. She shouldn't have done that. She should let me decide who to see."

He didn't need to know about her problems with the owner of the boarding house. "So you spent the night in the saloon with all the men celebrating whoever won the bet?" Why did that thought bother her so much?

"Sure. Eight men split over two hundred dollars, and they probably left all of it in the saloon. So what happened?"

He didn't sound hungover or drunk, and he didn't smell like whiskey. Tobacco maybe.

"I quit," she said after a moment.

"Why?"

"She tried to control my private life."

"So what are you going to do?"

"I'm going home."

"You can't go back out there by yourself. Sell it, Norah. Stop being stubborn, show some sense, and sell it."

"Would Mr. Van Cleve give you a bonus if you convinced me to do that?"

"I'm not working for Van Cleve any more, haven't been for some time."

Astonishment broke through her determined stoicism. She stopped staring at the street and looked at him. The familiar two-day stubble covered his lean jaw, his mouth was tight with aggravation over a woman who wouldn't do what he thought she should, and once again he was proving brown eyes could be cold.

If she listened to him and showed some sense, she'd be afraid of him. Instead, against all reason, the world seemed less bleak than it had a few minutes before.

"What happened?" she said.

"I quit."

"Why?"

"He tried to control my private life."

That did it. She smiled. "Aren't we a pair."

His expression softened too. "A sorry pair. Look, you don't have to sell to him for next to nothing. Sell it to me, and I'll pay you what it's worth. You can live on that for years."

"You. What would you do with a farm?"

"Live there. Work it."

"You're not a farmer."

"The only farm work I never did was pull a plow, and that's only because Uncle Henry couldn't find a harness small enough. I liked it in spite of him. I liked watching things grow, seeing what the land can do when you take care of it. Sell it to me, and we'll both be better off."

"Will we? Would Mr. Van Cleve leave you alone because you used to work for him or because of who you are?"

"No. We didn't part friends."

"Then you wouldn't be better off. The ones who are still holding out are like the Carburys. There are enough of them to put up a good defense, but you'd be alone. He'd win, and you wouldn't have your money any more, and I wouldn't have it either because it would run out and leave me right back where I am, only older."

"I can handle Van Cleve, and you can buy a smaller place close to town and raise your goats."

Could he handle Van Cleve? Norah shivered, only partly from the cold. "I don't need a smaller place close to town. I already have a place, and it's home."

"So you're going to go back out there and starve—or let them hurt you."

"No, I'm going to go home for a while and decide what to do and start again."

He turned up the collar of his coat and pulled it closer around his neck. "Let's go someplace warm and talk about this."

"I don't want to go anywhere. I'm fine here. If you have so much money, you can buy your own land. You can find land no one's trying to steal."

"Yeah, but I like your place."

"That's the problem. It is my place. You were only inside the house once. How could you take such an affection so fast?"

He looked away down the street, his voice dropping so low she could barely hear him. "I know the place pretty well now. I've been living there a while."

"You what!"

"After I quit Van Cleve I needed a place to stay, and it was sitting there empty, so I've been living there."

"Since when?"

"Since that first time I took you to the restaurant. I went back there that night."

"You, you...." She couldn't even think of anything bad enough to call him. "You were thieving the first time I set eyes on you, and you're still thieving. That's what it is, you know, moving into my house without telling me. You saw me again. You saw me more than once after that. Why didn't you tell me? Why didn't you ask?"

"I didn't tell you because I knew you'd get like you are now, and I didn't ask because you would have said no. I'll pay you rent. Decide what it's worth for the six weeks or so, and I'll pay it."

"A hundred dollars," she said furiously. "Since you're so rich you could buy the whole place and you weren't smart enough to ask first, you can just pay a hundred dollars rent."

He glared at her, and for a second she thought he'd refuse, then he opened his coat, pulled up his shirt, and started digging around underneath. She watched in fascinated horror. After a quick check up and down the street to see if anyone was witnessing the whole thing, she went back to witnessing it herself.

Finally he brought his hand back out, holding a small sheaf of bills. He counted a hundred dollars and held it out to her. She grabbed it and watched him put the rest back where it came from.

"Money belt," he said. "Under everything where it doesn't show."

A hundred dollars. She'd been sitting here feeling sorry for herself because she'd had to give up almost everything she'd earned and pay for two weeks at the boarding house to stay there at all. Now she had a hundred dollars in her hand, as much as Mr. Van Cleve would pay for her entire property.

She ought to give some of it back. She ought to feel guilty. She pushed the bills into her pocket on top of the few coins and bills left from her wages.

"You can live on that for a year, you know," he said, "but it's not enough. A woman could make a living on your place, but you'd need to start with enough cash to hire help, and I don't see so much as a plow out there. Did you hire everything done?"

"The day you came wasn't the first time Mr. Preston and his men came to the place."

"What does that...? Are you telling me they stole farm equipment?"

"They took everything except some of the small tools."

"I never saw a plow, harrow, or anything of the kind on the ranch," Cal said thoughtfully. "I suppose they'd sell it all. Preston might even have shared what he got with his men and never mentioned it to Van Cleve. How did you harvest? Contract with reapers?"

"Yes. Threshing too."

"Not much of a crowd standing in line for that in these parts any more."

"No, getting them to come may be a problem this year, but there has to be a crop for that to be a worry. We haven't had a full crop for three years. Maybe it was just as well because with the barn burned we had no storage. Sometime in there we stopped worrying about anything except getting by."

"Stop worrying at all. Sell it to me, live off the money, or buy some smaller place that suits."

"I have a place that suits. It's home, and you better be moved out before I get there."

"Or what? You'll throw me out? You're shivering and we need to talk about this some more. I'm hungry, and if you don't get up and come along, I'm going to drag you. You can try to stop me and get an idea of your chances of throwing me out before I'm ready to leave."

Norah didn't move, staring across the street but really seeing the man beside her as she had seen him that first day in her yard. "Caleb, I know you've killed more men than just the one I saw, and I know you're a thief. You're a liar too, aren't you?"

"When it serves."

"Would you lie to me?"

She heard an impatient huff of breath. "No. But I might not tell you something, like living in your house. Then again, maybe I'm lying now."

She knew that, knew it all too well, and asked anyway, "That day with Preston, if you hadn't recognized me, would you have tried to stop them?"

"No."

"Would you have—participated?"

"No."

"Have you ever hurt a woman?"

"I did my best to kill two women once. I didn't, but I messed them up real bad."

"The prostitutes? In the place your mother used to work?"

She whirled at the sudden deep throaty sound he made, saw his face shut down, and wished she hadn't asked.

"How do you know about that?" he growled.

"Becky's husband's grandfather knew Henry Sutton. I talked to him."

"Did you. I guess you know some secrets then."

"I'm sorry. It was nosy of me, but I was...."

"Afraid."

"A little. I'm not any more."

"You should be."

"I know, but I'm not."

"Get up. We're going to the restaurant to have breakfast."

In spite of his words, he didn't move.

"We could be partners," Norah said at last.

"Partners."

"I have three hundred twenty acres and a house you want, and you have money and—abilities I need. We could be partners and both have what we want."

"And how would that work? I'd put in cash and labor and get some part of the profit if there was any, and you'd still own everything? I've already done too much work for nothing in my time."

The bitterness in his voice pierced her, and maybe that's why the next words popped out of her mouth before she thought it through.

"We could get married. You'd own it as much as me then, more probably. That would make it a real partnership."

He recoiled as if he'd been burned, managing to put several extra feet of the walk between them before she finished speaking. "You're out of your mind. You don't want to be married to me."

No, she didn't, but it wouldn't last very long. He might stay long enough to get in a crop this year, but farming would bore a man like him in a year. Two at the most.

"You could just say no. You don't have to jump around and make excuses."

"I'm not jumping around, and I'm not.... You don't mean a real marriage. You mean just—a partnership."

"The only kind of marriage I want is a real one," Norah said, amazed at the strange words that kept coming out of her mouth.

Her shivering had turned to shaking. He stood and held out a hand, face stony. Too stiff to get to her feet without help, Norah reached out and let him pull her up. Neither one said another word as they walked to the restaurant.

HE'D PRETEND SHE never said it.

Desperation had driven her to say it, and if she wasn't already in a panic over her own foolishness, she must regret it and be wondering how to back out.

Except she didn't look particularly panicky, desperate, or regretful at the moment. More like calm and downright pleased with herself. And she had every right to be pleased. After slaving for months to earn twenty dollars, she had lifted a hundred from him in less than a minute.

Whatever else that boarding house did, it gave her a decent place to sleep. She looked better rested than he'd ever seen her.

In fact now that she was warming up, no longer shivering and blue around the lips, she looked good enough any man she just proposed to should be shouting yes and doing whatever she wanted, ignoring any attempt she'd make to change her mind. Any husband-material kind of man.

The first time he'd seen the new dress, he'd let her know in no uncertain terms how much he liked the look of her in something other than gray. Even though he'd have chosen real red if given the chance.

Today, with cold gray light from the windows blending into the softer yellow light of the lamps around the room, he couldn't imagine any woman looking better in any dress. Her hair looked darker and shinier, her eyes bluer, her cheeks a more delicate pink.

The best part of the dress was the line of buttons that started right under the lace collar and marched down over the tempting curve of her breasts and on further into the tuck of the waist that had fit his hands just right when he'd held her at Christmas. The buttons didn't stop there but continued past even better territory until they ended where the material bunched into some decorative something halfway down her skirt. About where her knees must be.

Not being husband material, Cal's ideas about those buttons had nothing to do with fashion and a lot to do with popping, ripping, and tearing. He gave serious consideration to hauling her off somewhere and showing her what marriage to him would be like, which would scare the idea right out of her. Her voice jolted him back to reality.

"I meant what I said. You can just say no. I won't cry or have a conniption. It was a thought as to how we could work things out, but if you don't like it, you don't. Are you married already?"

"No."

"Stop glowering at me. Say no, and let's enjoy breakfast."

How could she tell he was glowering when she wouldn't look at him? She stayed focused on the menu board as if the few items listed needed studying.

"How lumpy is the porridge?" she asked.

"Very."

"That's too bad. I guess flapjacks then. And bacon?"

Marrying her was absolutely out of the question. He leaned forward, his arms on the table.

"You're being as stubborn and stupid as when you sat alone out there trying to starve and pretending you weren't. Sell it to me."

She pressed back in her chair, her smile disappearing, and finally met his eyes. "No. See how easy that is to say and be done with it? I'm not selling it to you or anyone else. No."

His jaw tightened, and he forgot about buttons. In the last days he'd come to believe not only would she sell the farm to him but that she'd be happy to do it, grateful even. Her stubborn refusal to do what any sensible woman would do infuriated him. He ought to marry her just to teach her a lesson.

The flapjacks were dry and tough, but enough syrup made them edible, and the bacon arrived crisp and without char.

They ate in silence, but he couldn't mistake the muley look on her face. Neither intimidation nor persuasion was going to get him anywhere. Not having to buy the land would mean starting out with a much bigger cushion of cash. He banished the thought, and his mind skipped on to others even more treacherous.

Now that she looked and acted the way the woman who had been the Girl should look and act, if he wanted a wife, she'd be the one he'd want. To marry the Girl. After all the dreams and all the years. Partners. A real marriage. He took several deep breaths to steady himself.

"When a man proposes to a woman, doesn't she get to take as long as she wants to answer?"

"I didn't pro...." In other circumstances the look on her face as she realized that's exactly what she had done would be funny. "Yes, we get to take as long as we want, but you only have until I find someone to give me a ride home."

When she first mentioned partners, all he could think of was sharecropping, feeling like an indentured servant again, Jake Kepler and "next year." Marriage would be different. A husband owned everything, including the woman. She was crazy to propose it. He was crazy to consider it.

He could keep her safe, which was all he'd started out to do, but how miserable would he make her? How miserable would she turn around and make him? Would it kill all the peace he'd found out there, walking over the land, making plans, and daring to dream of a different life?

They walked back out in the cold, and he knew that if they parted and she went back to sitting by the store or to the boarding house, the decision would be made by default, and it would be no.

"All right," he said. "How do we get married?"

She crossed her arms and tipped her head at him, "Are you sure? If you marry me you can't have someone else later, you know."

"I know."

"Are you sure you don't want someone younger? Some beautiful young blonde?"

"Now who has cold feet? If you've come to your senses, say so."

"I haven't.... We are a sorry pair, aren't we? We need to find Reverend Densmore, and on a day like this he's probably home close to his fire."

Getting married was all too easy. In Cal's opinion something that life-changing ought to take longer and present a lot more difficulty.

Instead, Densmore rounded up a couple of wide-eyed neighbors as witnesses, stood them all at the front of the church and, sounding all too much like Henry Sutton, read biblical words out of some other book. The man intoned rather than spoke, as if the words required emphasis. Which they didn't. Those words could be whispered and make a man's blood run cold. If he meant them.

Cal had never considered promises—his own or anyone else's—much of a burden. No one had ever kept a promise to him, and he kept only those that were easier to keep than break. These promises had a disturbing weight to them. He told himself once outside the church the feeling would pass.

Till death. The only thing that kept him from walking out before the final amen was the look of her in the rose dress. A partnership. A real marriage. Norah.

He had no ring. Why hadn't she mentioned a ring? Hawkins probably gave her some shiny thing, and where was it? She'd have a collection soon.

The female stranger who had agreed to be a witness, looking all misty-eyed, pulled the ring off her own finger and handed it to him so he could put it on Norah for those few minutes.

By the time it was done, he was impatient with it, ready to forget the strange feelings and start the long list of things he had gone over and over in his mind these last weeks.

"It's late to start home today," Norah said tentatively. "There are no married couples at the boarding house, but maybe Mrs. Pollard will let us stay there just for tonight. When she finds out we're married, she's going to feel bad about not admitting I was there when you asked."

"We're only going to the boarding house long enough to make that woman give you back most of your money. There are better places to spend the night, and we've got a lot to do before then."

"I'm not spending the night in a saloon."

"Didn't you just promise to obey?"

She gave him the first of what he knew would be many unhappy looks.

11

"It is a boarding house, not a hotel," Norah said, as she hurried down the street after Caleb. "I couldn't stay at the hotel by myself, and everyone says it's terrible anyway. I couldn't stay at the saloon like you."

"For what she charged, you could. You'd need a gun to discourage any customers who mistook you for one of the regular women is all."

"Are you telling me I look like one of those women?" She remembered about his mother after the words were out and flinched inside, but he didn't take offense.

"Not to a sober man."

"Oh." She didn't care whether he meant she looked better or worse to a sober man, specifically to his sober self. She really didn't.

"Well, I don't like her, but I don't think Mrs. Pollard did anything wrong. I needed a safe place to stay, and I agreed to her terms."

In the end. After all but swallowing her pride and begging to pay for only one week instead. Still, did the woman deserve whatever Caleb had in mind?

"She took advantage of you, and she lied to me."

Norah half-wanted to ask why he took offense at someone lying to him when he admitted he was a liar himself. Her other half was smarter than that.

He stopped, and for a moment she dared hope he'd changed his mind. He hadn't. "I suppose you have things in your room at that place you need to get out."

"No, Mr. Lawson let me have my trunk brought to his store and put in his storeroom before I knew where I was staying yesterday, and I brought the box with my other things with me this morning, hoping I'd get a ride home today."

"He won't let you buy anything in his store, but he let you use the place for storage?"

"It's only one trunk and one box. He's a nice man really, but he has to make a living. The stores in town haven't exactly flourished with so many people leaving these last years. He can't give credit like he used to."

"Norah.... You don't need a partner. You need a keeper." He gave her a smile she didn't like the look of. "I guess that's what you've got now, isn't it? Let's get this done so we can get on to more important things."

Norah watched in awe as Mrs. Pollard, a tall, heavyset woman who had been so unyielding two days ago, refunded twelve out of fourteen dollars without an argument.

Caleb never made a threat. Of course between pounding on the boarding house door with his fist the same way he did on the soddy door and then standing there with his coat open and tucked back, one hand on a hip and one on the butt of his pistol....

In spite of her previous defense of Mrs. Pollard's business practices, Norah took guilty pleasure in her new husband's performance. In fact she had to suppress a childish urge to stick her tongue out at the other woman.

"Here," Caleb said, handing her the money. "You're going to need this for better things."

She had almost a hundred and twenty dollars in her pocket, and spending it on better things had an ominous sound. Pushing the money down deep, she kept her hand on top of it, liking the feel.

Ogden's stable was in sight when Caleb ducked between two buildings and went through that digging under his clothes routine again to extract money from his hidden supply. This time Norah watched with less fascination for the process and more curiosity about the result.

"How much do you have?" she asked, expecting the same kind of hard set down her father or Joe would have given her for asking such a question.

"I haven't counted for a while. Three thousand, give or take."

Thousands! She gaped at him, astonished. "You really are rich."

"Rich would laugh at this, but it's enough for a decent start. Not having to buy the land helps."

"You're going to put in more, aren't you? All I have is the land, but you're going to put in what it's worth and more."

"You're going to put in more too, partner. You just don't know it yet."

As they walked the rest of the way to the stable, Norah's heart raced as she worried about what he could mean by that. He couldn't mean.... People didn't talk about that. Then again, maybe a man raised in a brothel would. Oh, she'd be better off if she'd never talked to Grampa Butler, but she couldn't cut the knowledge out of her mind.

Arriving at the stable was a relief. She knew nothing about horses or wagons and would find a warm corner out of the weather and wait there while Caleb took care of buying both.

He had other plans. Partners did not sit in warm corners. They marched out back with the man selling the wagons and horses and examined the goods.

"I bought them before I realized what was going on." A bandy-legged little man with weathered skin and a morose expression, Teddy Ogden sounded as discouraged as he looked. "The way things are, it's all selling and no buying, but every one of these is a good wagon. You'll never get a better deal."

Norah didn't know what to look for in a wagon. She couldn't help, and Caleb couldn't possibly believe she could. He just wanted her to be as cold as he was.

Except—"Oh, that's our wagon."

Both men swiveled their heads toward her as if they'd forgotten her presence, but while Ogden's face stayed blank, Caleb caught her meaning.

"Are you saying this is the same wagon that killed your husband?"

The very question brought a surge of old anger. "The wagon didn't kill him," she said. "Mr. Van Cleve killed him, at least his men did."

Ogden didn't like it. "You said she was your wife."

"She is. We got married today. Until about an hour ago, she was Mrs. Joseph Hawkins."

"You can't just take that wagon. Maybe I didn't buy it, but it was abandoned here one night with one side all stove in, and I fixed it good as new, and I've been storing it here for months."

Storing? The wagons all sat in the open behind the stable. Not that the wagon had ever been under cover at home either.

"We may not take it at all," Caleb said. "Give us a minute." He pulled Norah far enough off to be sure Ogden couldn't hear. "How did it get here?"

"I don't know. The neighbors who brought Joe's body home found him crushed under the empty wagon and everything gone—the horses, the supplies, his rifle, everything. Maybe they went back and got the wagon, but why would they bring it here? Finding Joe scared them. They sold out and were gone within days."

"Maybe they used it, left it here, and hopped a train out of town. However it got here, we might get it cheaper than buying another one outright. How much would that bother you?"

"It wouldn't. I told you. The wagon didn't kill him."

"I know. Believe me, Norah, I know. They killed him. You don't have to convince me."

Relief flooded through her so strongly her knees wobbled a little. No one had ever believed her. At least no one ever admitted it. The sheriff said it was an accident and refused to investigate, and everyone else agreed.

"The road is straight as a ruler there," she said. "Our horses were just big saddle horses. They could barely pull that wagon loaded. They didn't run away, and the wagon didn't just tip over out of the blue and greedy neighbors swarm over it like locusts and carry everything off."

"I know, but you be sure you don't mind seeing it every day, using it again."

"I don't. Really. Do what you think is best."

In the end, Ogden swallowed his disappointment. Caleb agreed to the cost of fixing the side of the wagon bed and extra for storage, and if the total was less than half the price of a wagon, Ogden couldn't hide his relief over getting that much instead of dealing with accusations of theft and demands for the wagon's return free of cost.

Her husband had a strange way of doing things, Norah decided. He demanded twelve dollars back from Mrs. Pollard and got it, yet he paid Mr. Ogden what the man claimed he was owed without argument. Caleb didn't like Mrs. Pollard of course, but he didn't show any signs of liking Mr. Ogden either.

It had something to do with his concept of obligations owed and debts incurred and the need to repay. Someday she'd figure it out. Until death do us part. For better or for worse. She smiled a little, thinking of the look on his face at the sound of those words and the others.

They moved on to the horses, and Norah couldn't stop a small, sad, "Oh, dear," from escaping at the sight.

"They're just like the wagons," Ogden said defensively. "I shouldn't have bought them, but I didn't know. I should have put them on the train and sent them for auction, but it's too late now. The dog man comes and gets one whenever he needs meat, and I feed them as much as I can afford. I got some decent saddle stock heavy enough to pull a wagon around front. That's what you want."

Caleb ignored the man and walked up to the corral fence. The big horses were all thin, their ribs and hips poking sharply through rough winter coats, their eyes hollow.

"Joe always said that same thing," Norah whispered. "He said these big horses eat too much."

"Any horse eats too much for your place. The only feed around is grass, and if you turned them out they'd be off to the V Bar C now and in the crops eating themselves to death in the summer."

"Joe staked them out on the grass. They did all right."

Caleb made a disbelieving sound, and Norah knew he was right. Their horses had never looked good.

"Those look like two of Mr. Fleming's Percherons," she said, pointing at a pair of grays nuzzling each other. "He used to brag about his horses winning prizes at fairs back where he came from. Oh, I hate this."

"Can't say I'm having a good time myself," Caleb muttered.

Norah listened as Caleb sold a packhorse and bought the Percheron team and their harness. Sad and sorry as those animals looked, he and Ogden hitched them to the wagon. Caleb helped her to the seat, climbed up beside her, and drove toward the feed store.

"Can these horses even make it home?" Norah asked.

"The difference between a horse big enough to do the job and one straining at it, is yes, even half-starved like this, they can pull a loaded wagon to your place, especially after getting enough to eat tonight and tomorrow morning."

He gave her the closest thing to a regular smile she'd ever seen. "Skinny can be stronger than it looks sometimes."

The reference to his own surprising strength that night years ago, if that's what it was, made Norah smile too.

"Mr. Flood's arm did swell up and get red and drain for a while after you bit him. I think it almost scared him to death. He was sure he had hydrophobia and was going to die."

"Good."

Norah had been in the feed store a few times with her father and Joe, and it was one of the places they'd run up a considerable debt. She didn't want to stay out in the cold, but she didn't want to chance grumpy Mr. Huber recognizing her and dunning Caleb either. She offered to wait outside, but Caleb was having none of it.

Mr. Huber didn't have a chance to recognize her. Caleb introduced her. "My wife wants to pay her debt here, Mr. Huber. If you'll tell us how much is on the Hawkins account, she'll settle up."

Huber's dour face actually lit up. "That's an account I never expected to see another penny on."

He bent down to get his ledger from under the counter, and Norah made faces at Caleb.

After considerable page flipping, Huber pointed with one grubby finger. "Right there. Eighty dollars and thirty-two cents."

Norah pulled out the money she'd so recently pocketed and paid, watching Huber's notation of paid in full like a hawk.

Her husband then bought more oats than Norah believed the farm had produced the previous year.

"What are we going to do with all that?" she asked as they drove away.

"Feed horses."

"I'm not getting a good feeling about your business sense."

"If I can't make a living farming, I'll go back to killing people. It's easier anyway."

She had nothing more to say to him after that. At least not till they pulled up at the general store. "I don't have enough to pay the account here, so you can't make me do it."

"Give me what you've got, and I'll pay the difference. Keep twenty for yourself and sew it in your foundations for emergencies."

"What emergencies?" she asked suspiciously, digging out all her lovely money and handing over everything except one pretty gold piece.

"If I knew that, they wouldn't be emergencies."

Purchasing supplies without having to weigh the value of having one thing over another and keep down cost any way possible was a new and intoxicating experience for Norah. By the time they finished, she was dizzy with it.

"It's been so long I'm afraid I forgot something," she told Caleb.

"You have all night to think of anything we missed. We can get it before we leave in the morning."

She would have all night to think? Tonight was their wedding night, even if the wedding was a little—different.

The thought of the saloon or the hotel brought on another kind of dizziness. She couldn't bring herself to ask Caleb what he planned. Crawling under the tarpaulin on the wagon and freezing probably.

Darkness enveloped the town, and even the saloons appeared quiet from the outside by the time they finished every chore. Caleb groomed the Percherons while they ate the small portion of oats he decided was safe for animals in their condition, and he gave her a brush and expected her to help.

They left the horses munching hay heaped high in their mangers and walked to the restaurant. Norah's stomach growled in approval.

"I can't eat in a restaurant like this," she complained. "I smell like a horse."

"So do most of the folks in there."

"Not the women."

"There's a place you can wash up back by the kitchen."

Too tired and hungry to object, she nodded.

"Please tell me we aren't going to spend the night in a saloon."

Walking out of the warmth of the restaurant into the frigid winter night made Norah wish she could still cry.

"We aren't."

"The hotel?"

"I'd rather sleep in the street."

That seemed to be the only choice left, but Norah couldn't bear to say so. She followed Caleb in the dark, not understanding when he led the way between two buildings and then along behind the stores on the main street. She did understand when he stopped and tried a locked door, the rattle loud in the night.

"You're not breaking into one of these stores," she whispered furiously.

"Sure I am. We need a place to spend the night, and here's an empty place with a stove with a banked fire in it and everything we need."

"You can't...." But he could. She heard a crunching and tearing noise, and the door opened. She tried to balk, but he grabbed her arm and yanked her inside.

"Stop fussing. We're not going to hurt anything."

"You already broke the door down. This is like moving into my house without a word. It's stealing."

"Stealing what? We're not going to take anything. We'll burn a little extra coal, and I didn't break the door down, just did a little damage around the edges. We paid a debt he never expected to collect here today. What's he got to complain about?"

She wanted to screech at him, but someone might hear, and she'd probably go to jail with him. And she was too tired anyway, and how did anyone sleep in a general store where every square foot was filled with shelves and one thing after another?

There was some empty space around the stove, but it was the *floor*. How could he expect her to spend her wedding night on the floor in a store where he'd made her pay her father's and husband's debts earlier the same day?

Light from the stove as he added fuel showed shadowy shapes all around. The door grated softly as he closed it, and almost total darkness returned. Norah jumped as something soft brushed by her, falling to her feet.

"There. Make a bed out of those."

"Those" were blankets. Dozens of them by the feel. "Caleb...."

"Didn't you promise to obey today?"

She didn't answer.

"Make a bed out of those blankets. Be quiet and go to sleep."

She smoothed out the blankets as best she could, hearing him doing the same nearby. The thick pile did make a decent mattress, and she was warm, and her stomach was full. That was how she'd gotten herself into this mess to start with, thinking about only the good things.

When she had suggested—all right, proposed—marriage, she had thought about the good things. How he was the Boy and in spite of everything that had happened between them recently, what happened so long ago was important and had forged an enduring connection. How he brought her food and wood even if she didn't want them, and didn't shoot her, hit her, or even yell at her when she behaved so dreadfully in return.

She'd thought about him checking to see how she was doing at her new job and taking her for her first meal in a restaurant. Not making fun about the goats. Holding her when she needed to be held so badly. Looking for her when he heard she'd quit.

She had to stop trying to paper over the bad things, though. No matter the reasons, he saw the world in a twisted way. Yes, she thought of him as a thief and a liar, but she had to stop letting her mind skitter over the worst things, the really bad things.

He was a killer, a murderer. He could kill without a flicker of emotion crossing his face, and he had joked about it today—if he was joking. With a man who smiled seldom and as far as she could tell never laughed, it was hard to tell.

If they were caught here, they'd deserve to go to jail. Caleb was the only one who deserved to go for breaking into the store and using Mr. Lawson's coal and throwing brand new blankets on the floor and sleeping on them smelling of horse. She deserved to go for being criminally stupid, a charge Caleb had made several times, although not for the right reason.

Depending on what Mr. Van Cleve did next, Caleb might just save the farm, and her. With so much cash to burn, he'd leave her in a position to hire help next year.

Because he would leave. Farming would bore him soon, and he wouldn't honor marriage vows any more than any other promise. He would leave her better off, though, debts paid and equipment purchased.

She thought she could feel him close in the dark. Thoughts of what conceiving a child would involve rose unbidden, and her body reacted. Her fingers twitched, but wool blankets were not what she wanted to touch. Would he be gentle? Rough? Indifferent? How foolish was she to trust him?

I don't care. Let him leave me with a child. If that happens, nothing else matters.

For better or for worse. She'd keep her side of the bargain, but only this side of a jail cell. No more of this thieving business. He would lie, but she wouldn't, and she most certainly wasn't killing anyone. Decisions made and clear in her mind, she fell asleep.

12

CAL WOKE AT first light, rose, folded the blankets he'd slept on, and returned them to the table where they belonged.

On his own, he'd walk out of here without looking back, but with Norah along, disapproving of every move, he figured to smooth things over as best possible. The ride home was a long one and would be longer beside an angry woman. Home. Truly home. Worth folding a few blankets to keep a wife, if not happy, at least less unhappy.

He crouched to wake her, then hesitated, taken with the sight of her in sleep. With all the worry gone from her face, she looked content, her mouth soft and curved in a half-smile. Dark lashes made lacy fringes on eyelids that fluttered as her eyes moved underneath. Smooth skin invited a caress, dark arches of eyebrows the stroke of a fingertip.

He accepted the second invitation. A sound like a word not quite formed escaped her. Instead of springing awake, she turned on her side, curling a little and snuggling deeper into her pile of blankets.

He tried again. Two fingers this time. One along her eyebrow and the other on the fragile skin below. Her eyes opened, taking in first him and then everything else around them.

"Up and at 'em," he said. "Sleeping free means being gone before anyone else is awake."

She gave him a sleepy smile that took his breath away. "Good morning."

Keeping control of the situation around her might turn into a full time job. She sat up, yawning, folded blankets and stacked them beside the others without comment.

Catching sight of a curious gleam on the front counter when he checked one last time to make sure nothing remained to identify them was actually a relief. She hadn't changed into some different, compliant woman after all.

He retrieved the twenty dollar gold piece and gave it to Norah. "Don't do that again."

"Or what."

"Or nothing. Don't do it again. No wonder you lost most of your money within a day of quitting your job. We're talking partnership money now. Argue with me if you have to but don't go throwing gold coins around like we're made of them."

He slapped a single dollar down where the gold piece had been and herded her out. Her muley look returned, but he wasn't paying nineteen dollars to be rid of that.

She chatted easily enough through breakfast about what they'd bought and visiting the Carburys to retrieve the household goods she'd stored with them months ago. He hoped she'd put aside the subject of his sins for a while but wasn't counting on it, and he risked making it worse with his last words to Ogden, which felt a little like a betrayal, even to him.

"Why don't you get word to Van Cleve about those big horses? He hauls a lot of timber from the hills up north and some stone from the quarries there too. If he knew he could get good teams for dog meat prices, fatten them on grass, and have them ready to work in a month or two, he might help you out."

Ogden started to say something, glanced at Norah, and said, "I guess you'd know. I'll do it. If he takes one it's better than none."

He offered his hand. Cal shook his head slightly, and climbed to the wagon seat.

She didn't seem angry but sad. "You like horses better than people, don't you?"

"Yes."

The way she fidgeted on the seat prepared him for more serious talk, but not the line she took. "I don't feel like a partner, you know. I don't even feel much like a wife. Even my mother—she lived that verse from the Bible 'wives be submissive,' but at least she knew what she had to be submissive to before it happened. You're always ahead of me, and I run along behind as fast as I can, and when I catch up you do something so surprising I wish I'd run the other way. Do you think you could warn me—we're going to pay your father's old debts, don't worry about a saloon or the hotel, we're going to spend the night someplace we shouldn't but it will be warm and dry?"

"If I told you ahead of time you'd fuss."

"I fuss anyway only afterward instead of before. And afterward I'm not only upset because I think you're wrong, I'm angry because you did it without telling me. Like right now. We're headed in the wrong direction to go home."

The wisdom of keeping plans to himself had been beaten deep into Cal a long time ago. Everything inside him resisted the idea of trusting anyone with plans. Right now he could give her what she wanted, though. Where they were going now wasn't a secret that needed keeping.

"We're going to see the dog man and get a dog before we head home."

"A dog! We don't have sheep. What do we need a dog for?"

"Van Cleve is going to come after us hard and probably before he wastes time on anyone else. If he can show the others who are holding out that he can run someone like me—like us—off, then everyone may fold. You know why I believe he killed your husband?"

She shook her head.

"Asa Preston told me he killed my uncle. He laid in wait out in the yard, and when the old boy went out in the night to use the privy, Preston snatched him and threw him down the well. I've got no sympathy for Uncle Henry. I hope he died hard, and I regret I'm not the one did for him, but that tells me the way Preston's mind works. I don't want him able to sneak up on us in the night and kill you, me, or the horses. A dog can hear things we can't. If we get the right kind of dog, no one will be sneaking up on us."

He could see her chewing that over and didn't like it that she saw more than he wanted her to.

"That's why you insisted I buy a red scarf and that red-striped material for a coat yesterday. You want to make sure if Preston tries to shoot you from a distance, he doesn't make a mistake."

"I like bright colors is all. The land is pretty flat for that kind of sharpshooting. There's not many places to set up."

"I've heard buffalo guns like yours are accurate for more than half a mile."

"They are, but only a handful of men in the country are. I'm not, and I doubt anybody in the State of Kansas right now is. Don't worry about it."

"I suppose you like dogs more than people too."

"Always have."

"Maybe we should call it Ears."

"That would be telling."

"Early then, for early warning."

"That's good. If anyone asks, tell them your people admired Jubal Early, and we named it after him."

He didn't expect Norah to recognize the name of the crusty old Confederate, but she did.

"I'm sure General Early would be honored."

THE ROAD THEY had first taken out of town wasn't in bad shape. The one Caleb turned onto after that hardly qualified as a road. When he left the ruts to follow faint tracks over unmarked prairie, the ride smoothed out again, and Norah relaxed.

"How do you know the way?"

"Ogden's delivered now and then. He gave me directions."

A cluster of ramshackle buildings came into sight seconds before a pack of dogs raced from behind the buildings, barking, snarling, and snapping. They looked intent on eating the horses still alive and on the hoof.

Terrified, Norah choked back a scream and held on for dear life. The horses had enough spirit left to throw up their heads and attempt to run.

Caleb cursed in soothing tones and held them, his voice barely audible over the din. A shrill whistle sounded. She looked up from the slavering pack of dogs to see a figure by the buildings.

The dogs turned into a friendly, tail-waving escort. The horses calmed, and Norah turned on Caleb angrily. "You knew that was going to happen, didn't you? You knew, and you didn't warn me."

"Ogden said the dogs ran out and greeted visitors and Quist would call them off. He didn't say it was that bad. Maybe he was getting even over the price of the wagon."

She studied the side of his face, but gave it up. In time she might learn to detect signs of a lie in those hard lines, but today she never would.

Getting down into that panting, hairy mass of dogs held no appeal. Neither did sitting in the wagon behind nervous horses tied to a hitch rack that didn't look as if it could hold a sick pony. In the end she decided to stay close to Caleb, which meant taking her chances with the dogs.

"What do you two want?"

Josiah Quist was not someone Norah would be willing to meet on her own, even in town. He stood unmoving on the decrepit stoop of his house, dark eyes full of suspicion glaring from a face hidden by his gray-streaked full beard and wild tangle of long hair. The dogs looked cleaner.

"We need a dog," Caleb said. "Young, a good watch dog."

"You think I'd let someone with horses in that shape have one of my dogs?"

Caleb's hands went to his hips. Instead of explaining, he was going to meet belligerence with belligerence. For heaven's sake, did he plan to shoot this strange old man over a dog?

Norah tugged on his sleeve. "Let me talk to him," she whispered.

"Don't you dare go begging this crazy old coot for one of these curs." At least he lowered his voice.

"Do we want a dog, or don't we?"

"No begging, and no throwing around twenty dollar gold pieces either."

"Try to look like a man who just got married who at least *likes* his wife."

She stepped past him, pretending the growling sound behind her came from one of the dogs.

"Mr. Quist, I'm Mrs. Caleb Sutton, and this is my husband. We bought the wagon and team from Mr. Ogden yesterday. He's the one who told us about you. Please look at my husband's saddle horse behind the wagon. That's how you can truly see how he cares for livestock. We would take good care of a dog."

Quist stepped down and walked around the wagon. Every dog in the pack pushed at the others trying to get closer to the man.

Norah noticed the way his hands automatically touched each hairy head that came within reach. He stopped a few feet from the horse and took a good look. Caleb's saddle horse was an undistinguished bay gelding, but he was in good condition and everything from the way he was shod to the shine of his winter coat attested to good care.

"What's his name?"

Norah turned to Caleb, hoping he either had a name for the horse or enough sense to make one up forthwith.

"Forest."

"Huh. What you want with a watch dog?"

"We live a day to the west," Norah said. "I get nervous out there alone. Even though Indians aren't a problem any more, I worry, and Caleb can't be there all the time."

Oh, blast it, was she already turning into a liar too? No. Absolutely not. She did get nervous. Caleb couldn't be there all the time. She had never wanted a dog and didn't believe one would be much use, but she wasn't claiming she wanted the dog. Was she?

Quist stared as if he could read her thoughts, did the same to Caleb, dove into the pack and emerged seconds later carrying a large, hairy black and white bundle. "His mother's as good a watch dog as there is, and he's like her."

The bundle was a dog young enough his paws still looked too big for him. Caleb took him from Quist and hoisted him up eye to eye. Black ears tip-tilted at different angles over a face white except for the ring around one eye. Splotches on his body suggested a paint can had been knocked over near him.

"He'll do." Caleb looked at Quist. "How about some help with dog food?"

The old man nodded, and Norah watched the puzzle who was now her husband hand over five dollars for the strange-looking mongrel.

They left Quist's place with the dog tied on top of the supplies. Norah said nothing until they were back on the town road, heading in the right direction for home.

"You told me not to pay for a dog, but then you did."

"I didn't pay anything. He's a crazy old man who takes in every stray dog he hears about and does without to feed them. He gave us the dog, and I gave him enough to help him out a little without offending his pride."

The difference was too subtle for her. She changed the subject. "Is your horse's name really Forest?"

"It is."

"Did he come from a place with lots of trees?"

"No. Nathan Bedford."

Nathan Bedford Forrest, the extraordinary Confederate cavalry general that would be. General Jubal Early. "Where exactly did the Suttons come from?"

"Indiana."

If she asked, she wouldn't understand the answer. If he gave one. "I think Mr. Fleming always gave his teams plain names. These two were probably Bob and Tony, something like that."

Caleb pointed to the horse on the left. "Jeb." To the one on the right. "Stonewall."

More Confederate generals. "Your Uncle Henry was a Union man."

The corner of his mouth curled up. "Not enough to put on a uniform, but enough to rant about it between Bible verses."

Norah smiled, pleased to have figured one thing out. If only figuring out the rest of him would prove so easy.

13

THEY ARRIVED AT the soddy with enough light left to unload the wagon if they hurried, and they hurried. Cal tied Early out of the way.

"Can't let him off the rope until he knows he lives here."

"What about coyotes?" Norah said.

"Can't let him off the rope until he grows into those paws then. At least not at night."

Cal watched her examining the house for signs of damage or changes. He'd told her he hadn't damaged anything, hadn't he?

She frowned at the wood in the box he'd made but said nothing. His battered coffee pot and frying pan sat atop the stove, and she touched them lightly.

"I won't have my pots and pans until we get them from the Carburys tomorrow," she said, sounding wistful.

"You're tired. Let's finish that loaf of bread from the bakery with butter and jam and that's enough for tonight."

"Not that tired," she said shyly, her words full of double meaning. "We have a dozen eggs. We can have fried eggs with our bread. Do I need to waste an egg on Early?"

"Two."

"And I can warm water enough to wash in the metal basin. I'm glad I left that."

She bent to rummage through the boxes of provisions, and Cal studied the way her rump swayed under her skirt. He as good as owned her now. He could use her or abuse her in any way he wanted, and she'd have no recourse except to run.

They'd spent less than half a dozen hours in each other's company these last months and most of that arguing. How could she trust whatever tenuous thread bound them from that night so long ago enough to do this?

She should know better than to trust him at all. She should be afraid of that part of him that resented having to marry her to get the land. Hell, she should be afraid of him period.

She'd loved Hawkins enough to grieve almost to death over him. That probably explained everything. She needed a man, and one she'd never feel that way about would be safer.

Disturbed by his own thoughts, he returned outside to unload the feed and other supplies in the shed and take care of the horses.

Buttered bread, jam, and eggs fried the way Norah did them were a feast. He had to admit to looking forward to her cooking three times a day instead of his own.

Rejecting the urge to just throw her on the bed and satisfy himself, Cal decided to give her time alone in case there were preparations wives made.

"I'll take the dog out and make sure he's empty for the night. Walk him around a while."

"I'll leave the basin close the stove to keep the water warm and set out washing things for you right here on the table."

The high color on her cheeks wasn't from the stove, but her eyes were shining and voice calm. Hawkins had probably given her expectations of husbands. Cal had no intentions of competing with a dead man who had already won.

The wind had died to what would be a breeze in spring, but the temperature had only plummeted lower. He walked without attention to direction. His ghosts appeared, hazy presences bearing him nothing but ill will. The false, high laughter of whores swirled around him. *"You'll like it, honey. You know you will."*

Jake Kepler's bellowing laugh drowned them out. *"Get drunk. Have a woman."*

Having a woman meant paying, lying, and cajoling. Having a woman meant a burst of pleasure and relief and—nothing.

Around Norah, the calculated indifference he'd felt toward women all his life disappeared. She provoked temper and impatience and desires that had the ghosts howling with glee. He shoved them back down in the dark place they'd escaped from.

Early whimpered, pulling back on the rope. Cal stopped and looked around, spotting the faint light from the house in the distance.

"She already knows there's a lot wrong with me, just not how much. After all, you've known me less than a day and you've figured it out."

A few soft words and the young dog stopped pulling and followed him back to the house.

The lamp glowed on the table, the wash things set out as she'd said. In the shadows by the bed, he could only see the back of her head and the outline of her form under the blankets. He stripped and washed, carried the lamp to the bedside table and doused it.

Lifting blankets, he encountered the smooth texture of sheets. She'd thrown some of his money around wisely. He slid in beside her, the desire to mount her like an animal, drive himself deep inside, and thrust with crazed abandon pounding in his head and blood.

She turned and touched his cheek with a tentative hand, the other light on his shoulder. "You were a long time." Her voice was low and husky, her body soft and vulnerable.

Oh, damn. Hawkins wasn't even one of Cal's ghosts, and he'd end up laughing with the ones who were tonight.

Her hair was as long as he'd imagined and as soft. It slipped and slid across his palms and curled around his wrists. He ran his fingers along the sides of her jaw to her temples, into the silken mass, cupping her head in his hands as he kissed her.

First a light brush of lips, a test. Then a real kiss, holding her, sliding his tongue along the seam of her lips. When she gasped, he took advantage and slipped inside, caressing the insides of her lips and along her tongue. Her willing but hesitant response gentled him. Whatever Hawkins had done, he hadn't kissed her much.

She tasted of the same cinnamon-flavored tooth powder Cal had used minutes ago, a good taste as unlike whiskey or tobacco as possible. She smelled clean, no trace of cloying perfume, stale sweat, or other men. He left her mouth, ran his tongue behind her ear.

"Caleb!"

In the sound of his name he heard surprise, delight. Small flashes of light exploded behind his eyes. The night changed.

Nothing before now mattered, for her, for him. He wanted her to want as fiercely as he did, to feel as much pleasure, more. Woman, wife, the Girl, Norah. He kissed her face and her eyelids, feeling the same flutter he'd watched that morning as she slept.

She had some long soft thing on, and it had to go. He yanked at it.

"Wait."

She had it off in seconds, and her arms welcomed him back to her, hands kneading his back, exploring, caressing.

He reached her breasts, closed his teeth around a nipple and used his tongue. She arched to him, one hand moving to his hair. Soft sounds of her pleasure blended with his own groan.

A little longer. He could hold on a little longer and give her something. He stroked her belly, his mouth still at her breast until her fingers digging into his back told him she needed more.

Massaging, testing, he cupped her sex with one hand, kissed down across her belly. She was a stranger to this.

Almost beyond thought or ability to know anything outside his own raging need, he knew no one had given her this before. The sound of her pleasure filled his head as the feel of it rippled in the belly muscles under his lips and jerked against the hand curved between her legs.

No more. The fever in his blood wouldn't wait for her to recover or for another word or kiss or touch. The way she opened to him, legs hooking around his as he drove into welcoming, wet heat intensified the pleasure, the almost unbearable relief.

Prolonging anything would be impossible, and he didn't want to. He gave in to his own greedy lust as he'd first planned, thrust as deep and hard, finished as quickly.

The end was as different from what he had known as the beginning. Instead of pulling out of her still erect, washing every trace of her from his body, and wishing he had a different place to spend the rest of the night, he kept the connection as long as possible, relishing the fan of her breath on his shoulder, her arms around him and hands spread on his back.

When he finally lifted his weight from her, he pulled her close, back to his belly, buried his nose in her hair, and fell asleep.

Soft whimpering from beside the bed woke Cal. He and Norah lay in a tangle of arms and legs, cocooned together against the cold of the house. Memories of the day and night before rushed back, together with awareness of the source of the whimpers.

Mentally cursing the fool who had thought a dog was a good idea and accepted one not much more than a puppy, he moved the arm Norah had around his waist to her side, pushed her leg out from between his, and eased out of the bed.

Trousers, boots, he didn't fumble for more but pulled on his coat, picked up his rifle, and staggered out into the cold, coming wide awake with the first shivering breath.

"I should push you out by yourself and let the coyotes have you," he muttered as Early gamboled around his feet. "I bet you think I should be grateful you woke me up instead of making a mess." Early jumped against his leg, and he fondled the dog's mismatched ears.

"I bet you think your life changed a lot today. Yesterday. You have no idea. First she won't sell, then she wants me to marry her for it, then she...."

Even talking to a dog, he couldn't say it out loud. What she'd done was give him a glimpse of something that scared the bejesus out of him, something never meant for men like him that could start a hunger that would eat away what little was left inside him that didn't need to be shoved into the dark place.

Even so, as he whistled the dog back to him he wondered how she was going to react to his cold body back in the bed, using her to warm up.

14

THE SLIGHT MOVEMENT of the bed as Caleb rose woke Norah.

She watched him move away, admiring the long lines of his back and taut, muscular rear. Joe had hung blankets on a rope to hide the bed from the rest of the soddy. So visitors wouldn't see he said, but the two of them used it to hide from each other too. She had seen his body, of course. She'd nursed him through an occasional illness, but he never slept without a night shirt, never rose naked in the morning light, and if he did, she would never have watched him the way she watched Caleb now.

The race horse–draft horse comparison came back to her, but it was more than that. Yes, Caleb was lean, his muscle well defined under the skin, the taper of broad shoulders to narrow waist and hips marked, but he was also sleek.

The light picked out a sprinkling of golden hairs across his chest and on his arms and legs, but the blond hair didn't grow in the kind of thick mat that had hidden Joe's chest and even covered some of his back and shoulders.

Caleb's hair didn't feel the same either, silky and springy instead of, well, like fur. Everything about him felt so male, but not in a crushing, smothering way. And inside. Her body had opened to him so easily, eagerly, with no dry burning rasp at first. Only the pleasure. Oh, the pleasure of having him.

He washed quickly with the water left over from last night. Her body reacted so strongly to the sight, she closed her eyes and bit her lip. Desire curled low in her belly, and she wanted to call out, pull him back to her, touch him.

Those things were for times when the darkness covered them, and not for a woman to be starting either. Lying here like a slug-a-bed wishing had to be wrong. She wanted him to touch her the way he had last night. Twice.

Eight years married, and she'd never known. Did other women know it could be like that, or did some live and die thinking that part of marriage a mild pleasure some times and a small chore others?

In town, the way he looked at her, at least those times they weren't quarreling, made her feel like a girl again, special, pretty. He'd even called her pretty. What he'd done last night made her feel wanton, female, desirable.

He couldn't have learned those things in the brothel. He'd only been ten when they'd taken him from there to his uncle. She didn't want to think about the magic of last night having anything to do with a place like that, but then she didn't want to think about other women either.

He'd come out of the saloon early the morning they married. He hadn't been drinking, and those kind of women worked there. Trying to get him to tell her anything would be a waste of effort. He only gave up the reason he headed out of town in the wrong direction yesterday when he had to.

She kicked out from under the covers and sat up, astonished at the direction of her thoughts. She couldn't be thinking of talking to him about what they'd done. Sometimes women alluded to such things, reassuring each other of their common experience, but no one *talked* about what they did in the dark. She shivered at the memory, his hands, his mouth, his body. Her breath quickened, nipples peaked.

This morning would be like yesterday, eating at the restaurant and not mentioning breaking into Lawson's. They would just be not mentioning a different thing.

That's the way things were between a man and a woman, husband and wife.

She had to call him to breakfast. He came in with his face closed down and his eyes wary. They ate in silence, and she couldn't think of a way to relieve the tension or why it was happening.

She'd been so delighted, but that didn't mean he was. He was probably used to women who knew about those things, who knew how to respond better.

"Caleb?"

The wary eyes met hers.

"I liked what you did last night. I liked it a lot, and if you didn't so much. If I need to.... If I s-should...." She stuttered to a halt.

"You liked it."

"Mm hm."

"A lot."

"Yes."

He took a swallow of coffee, regarding her over the edge of the cup, his expression slowly relaxing. "So did I. How about if we do it again right now?"

She gasped. "We can't. It's broad daylight."

He looked around as if checking to be sure she was right about that. "So married people don't do it in daylight?"

"N-no. At least I never—we didn't—I don't think so. Maybe I could find a way to ask Mabel Carbury when we go there."

He pushed away from the table and reached for his hat. "Let me talk to her first. I still have money. Maybe she'll take a bribe."

Norah didn't recover from her surprise until he was gone. His words made her throw something at the door again, but this time she laughed as she did it, and the towel she threw didn't make a mess.

THE TRIP TO Carburys' would be longer than five miles by road instead of straight across the fields, but Norah couldn't see any reason why it required Caleb's saddle horse tied to the back of the wagon or Early tied in the bed.

"Are you and Early going to ride away and leave me with the Carburys?"

"No, but we're not leaving anything alive behind either. We can rebuild anything Preston wrecks, but we can't raise the dead."

Norah didn't want to think about Van Cleve, Preston, or the inevitability of more trouble. The sunny late January day matched her mood, very cold, but crisp, not damp.

Joe's old coat would have to do until she could make up the new one, but the red scarf perked up even the dull brown. Mabel would love the rose dress. Becky had probably already regaled her mother with the story of selecting the material, but showing off a beautiful dress wouldn't be half as much fun as showing off a handsome husband.

Armed Carburys poured from the house and barn as Caleb halted the wagon in the yard. Norah called out and waved, slowing the rush.

"If they shoot me," Caleb said, "make sure you get the money belt off the body before anyone else gets it."

"That's not funny. No one is shooting you." She climbed down without help and started for Mabel and Becky.

"I thought you'd like to meet my new husband, but if I'm wrong, we'll just load up my things and be gone as quickly as possible."

Becky took a step back. Mabel's jaw dropped slightly. "Husband? You *married* him?"

"Of course I did. Archie told me to go to town and find someone who could put up with me, didn't he?"

Archie appeared from the other side of the wagon. "I believe I mentioned it shouldn't be Sutton."

"Are you sure? Why don't I remember that?" She knit her brow but couldn't keep the expression and grinned.

"Well, get him down and let's meet him."

"Come meet everyone," she called to Caleb, as if he were waiting for an invitation, not for assurance no one would pull the trigger on any of the rifles pointed at him.

She tried to see him as the others must. Several days of dark blond stubble still covered the lean jaw, but most men sported full beards this time of year. Even shaded by the brim of his hat, his dark eyes had a hawk's intense alertness, and no one would be fooled by his relaxed posture on the wagon seat.

Neither his agile jump down nor that no footprints way he covered the few feet to her side did anything to dispel the dangerous aura.

Even so, Becky had been sighing and fantasizing about a non-existent romance for weeks and surely had told her folks about Caleb's visits. Mabel and Archie must have changed her attitude. Becky stood with her arms folded across her chest, glaring daggers at Caleb. In fact, Archie, who had let his rifle barrel droop toward the ground, looked the friendliest of the whole family.

"Your horses look like crowbait," Archie said, giving the team a critical once over.

Before Norah could spring to the defense, Caleb said, "Ogden has a bunch like this he can't afford to feed. They'll fatten soon."

"Fatten on what?"

"Hay and oats now. Grass as soon as I can fence pasture."

Archie threw Caleb a sharp look. Having been to the farm to help Norah pack the day she left, Archie knew full well there hadn't been a speck of feed on the place. "Bring them along. Her boxes are in the barn."

Just like that the men left. Becky threw herself at Norah, hugging and almost sobbing. "What happened? Did he force you to marry him and give him the farm? I'll get Pa and the boys to shoot him dead. We'll bury him where no one will ever find him."

Norah pushed Becky back far enough to look at her. "Where do you get such strange ideas? I quit my position with Mrs. Tindell and asked him to marry me, and he did."

"You asked him," Mabel said, frowning.

"I did." *And he didn't jump at the chance either.* Friends didn't need to know everything.

"Even if you met him once long ago, it's no excuse. He's one of Mr. Van Cleve's men."

"He quit. He quit almost two months ago, and it was because of me."

"He's a bad one."

"Oh, Mabel, yes, he is. He's a very bad man, but he's a beautiful bad man."

"He is not," Becky said. "I thought he would be handsome. Ethan is handsome. You said he was scary looking, and I should have believed you. You're afraid to tell the truth is all. You didn't ask him to marry you. He scared you into it."

Ethan Butler was a pleasant-looking young man of average height with a nice smile, light brown hair, and a pale, town complexion. Norah decided against doing a point by point comparison with Caleb.

Mabel had seen more of life than her emotional daughter. Her face softened as she met Norah's eyes. "So it's like that, is it? You'd better come in and tell us about it."

NORAH WAITED UNTIL they were well down the road on the way home before asking, "Were they horrible to you?"

"Not bad for people who think I married you for the land and as soon as a little time passes I'll turn it over to Van Cleve and disappear."

"You did marry me for the land."

"Not just the land. There's the curtains."

"Curtains."

"Whatever makes the house feel like home. I think it's the blue curtains."

After another while of silence, Norah pulled off a glove and curved her hand around his thigh.

"Did you ask her about what's acceptable to do in broad daylight?" He kept his eyes on the horses, but she saw a slight curl at the corner of his mouth.

"No. I decided to follow my mother's advice instead."

"Your mother had something to say on the subject?"

"Wives be submissive..."

He gave a short bark of laughter. After a startled moment, Norah kissed him. After all she needed to practice this new way of kissing, broad daylight or not.

15

THE MORNING AFTER the visit to the Carburys, Norah washed up after breakfast with a smile on her lips, humming to herself now and then and close to breaking into song. Whatever she had expected when she proposed marriage to Caleb, it wasn't this.

Today she'd finish putting everything away and then start on her new coat or the blue dress material. Or the green. Or maybe it would be better to brighten the gray dress Caleb disliked so with trim. Blue trim. He'd like that.

The sound of the wagon pulling up outside surprised her. Caleb appeared in the doorway before she left her chores to investigate.

"I need some help today, partner. Come on along."

Curious as to what help he could need, she bundled up in Joe's coat and followed him out. Forrest was tied to the back gate again, Early and a pile of rope in the wagon bed. He didn't want help with some small thing close by.

She climbed to the seat before asking, "Where are we going?"

"I don't know the name of the place. It's a couple hours away."

Two hours. The only neighbors two hours away would be far more hostile than the Carburys. She might not know them well enough to reassure them.

"Do you think that's wise? Maybe we ought to ask Mabel and Archie to introduce you to some of the neighbors."

"Tell me about the buildings that burned. What was there? How did it happen?"

So he wasn't going to tell her where they were going. She studied his profile. He'd shaved before bed last night. She liked the feel of his smooth skin rubbing across hers as much as the feel of the bristles the night before. Very different. Very nice.

She put a hand on his thigh again and saw a trace of a smile. "Don't change the subject," he said. "How did the fires start?"

"You're the one who changed the subject, but all right, coal oil splashed all over that's how. Even days afterward you could smell it under the smoke."

"Everything went up at once?"

"As far as we could tell. By the time we got out, all the buildings were burning."

"So everybody got out safe."

"Everybody was just me and Joe. It was summer, so the horses were out. We got the pig out, but we lost most of the chickens. After we butchered the hog that year we never had much fresh meat again. Joe hated losing the house and moving to the soddy, but for me it wasn't the house. It was—everything."

"We can't have livestock until the trouble is over, but we can have fresh meat. I've seen enough rabbits to keep meat on the table for a year."

"Fresh meat, but not beef," Norah said, giving him a sharp look.

"Not beef." He hesitated a second then amended, "At least not often."

"Caleb...."

"You want me to lie?"

She pulled her hand away and kept it in her lap the rest of the way.

Soon after turning off the main road onto an overgrown track, Norah saw the charred remains of what had once been a house and barns. The resemblance to the blackened hulks on her own property was eerie.

Caleb circled the team around the barn, then backed them until the wagon touched the fallen wall.

"Come on. I'll show you what we're here for."

Norah followed him to the edge of the burned out building, where he crouched and looked under a section of fallen roof.

She stooped to look too. A plow. "You aren't going to take that out of there."

"It would be dangerous by myself. That's why you're here, partner."

"I'm not helping you steal a plow."

"We aren't stealing it. Look around. It's abandoned."

"Someone owns it, and taking it would be stealing."

He stood and headed back out to the wagon. "Fine. I'm stealing it. You're my wife, and you're going to do what I tell you because you promised to obey."

"That's not what obey means, and you know it," she yelled at his back, scrambling after him, catching her hem on a loose board and yanking it free without looking.

When she caught up, he had the rope out of the wagon and draped in a coil over his shoulder.

"I won't help you steal."

His face had closed against her again, and for a moment she thought he was going to brush by her without a word, but he leaned back against the wagon, crossed his arms, and admitted she was right.

"All right. Van Cleve owns it. He burned out whoever lived here, and he owns it now. All he wants it for is grazing and to boast of a bigger empire, so he'll let all this rot. We can use the plow and a lot of this lumber. There may be other good equipment under there."

Norah set her jaw. Hating a man didn't give you the right to steal from him, did it?

"He owes you, Norah. He killed your husband and took everything so you'd have to sell or starve, and you damn near did starve. He gave Preston a wink and a nod to go out there and make you sell. The way you felt then you thought what they were going to do to you wouldn't make much difference, but it would. Whether you died an hour or a lifetime after they were through with you, you'd never be the same."

"And what does he owe you?"

"Nothing. I don't like him, and I don't have your problem with stealing from people I don't like."

"You said you couldn't do it by yourself."

"Maybe I can."

"And maybe those beams will fall on you."

He shrugged. "You know where the money belt is."

"That's not fair."

"Most things aren't."

She wanted to hit him. She wanted to walk away and not look back.

"You're as bad as Mr. Van Cleve."

"Worse probably. I do my own stealing and killing."

"All right. Show me what to do."

He showed her how to stand in front of the horses, hold the reins close to their bits, and lead them forward as he directed by shouting from the barn.

"I can't do that," she said, horrified. "I've hardly ever held the reins in the wagon. They won't listen to me, and what if they spook and take off?"

"They'll listen fine. Just stay calm. If they take off, hold on tight so you don't fall under them. They have to stop eventually."

"I can't."

"Sure you can. Just hang on."

When they were done, his dark eyes glowed with pleasure over the free plow. Norah shook from head to toe and feared she might vomit.

He finally noticed, guided her around to the back of the wagon, and lifted her onto the gate. "Sit there a minute. I'm going to load up as much of the good lumber as I can."

She leaned over and put her head in her hands, the rosy visions of the morning overlaid with ugly reality. Magical nights would only be a small part of marriage to Caleb Sutton, and they would never make up for days like this.

NORAH WANTED TO be so angry with him she could hold herself apart, but it didn't work. It didn't work because she was honest enough to admit she'd married him because actions other men wouldn't conceive of to start with or carry out to finish with were ordinary for Caleb. So far as she could tell, he considered stealing plows and lumber from someone he didn't like a personally beneficial expression of disdain.

Not that she had ever wanted or needed a husband who would steal without compunction, but she wanted that toughness, that hard-eyed indifference to what anyone else thought—to danger. She wanted a man who could stand up to Asa Preston and half a dozen like him and make them back down, and that's what she had.

In spite of the other emotions he evoked, Caleb made her feel safe. Day after day he rousted her from the household chores she wanted to do and dragged her to one deserted farmstead after another salvaging (his word), or stealing (her word) anything and everything he considered useful, and she never worried about what would happen if Mr. Van Cleve's men found them.

The problem was he also made her feel complicit. The last time she'd struggled so hard with her own concepts of right and wrong had been the first time she'd seen Caleb, the night her life had changed.

After a week of it, she no longer tried to resist when he parked the wagon in front of the house and came to get her an hour after breakfast. She suspected he calculated carefully so that she had enough time to wash dishes and clean up and not enough time to start a project like laundry.

Sooner or later he'd have to give her time for necessities like that, but today when he came for her, she put on Joe's old coat and wrapped the red scarf around her head and neck, ready to follow him into the cold February morning.

"When are you going to have a decent coat to wear?"

"When you stop dragging me off to help you steal, and I have time to make it."

No wagon waited outside the door. "Where are we going?" she said, certain she wouldn't like the answer.

"You want to know plans. Let's make plans. Come on."

They walked to the site of the burned out house and out-buildings. Caleb had stripped everything of use out of here during the weeks he'd lived in the house alone, and she knew he hadn't found much.

"What was it like?" he asked now.

"A lot like what Carburys have. The house was two stories, a parlor, dining room, kitchen, and one bedroom downstairs and three bedrooms upstairs. You can imagine what it was like for us in the soddy when we first got here. My brothers slept outside in good weather, but that winter we were like logs one beside the other across the floor. So Papa spent a good part of the cash money he had to build the house and a barn and storage sheds the very next summer."

"And you didn't approve."

"I don't remember how I felt at the time, but later I realized if he hadn't spent that money on the house, he would have had it later and maybe he wouldn't have failed."

She stared at the ruins. "Probably he would have anyway. It would have taken a little longer is all. He wasn't much of a farmer. I think he really believed what the land agents said, that you could just sprinkle seeds on the ground, sit back

BEAUTIFUL BAD MAN   147

and watch things grow. He never admitted it, but I think he came to hate it. Every year he put things off longer, did them with less heart. I think he was glad when Mr. Van Cleve gave him an excuse to sell and leave."

"But your husband was good at it."

"Better. Papa had a small inheritance from his grandfather and came out here with enough money for a good start and wasted it. Joe's father was a farmer, and Joe was the third son. Farming was all he knew, and he homesteaded south of here. We lived there for the first two years we were married, but this is better land and there's more of it. When Mr. Van Cleve started trying to buy everyone along the creek out, well, you know how Joe got the place. Sometimes I thought...."

She stopped, unsure whether she wanted to admit the truth to him. "He never said it, but I think you aren't the first man who married me for this land."

"He didn't get it by marrying you."

"No, but he put himself in a position to get it when Papa failed, and I think he always knew Papa would fail."

"Maybe he just wanted the curtains."

"He hated the soddy and everything in it. Losing this house was the worst thing that ever happened to him." She heard the bitterness in her own voice and forced lightness instead. "Is this the plan, to rebuild the house?"

"Not for a while and barn first when we can. Let's take a walk."

They walked the boundaries of the land, and Norah felt ashamed of how few of his questions she could answer. Neither her father nor Joe had shared what they did with different fields with her. They most certainly never wanted to hear her opinions. Caleb did.

Before long he was pointing, telling her about different crops, different varieties of wheat he'd heard about. He spoke with enthusiasm of theories on letting fields lie fallow, cover crops grown for no reason except to enrich the land when plowed under.

She listened first with surprise and then with pleasure, feeling almost like a real partner.

"When we're through dealing with Van Cleve, we'll get your goats," he said, "and chickens and a pig. There's no reason to ever starve on land like this, even in bad years. We'll have a bigger house like Carburys' someday, but only if you make blue curtains for it."

He looked serious, so she didn't laugh, but she did agree with a light heart.

On the way back to the soddy, his arm rested around her shoulders as if it belonged there, hers around his waist in the same fashion. Back inside, working on what would be a late dinner, Norah remembered that plans such as the ones he'd shared with her weren't supposed to ever come true. Once the threat of Van Cleve was gone, Caleb would grow bored and leave. That was her plan.

If she'd been wrong and he stayed, she'd be living with a very bad man until death. She rolled out biscuit dough, cut out the rounds, and began to hum under her breath.

16

"COME ON, PARTNER, time to plant corn."

The first months of marriage destroyed Norah's comfortable ideas about Caleb working the farm while she tended to familiar household chores. Today she moved along the rows of a plowed and harrowed field with a sack of seed corn over her shoulder, enjoying the scent of freshly turned earth and warm spring air. Plunging her planting stick into the soil up to the mark the way Caleb had demonstrated, she withdrew it, dropped a corn kernel in the hole, closed the hole with her foot, and moved on.

No matter what he had said about knowing and liking the rhythms of the land, Norah had not believed him in the beginning. More and more she understood his feelings were unlike what she'd seen from her father and Joe.

She watched him now as he dropped his own planting stick, picked up a handful of dirt and squeezed it in his fist. He spread it over his palm, poked it with one long finger, and examined it. At last he tipped his hand to one side and let it fall little by little to the ground.

He wasn't evaluating the moisture content as another man might. He was admiring that dirt the same way he sometimes admired sprouting seeds.

"If you keep that up, I'm going to beat you to the end of this row," she called out.

"The only way you'll beat me is by distracting me with the way you look peeking out from under that bonnet at me like that. It's cheating."

"You look like a mysterious stranger under your hat brim yourself, so you're cheating too."

"Not me. I'm not pretty."

No, he wasn't. He was beautiful. Heaven help her. She had to remember he was also bad. Not evil maybe, but very bad. A liar, a thief, a killer.

He would work the land and enjoy besting Mr. Van Cleve. In a year, two at most, farming would bore him, and he would go back to his old life, and after all, that was what she wanted.

Norah left the fields first so she could have supper ready when he came in at sunset. On her way back to the house with a bucket of water from the creek, she stopped to admire her garden.

Caleb had plowed and helped her plant, but only after moving the plot from where it had always been near the house to here by the creek. Why had it never occurred to her or to Joe that taking the garden to the water made life far easier than hauling endless buckets of water to the garden?

Moving the garden was only one of his endless ideas. They'd never plant corn by hand again, he assured her. Next year they'd have a check row planter. He built shelves along the kitchen wall to replace the turned over packing crates she had used and muttered about wells and cisterns, a spring house, and an outdoor fire pit for summer cooking.

After a day in the fields planting, her father, brothers, and Joe had all eaten supper in silence and gone straight to bed. Caleb never did. He took one of the books from the crate by the bed and kept her company as she made up the new dresses or did other chores by lamplight.

The only book Norah had seen since leaving Baltimore was the Bible. Her curiosity about the books had been building steadily, and tonight it got the best of her.

"What are you reading?" she asked without thinking. "Oh, I'm sorry. I shouldn't interrupt, and I could look for myself when you're not reading, couldn't I?"

"You can read any of them any time you want." He looked down at the book in his hand again. "I don't suppose you have much time for it either, do you. This one is called *Around the World in Eighty Days*, and it's about a fellow who makes a bet he can do that and what happens when he tries."

With that, he flipped back to the first page and began reading aloud.

His hair was dark gold in the lamplight, his voice deep, sharing the story a gift. The scarred hands that cradled the book and turned the pages would run over her body soon and dissolve all the cares of the day into a pleasure she'd never imagined existed. Her needle stopped in the cloth.

This is the way it's supposed to be. Partnership, marriage. No matter what we call it, this is how it's supposed to be. I was wrong. I don't want him to leave. If he does, I'll never stop missing him.

MANY THINGS COULD start Early growling in the night—wind soughing around the house, coyotes or other animals. Cal no longer paid attention to the minor episodes and neither did Norah. When a deep, steadily escalating growl woke Cal in the middle of the night, he didn't have to wake Norah.

After yanking on trousers and stomping into boots, he reached for the rifle. "Bar the door behind me and don't open it until you hear my voice."

He moved as quietly as possible in the dark house and could see Norah doing the same only because her night dress was white. He found Early's rope, slipped it on past his ears, and let the eager dog out into the night ahead of him.

Pulling hard, the dog made straight for the horse corral, but Cal saw a match flaring over near the haystack. He snapped off a shot, the flame died, and Early's growls changed to frantic barking as he lunged against the rope.

A distinctly human shadow moved near the corral. Cal fired again. Running footsteps pounded away.

"Good boy." The dog whined under his breath. "Me too," Cal said, "but I can't see in the dark, and we don't want to be the ones shot."

Nothing smoldered in or near the hay. After checking the corral gate and the horses, Cal took the disappointed dog back to the house.

"Are you all right? What was it?" Norah's hands ran over him as if she expected to find a wound he didn't know about.

"I'm fine. At least two men were skulking around, one to fire the hay and the other after the horses. The way they ran, I don't think I got lucky."

"You were right about a dog."

"Try not to sound so surprised."

She laughed, and the husky, nighttime sound of it ran over him like a caress. "Let's go back to bed. Early can keep watch. You and I can do better things."

Cal found the burned out match by the first light of the sun. It had fallen onto bare dirt instead of into the hay.

"I guess we did get lucky after all," he said to Norah.

The hatchet dropped next to the corral gate affected him differently. Through the red rage, he heard Norah asking what anyone would use it for.

"Even without a dog, we'd hear someone chopping from the house. Why not open the gate to let the horses loose?"

After several deep breaths, he managed to answer in what sounded to him like his normal voice. "They weren't going to chop wood. They were going to cripple the horses."

"What kind of men...?" Her voice tapered off.

The anger raced hot through his belly, and he let it out on her. "Evil men. That's what kind. My kind."

She stared at him, silent and wide-eyed.

He picked up the hatchet and threw it as hard as he could. Early raced after it, tail waving, but Cal ignored the dog and his wife, and strode off toward the fields.

The sun was high overhead by the time he returned, carrying two rabbits. Killing hadn't put him in any better mood. Neither would butchering, but he dropped them on the table and pulled his knife.

Early had greeted him with forgiving affection. Norah didn't. The two of them worked in silence until dinner was on the table.

"I'm sorry," she said finally. "I know you wouldn't do something like that."

"You don't know anything of the kind."

"Yes, I do. You don't just like horses more than people. You like horses, and you don't like people."

He met her eyes finally and saw if not forgiveness, acceptance. She was right. With a few exceptions such as snakes, he liked pretty much everything on earth better than people.

The knot in his belly loosened a little. She didn't need to know it, but she was an exception too. He liked her most of all.

CAL OPENED THE door a few mornings after the nighttime attack, and Early bolted straight for the creek. Early usually trotted around the yard in the morning, and the behavior triggered alarms.

Whistling and calling, Cal finally lured the reluctant dog back to him. He pushed Early into the house, told Norah to keep him there, and set out to find the cause of such unusual behavior.

A dead coyote came into sight first, then a fox, then crows, one still in the process of dying. The beef that had killed them was farther along, half hidden in the bushes by the water.

Cal cursed steadily as he hauled enough coal oil and wood to the site for a pyre, cursed even more vehemently as he piled the bodies and the beef that had poisoned them, careful to touch them only with rags that would burn too.

"Strychnine," he told Norah. "I couldn't find but the one carcass laced with it, but that doesn't mean they didn't leave more somewhere."

"They'd kill one of Mr. Van Cleve's cows just to do that?"

"Preston has a free hand. He wouldn't tell Van Cleve he sacrificed a steer to kill our dog. They know they can't sneak up on us unless they find a way to get rid of him."

"They brought the carcass to the far side of the creek. I suppose Early heard them but didn't growl loud enough to wake us."

Cal nodded agreement, but his mind was elsewhere. "Can you shoot?"

"Yes." She hesitated before adding, "But I can't hit anything."

"We better start working on that then. I'm going to be gone for a while tonight. I'll leave you the pistol or rifle, whichever you do best with."

She didn't look happy. Neither was he when he found out how true her words were. She could probably hit the side of a barn if it was a very big barn and she stood very close.

He left her the pistol and rode to the V Bar C in the same small hours of the night Preston and his men favored.

The only way Van Cleve's ranch dogs would be effective against Cal was if they were replaced. During the time he'd worked on the ranch, Cal had established firm friendships with the animals, and they greeted him happily in expectation of handouts of bacon or ham.

He didn't disappoint, and they escorted him to the corrals containing the ranch's working horses. Opening the gates, he propped them wide so the horses could find their own way out nice and quiet.

The largest of the several barns on the ranch housed hay, equipment, and the big bay Thoroughbred stallion Van Cleve had purchased to improve his working stock. Cal risked a lantern rather than stumble over pitchforks—or into the jaws of the stallion, which had turned out to be so intractable, the hands all swore they'd quit before anything he sired was old enough to ride. Halfway to the stallion's stall, Cal jumped as something massive crashed into wood to his right.

A bull. Mean little eyes glinted red in the lantern light and showed clear intent to get to Cal and grind him into the dirt of the floor. This one must be so valuable he'd only go out on the range with the cows for a few months for breeding to minimize chances of injury.

Cal continued back toward the stallion, revising his plans as he went. Releasing the stallion without getting hurt was easy, and the horse took off at a run. Within minutes he'd be terrorizing the loose geldings so thoroughly, they'd be in Canada by morning. He'd have the few mares in the bunch rounded up and be ready to defend them against any and all intruders.

The stall the bull was in had been heavily reinforced. Two latches and two bars. Cal dropped the bars, opened the stronger-looking of the two latches, and ran. Behind him he heard a bellow and wood splitting. He kept running.

The dogs joined him, frolicking happily around as they escorted him back to where he'd left Forrest. He was glad of the company. He really wouldn't want to meet either that stud horse or the bull on foot.

17

Cal gave a self-satisfied grunt as he finished tamping the last post for a fence that would give the horses summer pasture and keep them out of the crops.

Tomorrow he'd start stringing the new wire that would save him more night trips to haul wood rails from the same source as the posts—Van Cleve's private lumber yard.

Leaning back against the post, he looked out over the greening fields with satisfaction. Three months now and everything was shaping up the way he'd imagined.

He had put the lumber and equipment salvaged from the abandoned homesteads to good use, but boards wouldn't do for fence posts. With the fence done and no more immediate need to visit the V Bar C, Norah wouldn't have any reason to make that muley face for the foreseeable future.

Norah. Muley face and persnickety attitude over what he should and shouldn't do and all, she might yet make him change his mind about humans in general. Years ago she had climbed into a wagon with him and freed him with no ulterior motive he had ever been able to puzzle out.

He had a notion she'd suffered consequences that family loyalty kept her from admitting. She fought him tooth and nail every time he wanted to do something she considered wrong, and she fretted over it too much, but she wasn't much of a grudge-bearer.

Having a wife who welcomed him in the night the way she did sure kept a man easy in himself. He never should have humored her over the horror of coupling in daylight, though.

One of these days he'd override that one because in daylight the way her dresses tucked in here and rounded out there the same way her body did made him think randy thoughts. Taking her against a building or flat in a plowed furrow with the scent of fresh-turned earth all around would make a nice change from the bed.

He straightened, picked up his tools, and whistled to Early, uneasy at where his own thoughts had headed. She was willing and a good cook. Former luxuries like clean sheets and clothes had become everyday items.

Still, appreciating a woman was one thing. The unfamiliar feeling that came over him more and more often at the sight of her was something else, something dangerous that could weaken a man.

The look of her as she served dinner put him more on edge. No woman who had spent the morning doing laundry should be able to heat the blood of a man who had spent the morning tamping fence posts.

When she first started getting prettier, he thought it was the new dresses, but right now she had on one of the drab old rags, the front still wet. The air out here must do something town air didn't because her skin glowed and her hair caught the light, and her eyes, which he knew for absolutely dead damn certain had been gray that first time he saw them, shone bluer than ever.

If she knew the effect she had, she'd use the power it gave her. Time to provoke the muley look.

"After all the years you lived here, you must have been stealing chips from Van Cleve's cows last winter. I didn't plow many under, and there are hardly any on the grass I'm fencing."

She sipped coffee, unprovoked. "You have enough stolen wood piled up we don't have to worry about it, and you know Mr. Van Cleve will renew the supply any day now."

That drove all thoughts of dresses, what was underneath them, and shining hair out of his mind. "What are you talking about?"

"It's almost time for his cows to suffer their spring attack of wanderlust. Hundreds of cows all over the place for days make a lot of cow chips."

No woman, no sane woman, could be saying such words as if they had no meaning. "He stampedes a herd through here every year, and you didn't bother to tell me?"

Her eyes widened, even though he'd kept his voice low.

"It's not a stampede. They gather hundreds of them a few miles from the property line and then drift them this way in the night. You worked for him. How could you not know that?"

"I worked for him for little more than a month in the dead of winter. Do you think he gave me a written history of everything he's ever done?"

"I'm sorry, but it's not as if you can do anything about it."

"The hell I can't."

"You can't. One man can't stop hundreds of cows. It took us days to drive them all off, and when we were almost done, Mr. Van Cleve's men showed up, apologized out of one side of their mouths, laughed out of the other, and rounded up the last few."

At least she sounded bitter. A little anger would be nice. She got angry at him for salvaging used lumber off land Van Cleve had all but stolen.

"So hundreds of cows ground everything to dust, and you stood there and watched them do it?"

"You don't have to yell. No, we didn't stand and watch them. We worked to exhaustion to move them back to the V Bar C from the minute we heard them. It was different every year, but last year about half the crops survived. Joe did some replanting."

Cal dropped his fork in his food, appetite gone. "You didn't tell me because I might do something to stop them, something you and some preacher wouldn't like."

"That's not true, and you know it."

"I'll tell you what's true. No one's running cows over those fields, not now, and not in the middle of the damn winter."

"How are you going to stop them, shoot them?"

"Whatever it takes. Glad you feel the same way, partner."

He paused long enough to take his Winchester down from where it hung by the door. He might need the Sharps before this was done, but not yet.

SHE HAD NEVER seen a man so angry. The day he'd gotten nasty when she'd said ugly things about prostitutes was nothing compared to this. Yelling and throwing things would have been better than the low voice, twitchy jaw muscles, and hard eyes.

Norah put her own fork down and rose to clear the table. Caleb had slammed the door in Early's faithful face, and the dog sat there, whining under his breath. Scraping her own leftover food and Caleb's into Early's battered tin dish, Norah ran her fingers through the rough white hair on the dog's neck, then tugged gently on one velvety black ear.

"It's me he angry at, not you, although mostly he's angry because he knows he can't stop them. He can't shoot hundreds of cows."

Except maybe he could. He'd been with buffalo hunters for years, and they shot hundreds a day. If only she could be sure cows were all he'd shoot.

Through the window she saw him lead Forrest out of the corral, saddle up, and head west toward Mr. Van Cleve's land. Of course it was V Bar C land in every direction except the creek now, but the main ranch lay west. He'd be going to see if they really were gathering hundreds, holding them in a herd, and getting ready for the invasion.

She prayed he'd find nothing, that this year it wouldn't happen. Except for the attempt on the horses and the poisoned carcass, Mr. Van Cleve had been strangely quiet since she and Caleb married. At first she'd hoped the rancher was afraid of Caleb after all and would leave them alone. She knew better now, but even so she forgot the threat for days at a time.

If Caleb shot hundreds of Mr. Van Cleve's cows, or heaven forbid, any of the cowhands, the sheriff would come out from Hubbell and arrest him. The same sheriff who wouldn't do anything about Joe's murder would do anything Webster Van Cleve wanted.

Caleb wouldn't let anyone arrest him. He'd fight, and they'd kill him, or hurt him and drag him away. If only she could make him stay home and safe. Foolish wish. Stopping the cattle would be easier.

When had Caleb become more important than the land or anything on it? She didn't know when and didn't know how, only that it had happened. She couldn't explain it to herself and had failed abysmally to explain it to Mabel Carbury when they'd visited last month.

"He's good looking in a mean way," Mabel had said, "but you've let female feelings get the best of you. What does it matter how he makes love if he's got the devil in his heart?"

Norah had never before heard that term used for what happened in the night. She liked it better than coupling or mating or breeding or any other way of thinking about it.

Of course there was no love between her and Caleb. She cared about him, cared more than was wise, but he cared more about the horses or Early than he did about her. He still referred to Joe as her husband, and almost always called her partner, not wife. No matter. She'd never say it out loud, but she liked thinking it. Making love.

She'd tried to tell Mabel all the ways Caleb was a good husband, better than Joe, but gave up when her friend argued. "It was an accident, Norah. Surely you can forgive him now that he's dead."

No, she couldn't forgive Joe, and even if she ever did, Caleb Sutton was a better husband. He was a hard man, but she preferred it to indifference. He shared the kind of plans with her that she considered dreams, and she could tell he believed he could make those dreams come true by the kind of work he did and the way he did it.

Once in a while he mentioned how they'd have goats or a cow and chickens when the trouble with Mr. Van Cleve was over, but he didn't whine about the rancher as if no one else had to move back into a soddy, as if losing a house was worse than losing....

She finished the dishes and hurried out to continue with the laundry. Caleb couldn't mean to shoot hundreds of cows. He couldn't mean to shoot the cowhands who pushed them. She didn't want him arrested. She didn't want him hurt. She wanted him *here*.

By nightfall, Norah jumped at every bird call outside or thump when Early stopped pacing and threw himself down for a short break. When the dog jumped at the door, tail waving, she followed him into the yard at a run. At least the dog got a greeting and a pat on the head. She hung on the corral fence as Caleb unsaddled and rubbed the horse down.

She walked to the house beside him. "Are you still angry with me?"

"No, but we have to talk."

In spite of his words, he showed no inclination to talk while she served a late supper and they ate. She filled the silence with nervous chatter, about how the dog missed him and how she had forgotten how it felt to be alone in the house after dark and other things so trivial she couldn't remember them seconds after they left her mouth. He looked so grim.

"What did you find?" she asked finally.

"You were right. They had about fifty bunched up when I first found them, and they added more all day. If you're right about hundreds, we've got no more than two or three days before they come."

"I'm sorry."

"Being sorry is the problem. I'm going to town tomorrow for supplies, not staying over but turning right around and coming back. If you want to stay at Carburys', I'll leave you there. If you want to come to town and stay with your friend until you find a place of your own, I'll give you what I was going to pay you for the land in the first place."

She gaped at him until words came. "No. I live here as much as you do. I won't leave unless you do. We could both go. You admitted you could find other land as good."

"Nobody is running cows across land I plowed and planted, and nobody is running me off land I own. I'm going to fight them. I'm not going to fight them and my own partner at the same time. You people, all of you, you sit on your land like rabbits, hoping the coyote will fill up on some other rabbit. Van Cleve will stop when he's dead or when he's convinced the price of this land is more than he's willing to pay. I'm going to convince him, or I'm going to kill him."

"You can't kill people over land."

"He killed your husband. Had it done. He killed Henry Sutton and probably a few others. Over land. Wake up, partner. We're in a war."

"I know what they did, but they're...."

"Evil? So am I, remember? Devil's spawn. You pack what you need, and I'll take you to town."

"I won't go."

"I'm not asking."

Norah lay awake beside him that night, her mind in chaos.

"What are you going to do?" she whispered finally, knowing he was awake too. He told her.

Sick fear flooded through her. She squelched every urge to tell him couldn't or shouldn't. They were beyond that.

"I don't want to go," she said finally. "I won't fight you."

"Will you help?"

"I don't know if I can."

"Fair enough. No arguing and no getting in the way."

"No arguing and no getting in the way."

She knew they wouldn't be making love tonight or for many nights, but when she reached out and grasped his hand, he let her take hold. It helped, but nothing felt right until he pulled her into his arms and against his chest. Her fear subsided enough she slept, waking at first light alone.

18

"You want to stay at Carburys'?"

Norah shook her head and climbed onto the wagon seat. Early hopped into the wagon, tail waving happily. The scent of the horses drifted back on the cool morning air as the big animals moved the empty wagon effortlessly.

Dew sparkled on every plant in the morning sun. Not for the first time, Norah marveled at how little the world around them cared about the problems of humans.

"Are you sure they'll have it in town?" she asked.

"If they don't, I'll steal it from Van Cleve. They use it in his quarries up north, and I've seen more than I need stored at the ranch. The drawback to that is someone might notice it's gone and start to thinking."

"I suppose they keep it right next to that handy supply of fence posts," Norah said tartly, and then wanted to bite her tongue. No arguing she'd promised. If he left her in town, she could find a way home but not quickly.

With no load one way and a light load the other, they made it to town and back in record time, arriving home in the early hours of the next day.

"What are you going to do first?" Norah asked.

"Plow."

"The horses are tired."

"So am I. So are you. You get some sleep."

She lay on the bed and stared into the dark until it lightened to day, then stared at the ceiling until sunlight pouring in through the east window painted that bright square on the soddy wall. If Caleb's plan worked, the men pushing those cows would be in danger. If it didn't work, Caleb would be in danger.

Norah gave up on sleep, dressed, cooked breakfast, packed it in a pail, and set off across the fields to find her husband.

Except for spotting the occasional huge footprint of one of the draft horses, she would not have had the courage to venture so far onto Van Cleve's land. Caleb had to be plowing virgin prairie at least two miles beyond the property line, and furrows running across the slight dip in the land had to be a quarter of a mile long.

He saw her long before she could distinguish his features, stopped the team, and waited. From the distance he had looked glad to see her, but maybe she had imagined it. When she drew close, his face was set in the same hard lines as the past two days.

"I thought you might be hungry," she said, lofting the pail.

"Starved." He left the plow and the horses and came to sit beside her on the grass.

"I couldn't carry anything to drink."

"I brought water in the wagon."

"Can you finish by dark?"

"Not as much of a firebreak as I'd like, but if they don't come tonight, I'll finish it tomorrow."

"I want to help."

He took another bite of biscuit, chewing slowly as if he hadn't heard her.

Finally, "Why?"

"I can't stand the thought of you out here alone against hundreds of cows and a dozen or more men."

"You think two of us changes the odds?"

"It changes things for me. You're my husband. I want you home in one piece, and if you really can turn them back.... I want to help."

"You can't heft those cans of coal oil, I don't want you touching dynamite, and you sure can't plow."

"I thought I could use the pail to spread the coal oil a little at a time. I could lay the fuse cord if you show me how."

He finished the last piece of bacon, stood, and offered her a hand up. "It's a deal, partner."

Long before sunset, Norah's back ached so viciously she wondered if she'd ever stand straight again. She didn't wonder but knew she'd never get the stink of coal oil out of her nostrils.

Caleb leaned on the shovel and looked the whole trap over with satisfaction. "It should turn them. If it doesn't, it's the Sharps, and I don't like shooting things in the dark."

Norah levered herself upright with a hand at each side of her lower back. "I suppose you like cows better than people too."

He gave her a wider smile than usual. "Better than some people. I might make an exception for a woman in blackface."

Rubbing a sleeve over her forehead, Norah looked at the smear of oily dirt with loathing. "I'm not going to wash this dress. I'm going to burn it. I'll save the scrubbing for myself."

"Don't go tossing that on the fire, bury it. I never liked it anyway."

With horror, Norah looked at herself and remembered that she hadn't put on one of her old dresses. She had on Mrs. Tindell's gray dress. Of course it had started to resemble the old ones even before this. She said a word most men didn't use around women, and Caleb laughed out loud.

"Come on, partner. We need to get all this equipment put away and get back here."

"What if they don't come tonight?"

"It will still be here the next night. Until it rains, it will stay good."

But they did come that night.

CAL HAD NEVER been in a fight where he cared what happened to anyone except himself. Small wonder men left women home when they went to war. Norah was quiet beside him, her hand in his small and vulnerable. He should have tried harder to make her go back to the house and leave the rest to him.

Her help could make a difference in achieving the effect he wanted, and she'd argued ferociously, but he shouldn't have given in. Right now he ought to pick her up, carry her back to the house and tie her there. She'd promised three times to follow directions exactly, yet the urge to risk her being angry at him for a year or two and take her home wouldn't die.

Too late. The sound of cattle drifted to him on the still air. His worry switched to his own calculations. The fuses would burn one foot every thirty seconds. They'd rehearsed, tried to time how long it took from lighting the first to the last, calculated the length for each one. The end of each fuse sat atop a square of white cloth so as to be visible in the dark, Norah's idea, and a good one.

No use worrying about any of it now. Norah lay stretched beside him, determined to do her part. The approaching sound became sensation, the rumble of hundreds of hooves background for the occasional bawl.

Shadows separated from the night. Good. They were coming slow, not too tightly packed as they ambled along.

"Go."

He struck the first of his matches, touched the fuse at hand and moved to the next, trying to concentrate, forget ideas of snatching Norah up and running. He could see matches flare as she moved away from him, lighting her half of the fuses.

Go, go. Finish up. Get on that horse and get away. For the first time since he was a boy, he did something close to praying.

The cattle were closer than he expected when the first of the dynamite-packed trenches he'd dug exploded and dirt fountained into the air under the noses of the herd leaders. His calculations had been good. The other traps exploded only seconds later. Fire shot across the grass, stopped at the plowed firebreak, but didn't stop burning toward the herd.

The leaders whirled, panicked. For a moment the front of the herd turned into a milling, confused mess; a few head broke free, running as if pursued by wolves. The rest followed, stampeding back the way they had come. Men yelled. Shadows danced against the flames.

He'd planned to watch and enjoy the sight. Instead he took off at a run. Once he knew Norah was safe, he'd come back and make sure the herd had run so far and scattered so thoroughly no one would be gathering them again in a hurry.

Victory celebrations with a female partner had a lot to recommend them. The problem seemed to be finding the strength of mind to untangle from the female partner before daylight and go assess what they'd done.

Cal slid a leg out from under one of Norah's, moved her arm from his stomach to her side, dressed, and left with Early at his heels. He saddled Forrest, tied Early to a corral post, and paused to rub behind the dog's ears a moment.

"Sorry. You can't come, and I don't want you whining and waking her. She'll be out and get you soon enough."

The fire had burned no more than half a mile back onto the V Bar C. Forced to choose, the cowhands had let the herd run and worked to stop the fire. The moisture still in the grass this early in the season would have helped. He heard voices calling back and forth, men searching for something—or someone.

Cal had studied the land long and hard before deciding this had to be the easiest route for anyone aiming to bring cattle onto his land from the herd's starting point. He'd also noted the rough terrain most likely to cause problems for crazed animals running in a stampede. That's where he found what the searchers were looking for, or what was left of him.

He lashed the body across his saddle and in the last hour of darkness wove his way undiscovered through Van Cleve's men. The body could spend the day under the tarp with the best of the lumber he'd salvaged from the burned farmsteads, a place Norah would never look.

Van Cleve's men would find it tomorrow, but they wouldn't find it where they were looking. They'd find it when and where he wanted them to find it.

19

EARLY'S PERFORMANCE OVER Preston's foray in the night had convinced Cal that Josiah Quist knew what he was talking about when it came to dogs. When the dog abandoned his constant hunt for field mice, ran a short way toward the town road, and stopped stiff-legged and growling, Cal didn't second guess him.

"Norah, hide!"

She dropped the cultivator and curled down in the corn without a word, untying her new blue bonnet and tucking it under her skirt. For once Cal appreciated the washed out old dress she wore. She wasn't invisible, but someone would have to get closer than he had any intention of letting them get to see her.

Wearing the gun belt while working the fields was wearisome. So was constantly moving the rifle to keep it close. Times like this proved the caution necessary.

Cal bellied down in a low spot at the edge of the field and waited. A lone rider. He watched the man stop at the house and knock. He didn't go in. Good sign. He left the house and rode into the field, riding along the edge. Another good sign. The closer the rider came, the less he resembled trouble, at least the expected kind of trouble.

Rising, Cal whistled Early close and cut across the field toward the man. The farther from Norah strangers stayed the better.

Although the rider sure didn't look like one of Van Cleve's men, Cal was hard put to decide what he was or why he'd be out here. He wore a derby, the narrow brim little protection against the sun. An embroidered satin vest hung open over an unbuttoned shirt and collar. Some equally expensive jacket was probably tied behind the saddle, one more concession to the rising heat of the late May day.

The rider reined to a stop a polite distance away. Cal kept the rifle trained on him. "Lost, are you?"

The man smiled the way a coyote would, or a weasel. "I suppose it's no surprise you don't recognize me, Caleb."

Close up he looked much younger than from a distance, barely old enough to grow so much facial hair. Dark sideburns turned into a short pointy beard that hid the lower half of his face, but something was familiar around the dark brown eyes, and no one but Norah called Cal Caleb.

"Eli?"

"Micah."

Cal didn't lower the rifle. "No, it's not a surprise. I heard you ran not long after I did. What are you doing here?"

"Unlike you, I visit family every now and then, see how they're doing. Jason told me you were back. Since you haven't seen fit to visit him, he'll be here sooner or later. He'll figure it's his duty to make sure you're all right and fix things if you're not."

Cal said nothing. He barely remembered Henry Sutton's youngest son and didn't like what he saw now.

"Any chance of a drink around here?" Micah asked.

"Water. You don't look like you drink much of that."

Micah threw his head back and laughed the kind of laugh that was all for show and had neither joy nor humor in it. Even so, if Micah Sutton was dangerous, Cal couldn't see it and figured he could handle it. He lowered the rifle, and Micah dismounted.

"Norah," Cal called, "you can come out now."

Her head popped up from amid the young corn plants, and she came toward them, stepping through the rows like an old hand. The thin fabric of her dress clung to her in a way Cal would appreciate if he were the only one watching.

One of those ugly big aprons wrapped right around her would be better at the moment. Then again shooting Micah, even a cousinly little shot in the foot, would stop the avid way he was watching what he had no right to watch.

Micah showed no awareness of his own jeopardy. "So you have a woman now."

"Wife," Cal said, low and hard. "You call her Mrs. Sutton, and you call me Cal."

The young man's eyes jerked back to Cal. "So it's like that. Jason's got a wife now too, you know. He'd been eying her for years, but he waited until the old man was safely dead. You know about that, I guess."

"Broke my heart."

Micah laughed again. Genuine this time. "You've never been to a funeral with so many dry eyes."

Cal had never been to any funeral, but he didn't say so. He introduced Micah to Norah and afterward said to her, "We got enough done today. I'll finish up myself."

If they were alone, she'd argue. The blue eyes met his, assessed Micah, and she smiled. "It's nice to meet one of Caleb's cousins, Micah, but if I neglect the house any longer, the dust will choke us in the night."

Cal watched the gentle sway of her skirt as she walked away, the blue bonnet swinging in her hand emphasizing the motion.

Micah was watching too, damn him. Cal ground out, "Don't. Unless you want a fist in the face, don't. What the hell are you here for anyway? Don't give me any malarkey about family feeling."

Whatever else he was, Micah wasn't a fool. He turned away from the sight of Norah's receding figure. "I came to ask you a favor, not for me, for Jason."

"He's old enough to ask for his own favors." Jason was also the only Sutton who would get any.

"He can't ask for this one because he doesn't know he needs it, and if he did know, he wouldn't come to you. He'd try to fix things himself and get killed or arrested."

Hearing it put like that, out in the open, was a relief. Micah's dark Sutton eyes widened at Cal's sudden grin. "So you want me to get killed or arrested instead."

"You won't," Micah said. "I'm not like you, but I spend enough time in the kind of places you do I've heard your name. Men sometimes ask if we're related."

"You look like a card sharp."

"I make my living gambling. A good living. Better than you'll make scratching in the dirt. I'd have bet no one could force you to follow a plow—or walk inside a soddy."

"So you're not as good a gambler as you think you are."

Micah's confident air slipped, and for a moment youthful uncertainty slackened the lines of his face. He went to the saddlebags on his horse, pulled out a letter, and handed it to Cal. The letter was addressed to Jason but had not been through the mail. It had been opened.

"I was at the house, visiting like I said. So I was the one who got this when some fellow stopped by and dropped it off."

Cal turned the paper over in his hand. "I suppose this fellow got the impression you were Jason."

"He might have."

"And you opened it and read it."

"I was alone at the house and was bored. It's from Grace. She was the one two years older than me, you know. Pa married the girls off to men like him. The others are doing well enough, no worse than Ma anyway, but Grace.... He's a preacher over by Fischer, and he might just be meaner than Pa. She was dying when she wrote that. Even without the letter, Jason will try to get Grace's daughters when he finds out she's gone."

Cal gave in, opened the letter and read. When he got to the end, bile climbed up into the back of his throat. He swallowed fast, used every trick he knew to keep from giving way to the nausea in front of Micah.

"Why aren't you doing something?" he said.

"I told you. I'm not like you. I'd get killed or arrested as fast as Jason."

"But I'm supposed to risk it. I don't remember anything about Grace except she had as big a mouth as the rest of you."

"I'm not asking for her or for me or for her girls. I know you wouldn't lift a finger for any of us, and I don't blame you. I'm asking for Jason."

"You've got no right to ask for him. Get out of here. Get off my land and don't come back, and don't even think of pulling some lady's gun out of your sleeve and pointing it at me."

Cal let the letter flutter to the ground, pivoted, and went back to where they'd left the cultivator among the corn rows. He heard the horse leaving but didn't look up until Micah was a dark spot in the distance.

The sun was low on the horizon when he quit for the day and headed for the house and Norah. On the way he stopped where the letter had fallen and pocketed it, feeling the poison of it every step to the house.

Norah had been cooking over the outdoor fire for weeks now. He yanked open the door on the cold stove and threw the letter in anyway. Let it be tinder for the next fire.

"I know he's your cousin, but I didn't like him," Norah said as she dished up supper. "That vest would be in poor taste on a woman."

"He's a gambler. He's showing the world he wins more than he loses."

"What did he want?"

"He wants me to kill someone."

Norah put down her fork with the beans on it still untasted. "And you're going to do it for him."

"No, I wouldn't do anything for him, but I'd do it for Jason. I owe Jason like I owe you."

"He helped you get away?"

Cal nodded.

"I would never ask anyone to kill someone, and from what I know of Jason Sutton he wouldn't either."

Cal shoved his plate away, rubbed his forehead even though the pain was too deep to reach, went and retrieved the letter from the stove.

"You should know it all, I guess. If I don't do it, Jason will try. He'll find out sooner or later, and when he does, he'll talk to the law and try to do it right, and that won't work. No one's going to help him take children from their natural father. In the end, he'll get himself killed or jailed."

Cal handed her the letter. Smoothing it out on the table, she held it close to the lamp, turning the paper one way and the other. Reading the spidery words had been hard enough in daylight. Cal didn't envy her puzzling it out, but he didn't offer to read it, knew he couldn't read those words again.

Grace had written to Jason five days after the birth of her third daughter, knowing she was dying of childbed fever. The neighbor woman who had helped her through the birth and was helping her die had promised that the letter would go to Jason without Reverend Abel Whales ever finding out.

She rambled, full of apologies for not writing, but her husband forbid it, for not visiting, but her husband forbid it, for being cold and unwelcoming the times Jason and Eli had visited, but her husband demanded it.

She always wished she could leave the husband she disappointed and live with Jason. She would keep house for him. She wouldn't be a burden. She wished her daughters could live there. They would work hard. She wanted Jason to come get her daughters, although Whales would never let them go.

Some parts of the letter were more legible than others, a testament to Grace's struggle with the fever. Toward the end, the scrawl skipped words, the lines wavered, maybe the fever, more likely what Grace had been determined to confess. For she wrote it as a confession, as if what she had glimpsed from her deathbed was her sin, not her husband's. Even at that bitter end, she was her father's daughter, the blame hers.

"Does 'interfering with' mean what I think it does?" Norah asked, folding the letter.

"Yes."

He expected her to tell him what he should do or what he shouldn't do. She reached across the table and put a hand over his, and they sat in silence.

"We just defended this place with everything we had," he said. "I don't want to walk away and leave it."

"I know, but maybe it will be a while before Mr. Van Cleve decides what to do next. Maybe he won't realize we're not here."

"More likely he will." Which made no difference in what he had to do. "I'll leave you with your friend in town."

"No, you won't. I'm coming with you."

He jerked his hand away, started to squash that idea, but she spoke over him. "How are you going to get three little girls, one of them a baby, from Fischer to here by yourself? Even if their father hands them over, they'll be afraid."

"I'll tie them up and throw them in the wagon."

She patted the hand he'd returned to the table, picked up her fork and began to eat. He watched her for a moment, the pain in his head and nausea in his guts receding.

Pulling his own plate back, he picked up his fork. "You sure look pretty in that blue bonnet."

She smiled around a mouthful of beans and swallowed. "I'll wear it in the wagon tomorrow."

THEY SPENT THE next night in Hubbell. Knocking on Becky's door and asking for shelter discomfited Norah, but Becky's attitude toward Caleb was what took all the pleasure out of the visit. He frightened Becky, and without being rude, Norah couldn't make the girl stop leaping to dramatic and silly conclusions.

She climbed to the wagon seat beside Caleb the next morning still tired and worried about where Caleb, who had left her at Becky's and disappeared, had spent the night. Asking would be foolish. Better not to know. She wouldn't ask him. Wouldn't.

"Where did you sleep last night?"

"In the wagon with Early. Ogden even let me clean up this morning at his pump. He didn't say, but he likes the way Jeb and Stonewall look, and Van Cleve bought two teams from him. The big horses he had out back are all gone now."

Jeb and Stonewall did look good. The dappled gray rumps a few feet away were round and muscled. The horses' coats gleamed in the sun. They felt good too, able to trot for long stretches.

For the first time since Micah's visit, one corner of Caleb's mouth curled up slightly, his brown eyes danced with amusement. "So you were afraid I'd break into Lawson's again."

"No, not really." Oh, why not admit it? "A little, and I also wondered, that is, I didn't think you would, but I didn't want to think...." Deep breath. "The morning we got married, I saw you coming out of the Royal Flush."

"We weren't married then."

"I know. I shouldn't have mentioned it. I'm sorry."

"You apologize too much."

"I know. You tell me. I'm sorry. I mean...."

He laughed at her, and she couldn't help laughing too.

"I bribed the barkeeper to let me sleep in a storeroom because it's clean, and the hotel isn't. No woman that night, but you know...."

"Yes, I know," she said quickly stopping him, not wanting to hear.

"You don't imagine I much like thinking about Hawkins, do you?"

The thought had never occurred to her, but she liked hearing it. She should tell him she didn't much like thinking about Joe either. She would tell him. Someday.

They reached the town of Fischer in early afternoon. A few stores and a saloon lined the town's only street.

"Hubbell looked like this about ten years ago," Norah said. "How do we find him?"

"Let's see if we can just spot a church. Can't be many in a place this small, and I'd rather not ask around."

"Maybe he'll give us the girls. Raising them by himself would be hard. Maybe he'll give them up rather than have anyone know."

"Sure. That could happen."

The day was hot and the sun bright. Caleb's tone slid ice over the back of Norah's neck and down her spine.

20

CAL SPOTTED A plain white building with a cross over the door among the scattering of houses outside the town. Even if this was the right church and Whales lived close, finding him might require asking. What Cal wanted was to get in and out of town unremarked, but he could already tell that wouldn't happen.

He parked the wagon beside the church and left Norah there with Early and orders to stay, no matter what she heard. He had more faith in Early obeying—he tied the dog to the wagon.

A woman came to the first door he tried. No more than Norah's age, she had two boys hanging from her skirts and a pleasant smile on her face.

"Reverend Whales lives in the house behind the church."

Cal thanked her and turned to leave. Before he'd taken two steps, her voice stopped him.

"Mister? Excuse me, but you don't look like someone who would be inquiring about joining his congregation."

On another day he'd find that humorous. "How would a person like that look?"

She hesitated then blurted, "You should stay away from him. He's not just fire and brimstone. He's mean."

He had pictured the woman who tended to Grace as older, gray-haired and grandmotherly. "Did you know his late wife?"

"I did." She stepped out closer to him, her hands on her boys' heads. "Are you her brother?"

So much for not leaving tracks. "Cousin. I've come for the girls."

"Oh, I'm glad. So glad. He won't want to let you have them, you know." Her eyes left his and went to the gun belt, the rifle. "He has a shotgun. I've seen him threaten people with it. Be careful."

Abel Whales didn't look like anything to be careful about at first glance. Short, thin, hair and full beard streaked with gray. His eyes were gray also, not brown like Henry Sutton's, but the fanatical gleam was so much like his uncle's Cal froze at the sight.

"If you've come to find Jesus, you get rid of those guns and come back," the old man said.

Thin and high, the sound of his voice broke Cal's paralysis. How could anyone sit in a church and listen to that preaching at them?

"I'm Cal Sutton, and I've come for Grace's daughters," he said.

Whales snaked a scrawny arm back into the house. Without the woman's warning, Cal might have been too slow, but he had his pistol clear by the time Whales brought the shotgun to bear, the hammers on both barrels back. Cal's chest shot knocked the man back through the door, the shotgun blasting upward as he fell, bringing down shards of wood and plaster on top of the body.

Picking up the shotgun, Cal eased the hammer down on the second barrel, then moved into the doorway to check Whales. Dead. Behind him he heard Norah running, calling his name. In front of him, inches from her dead father's head, stood a small, dark-haired girl clutching a rag doll.

Cal straightened and leaned against the door frame, still dealing with his blood buzzing wildly through his veins, pounding in his head. He'd never come closer to being the one on the ground, blood no longer leaking because the heart was no longer pumping.

Norah reached him, and he felt her hands, patting, stroking, checking for damage.

"I'm fine."

"That boom was a shotgun, wasn't it?"

"It was, but I'm fine. If you want to help with the girls, you need to start."

He jerked his head toward the doorway. There were two of them there now, not crying, not making a sound, just staring. For the first time memories of Grace and her sisters floated from the dark place in his mind, the silent acceptance of whatever went on around them, the blank stares.

"If there's a back door, meet us there," Norah said.

For a woman who had thrown fits over salvaging wood from abandoned farmsteads, Norah stepped over a dead man with remarkable calm. Cal stayed in the doorway a moment, staring at the place where she had disappeared from sight and marveling.

Heart slowed almost to normal, Cal went back to the church, let Early loose, and drove the wagon to the back of the house. Norah had both girls outside with her, boxes filled with their clothes at her feet, and a baby in her arms.

"This is Deborah," she said, touching the bigger girl on the shoulder, "and this is Judith." She pointed to the one with the doll. "And this little sweetheart is Miriam." She jiggled the baby in her arms, smiling down at it.

Cal didn't care what their names were and didn't want introductions. What he did want was away from this town as fast as possible. He lifted the girls into the wagon, threw the boxes in, and all but shoved Norah, still cradling the baby, to the wagon seat.

"You have to get the cow," she said, arranging her skirts.

"What!"

She pointed to a small brown cow in a pen beside a shed. "The baby needs milk."

"We can't be hauling some cow around. We need to get out of here. Fast."

"Why?"

"Because I just killed a preacher."

"He tried to kill you."

"I don't want to explain that to some lawman. It's always best to be as far away from bodies as possible when someone finds them. Believe me. I know about this."

Muley look. "We can't flee in a wagon with two little girls and a baby. And a cow. We'll just stop at the sheriff's office and explain. He needs to send someone to take care of things here anyway.

"We're not hauling a cow back with us, and we're not talking to any sheriff."

Her hand closed over his arm. "If you want to run, take Forrest and run. I can drive the wagon. I'll drive home, cow and all."

She had never driven the wagon a single mile, and holding the Percherons to a cow's pace would take some doing.

"I'm not running," he growled. "I'm making myself unavailable, and you're not bringing any of them home. They're going to Jason."

Her hand went from his arm back to the baby. She shifted it a little on her lap, her touch—possessive. Damn it. If he didn't stop her now....

"Taking a cow that's not ours is rustling," he said.

"The cow belongs to the Whales family, and this is the Whales family," Norah said, pointing to the children in the wagon.

He didn't like it. Didn't like any of it. Most of all he didn't like her thinking he was running. "All right. I'll get the cow, and we'll find the sheriff, but they're going to Jason's. Don't say another word about it. Not one."

He tied the cow behind the wagon next to Forrest, who snorted and tried to pull away. At least the horse understood. It would take a year to get to Jason's with that milk cow along, maybe two. And why was he worried about it, Cal thought savagely. He was going to be in jail, waiting to hang.

The sheriff's office was in a handy place right across from a saloon. The baby started crying as Cal pulled up. According to Norah it needed its pants changed, and it needed a drink. He was almost glad to leave the fuss behind and do the suicidal thing Norah had shamed him into doing.

The sheriff behind the desk was the type Cal most hated. Middling size, a deep tan emphasizing the honed-down rawhide look of him, and sharp blue eyes that would never miss anything you wanted them to.

Ah, who was he fooling. Hating anyone with a piece of tin on his chest was just smart if you were Cal Sutton. If you were Cal Sutton and about to commit suicide because of a muley woman, there was no reason to ease into things.

"I killed Abel Whales a few minutes ago. He threw down on me with a shotgun because I came to take his daughters to kin the way their mother wanted. They're in my wagon out in the street there."

The sheriff looked through the window. "That your woman with them?"

"My *wife.*"

"Will the girls tell me you're kin and they want to go with you?"

"No. They don't know me."

Cal pulled out the letter and handed it to the sheriff. After another glance outside, the man began reading. He took his time, went back over parts. When he was done, he handed the letter back.

"You're not Jason Sutton."

"No, I'm Caleb. The girls' mother was my cousin."

The small attempt to avoid recognition didn't work. This time the sheriff's head-to-toe examination all but peeled skin.

"I've heard of Cal Sutton," he said.

Nothing good. Cal kept quiet.

"Let's go take a look at Whales."

At least Norah looked a little worried when he told her what they were doing, but she was too busy holding a bottle for the baby and talking to the girls to say more than, "I'll wait here for you."

Nothing had changed at the house. The shotgun lay where Cal had thrown it, and the body lay where it had fallen. The sheriff took it all in, including the shotgun pellets embedded in the door frame.

Cal heard someone approaching and whirled. The woman who had warned him of the shotgun stopped a little distance away. "I heard the shots and was afraid to come, but when I saw you, Sheriff.... Is he dead?"

"He is."

"And you're all right," she said to Cal.

"I am, and I owe you for the warning. Without it I might be the dead one."

"Let's see that letter again," the sheriff said, and Cal handed it over. "Is this Grace Sutton's handwriting, Mrs. Duncan?"

"Yes. She finished that letter the day she died and gave it to me. My husband paid a man he knew who was traveling to Hubbell to deliver it in person."

"Do you know if this man is really her kin?"

Mrs. Duncan studied Cal again. "No, but he has her eyes. He has eyes like Grace's."

She turned to leave, but Cal stopped her, offering her a gold eagle. "You shouldn't be out of pocket for that letter."

"We only paid a dollar, and we did it for Grace. I can't take that."

"You probably saved my life today. Take it and buy something pretty. Buy something for your boys."

She looked at him uncertainly, then at the sheriff. In the end she took the money. "Tell the girls.... Tell them I'm happy for them, but I'll miss them."

Cal and the sheriff were halfway back to his office when the sheriff spoke.

"Nobody's going to miss him. He would have been moving on again soon anyway."

"They weren't here long?"

"A year maybe. Came to replace a fellow who died. Real boon for the other churches around."

Remembering the voice and the zealot's eyes, Cal had no trouble understanding the sheriff's meaning.

"Since you're kin, I expect you'll want to pay for a funeral."

"I'm kin to the girls' mother. I don't care if you dump his body outside town and let the coyotes take care of him."

"Let me put it a different way. Since you killed him, I expect you to pay to bury him."

Cal handed over a double eagle this time, but it was worth it. He began to believe he might be leaving town today.

Back at the wagon, the sheriff nodded to Norah and addressed the girls where they sat side by side in the bed.

"Did either of you see what happened today? Did you see what happened to your pa?"

The older girl looked away. After a moment, the younger one said, "I saw Pa open the door. Then he got his gun and tried to shoot him." She pointed at Cal. "He's our cousin. Norah's our cousin too because she's married to him. We're going to live with our Uncle Jason. Mama wanted us to live there."

"You know your pa's dead?"

The girl nodded, her face taking on the same blank expression as her sister's.

The sheriff stood for a moment as if unsure, then whacked the side of the wagon with his palm. "Go ahead. Take them and get out of here."

Cal got out of there.

THE ONLY THING his uncle preached that Cal believed was the certainty of hell. Spending eternity in flames would be worth it if Henry Sutton suffered the same.

The trip back from Fischer made Cal revise his mental picture of perdition to an eternal wagon trip with a baby, two young girls, and a milk cow.

And a stubborn wife. He couldn't leave her out.

"Jason and his wife don't even know they're coming. They haven't been married long. Maybe they won't want three little girls." Norah whispered the last.

Cal didn't whisper. "We haven't been married long, and I don't want three little girls."

"Sssh. Of course we do. Let's go home first and send word to Jason."

"No. We're going to Jason's, and we're handing them over."

"But...."

"It's what their mother wanted." There, that ought to end it, he thought with satisfaction.

Not a chance.

"She didn't know about you. Or me. If she knew, she might have thought we'd be a better choice."

"I killed their father. You've barely promoted me from evil to very bad. Jason is good. He's as close to a saint as people get. We're taking them to him."

"But...."

"Didn't you promise to obey?"

Hell. A wagon trip with a baby, two young girls, a milk cow, and an angry, not-speaking wife.

From home to Fischer had taken a day and a half. Fischer to the Sutton place took three days.

Cal expected the sight to do bad things to his stomach, but nothing looked too familiar. The fencing was new. A few trees had gained a hold along the farm road. The house was no longer white but pale yellow, and the sod buildings were gone as if they had never existed.

A thin young woman with reddish hair opened the door as they approached. She clutched an old Star pistol in shaking hands.

"I'm supposed to shoot this when I see strangers so Jason and Eli know to come, but when I saw a woman and a baby, I—I didn't."

Good. Cal didn't want to see either Jason or Eli. "You don't need to call them away from their work. I'm Cal Sutton, and this is my wife, Norah. We've got Grace Sutton's girls out in the wagon. She's dead, and she wanted you to have them."

Cal handed her the letter. The woman stared with her mouth open, and Norah pushed past him.

"See? I told you. It's too much for her. She can't manage three little girls dropped on her out of the blue."

To the woman she said, "Don't let him scare you. That letter does say Grace wanted Jason to have her girls, but they can come with us. You don't have to feel obliged. We can take them. In fact I'd love to have them."

Cal was going to have to push those girls out of the wagon, and maybe he'd leave Norah here too.

Jason's wife saved him by recovering. "Grace is gone? That will break Jason's heart, but her children.... Of course we'll take them. He frets all the time because Grace won't leave that man and bring them here."

Emma Sutton put the pistol on a high shelf, and in minutes she and Norah had the girls in the house, seated at the kitchen table, eating sugar cookies. The baby went into a drawer pulled from a bedroom chest, and Emma started worrying about her husband.

"I'll just shoot the pistol, and Jason and Eli will come, and you can talk. They'll be glad to see you."

No, they wouldn't. "No, thank you. We need to get home before dark. I'll talk to Jase another time." Cal had to all but pick Norah up by the elbows and carry her to the wagon.

Free of the cow, he headed the team for home at a smart trot. Norah was speaking to him again, but that wasn't a good thing.

"You should be ashamed of yourself. That was rude. Worse than rude. We won't be home until after dark anyway. Those little girls must feel like unwanted baggage, and Emma must think you're...."

"Devil's spawn?"

"Stop saying that like you're proud of it. Stop saying it at all."

"Grace wanted Jason to have them. They need someone like him. That house is big enough they won't be laying on the floor like logs. I killed their father."

"All right! You're right! They're better off somewhere else. Happy?"

He put a hand on her knee and rocked gently. "No. It's not like I want to make you miserable. I just—do."

She stayed stiff for a while then relaxed and put her hand over his. "You didn't do it. I did it to myself. Coveting. We'll see them again, won't we?"

"Sure." It would happen whether he liked it or not, so he might as well agree.

THE HOUSE, THE shed, the corral—nothing showed signs of damage or even any stranger's presence in the days they'd been gone. Cal's tight nerves didn't relax.

Destruction of any of those things would be revenge and retaliation. By the thin light of a new moon, he couldn't see the fields. If Van Cleve's men had gathered another herd and driven them over the crops, cloven hooves trampling and tearing the land and the growing plants, it would be more than revenge, it would be destruction of a year's work and hope, the heart of the farm.

He couldn't stand it. While Norah fussed around the house, putting things away and deciding what to rustle up for a late supper, Cal took Early for a walk the length and breadth of the land.

At first he held firm to the belief that the darkness concealed damage. Again and again silvery moonlight revealed sturdy young plants reaching for the night sky.

Whether Van Cleve had stayed his hand out of ignorance that the place sat empty or to plan some different kind of harm, Cal didn't care. The healthy, unharmed plants, the quiet night, and sweet summer air all brought a surge of well being.

Of course letting his guard down also brought the ghosts. Whores laughed and lured. Jake Kepler lied. Men known and unknown cursed and condemned. Henry Sutton joined Abel Whales with assurances of damnation, their zealots' eyes burning.

Early came from behind, his cold nose against a dangling palm breaking the spell. Cal rounded up the ghosts, threw them in the dark place, and slammed the door shut behind them.

The dark place had no lock. The ghosts would escape again, but not tonight. Tonight there was only Norah, and she'd forgiven him again.

21

Working in the garden Caleb had insisted she move close to the creek, Norah admired the ingenious irrigation system he'd dug for her as she did every time she used it. Mabel would change her mind about Caleb if she saw this. Next time the Carburys visited....

As if her thoughts conjured him up, Caleb charged into the yard astride Stonewall, Jeb following loose, and Early bringing up the rear.

"Norah!"

He saw her running toward him, met her halfway, and scooped her up onto the horse as if she weighed nothing. She barely had time to absorb how much it hurt to be belly down across his thighs on a galloping horse before they reached the house. He pushed her off onto her feet, jumped down beside her, and hustled her inside.

"What's wrong?"

"Early says we've got company coming."

Caleb stood in the doorway with the Winchester, the dog stiff and growling beside him. "Take the Sharps off the wall and lay it on the table. There's field glasses in a pouch on the side of the case. Let me have those."

She had never touched the big gun before, and it was heavier than she expected, the elkskin case softer. Untying the flap covering the pouch, she pulled the glasses out and handed them to him. The tension melted off his shoulders as he scanned toward the road. "Looks like neighbors. I'll catch the horses and put them up."

He gave her the glasses back, and Norah looked for herself. Sure enough. She saw Archie Carbury and several other men she recognized. Some rode, some drove farm wagons. She put the glasses back in the case and returned the Sharps to its place on the wall, but she noticed Caleb kept the Winchester with him when he went for the horses.

Norah carried the water bucket and dipper outside. The June day was hot, and some of those men had come a distance. Like Jason Sutton.

She waited beside Caleb until they all pulled up in the yard and dismounted or climbed down from wagon seats. Archie took it on himself to introduce the others to Caleb.

"And you know Jason," he finished.

Caleb nodded and said nothing.

"We're here because word's out about what you did out here. One of Van Cleve's men quit and did some talking in town. They've pulled that trick with the cattle three years running, but this year none of us has seen a single cow. The fella who quit said the regular hands refused to try it again. Finding that body hanging the way you left it spooked them. They figure the men drawing fighting pay can earn it."

Norah's head whipped from Archie to Caleb. With an effort, she choked back the question forming on her lips.

"This quitter claims he saw me do something with a body?" Caleb said.

Archie grinned. "No one saw you do anything, but for some reason they think it was you, not hobgoblins." The grin faded. "He's offered a bounty on you, a thousand dollars for proof you're dead. We came to see how we can help."

"Telling me about it instead of trying to collect is a good start."

"Nobody here wants to collect or see anyone else do it either. If you can beat him, or fight him to a standstill, we all win, so how can we help?"

Norah listened to them bandy it around for a while. Aside from passing on warnings and information, the remaining neighbors couldn't help. If Caleb had plans, she knew she'd be lucky if he shared them with her much less strangers.

For once she agreed with his attitude. While Archie and a few others exuded genuine goodwill, some of the men stayed quiet, their reservations plain on their faces.

The settlers began to get back on their horses and in their wagons. Jason Sutton didn't leave with the others. He shifted from one foot to the other a few times, then approached Caleb.

At first Norah saw no physical similarity between the cousins. Dark-haired and swarthy, Jason was almost as tall as Caleb, but he looked thin and bony rather than lean and muscled. On second thought, maybe he would be as tall if he stood straight instead of stooping like that.

A nice-looking man, nothing distinguished him the way the hawkish nose and prominent, stubborn jawline did Caleb. Yet when Jason and Caleb stood close, she saw the family resemblance in the wary dark eyes, the cheekbones below them and winged brows over them.

In spite of the tension between the men, she couldn't help asking, "How are the girls? I think of them all the time and hope they're recovering and doing well."

"They think of you often too," Jason said somberly. "They talk about how Cousin Norah came and got them. Judith especially. They'd like to see you again."

"Caleb is the one they should be grateful to," she said. "When they're older, they'll understand that."

Jason nodded, and no one said anything, the silence uncomfortable.

"I just remembered. I left the sluice gate open and creek water running into the garden," Norah said. "It was nice to meet you, Jason. I hope we can visit soon."

As she walked away, she heard Jason say, "I wanted to believe you made it, but I never did until I heard you were back."

If Caleb answered she didn't hear. From the distance of the garden, she watched the two men, tense and not saying much. When Jason rode away, Caleb never looked toward her. He pulled the horses back out of the corral and returned to the fields.

If he didn't want to talk about Jason, she wouldn't try to pry it out of him. She was going to know about the body before bedtime, though. And the bounty. What was he going to do about the bounty?

JASON LOOKED LIKE hell. Like some kind of beaten down farmer trying to eke out a living on land that was all rocks. Cal didn't know why that surprised him. How had he expected anyone who lived his entire life under Henry Sutton's thumb to look?

Dead. That's how. Jason only looked half dead so he'd managed pretty well. Maybe he'd even bounced back some since the old man died.

Seeing him again, listening to him go on about his thoughts over the years, even forcing out an expression of gratitude didn't change Cal's mixed feelings. Just as well Jason lived far enough to the north there wouldn't be much of that. Some things when they were done, were done. Letting sleeping dogs lie and all that.

There were a couple of other things those helpful neighbors had slung around he wished they'd left prone. He should have made Norah stay in the house somehow. She'd be after him about the body until he told her, and the bounty.... He couldn't come up with any ideas to deal with that except a bullet between Van Cleve's eyes, and that meant finding a way to do it so Archie's hobgoblins would get the blame.

He washed up and watched Norah bustling around, putting supper on the table. She'd not only cleaned up but redone her hair and put on his favorite of the new summer dresses she'd made.

So much for his expectation that she'd be banging around, angry and demanding to know about the body. She was focused on the bounty, upset and fretting. He wanted to smooth that worried look away, and didn't know how.

She waited until the food was on the table. Rabbit stew. Very good stew. He wondered how much he'd get down before losing his appetite.

"You weren't going to tell me about the body, were you?"

"No."

"What kind of partner is that?"

She surprised him. He met the blue eyes for the first time since he'd sat down, saw only determination.

"Not a good one, I suppose," he admitted. I didn't want you going on about how we killed someone."

"We did."

"We made what they were doing dangerous. We didn't force them to do it. Van Cleve didn't force them to do it. They can quit. One of them did."

"What was that about hanging the body?"

"He's got one of those overhead signs at the end of his ranch road. I left the body hanging there."

She hid her face in her hands. When she spoke, her voice was muffled. "Do you know what? If I were Mr. Van Cleve, I'd put a bounty on you myself. What are we going to do about that?"

He wasn't going to let her do anything, but he liked her new attitude. "I'm not sure what to do about it yet, but I'll think of something. He's getting tiresome."

"How close to dead is tiresome?"

"Pretty close."

She took her hands away from her face and began eating again. Not, in Cal's opinion, with the enthusiasm the food deserved. Probably nothing would take her mind off the image of a dead man hanging in the breeze like forgotten laundry, but he couldn't keep from trying.

"Is the garden a muddy mess?"

"No, the irrigation water wasn't really running all that time. I thought you'd like to talk to him alone."

"He didn't say much. Glad I made it. Wondered about me over the years. Wasn't sure it was really me back here at first. That kind of thing."

"Did he help his father—hurt you?"

"No. I told you. He's like you. He's a reason I'm still alive."

Her hand stopped with a piece of bread halfway to her mouth. "I know you said that. I know you feel an obligation, but the way you looked at him, I didn't think you liked him much."

She smiled, not much of a smile but better than none. "Of course you didn't look at me very friendly when you first saw me again either."

"That was different. I never knew you. I just had ideas about how I thought you should be, and when you seemed different it made me mad."

"So Jason is different than you expected?"

"No. I knew Jason, the core of him, and there's no way that changed. He's good, the exact opposite of devil's spawn like me."

"I'm going to start doing something violent every time you say those words. You know it's not true of you or anybody else. Even saying it gives your uncle credence he shouldn't have."

"It probably is true," Cal said. She looked so worried. If it would take her mind off bodies and bounties, he'd even tell her about some of the things he'd kept shoved down in the dark place all his life.

"My mother was a seventeen-year-old farm girl brought up as strict and sheltered as possible. She never said a word about my father. He must have been a stranger who forced her."

"Or maybe he was a young man who planned to marry her, but he died. Maybe she quarreled with a lover, and he joined the army or moved away, but if he'd known he'd have come back. It would be bad enough if he was a married man who seduced her with sweet lies. You don't need to reach for the most terrible explanation."

"You always want to put a pretty face on things."

"You always want to think the worst."

They ate in silence for a few minutes before Norah asked, "What did he do?"

Cal didn't pretend not to know who she meant. He only hesitated long enough to swallow the last of his stew. Then he told her.

SHE HAD ALWAYS known all his secrets were bad. People talked about good memories and happy times. Secrets were about pain. Her own secrets were about pain. He'd stopped looking at her, his voice low and dull.

"Living with Uncle Henry was better at first. Better than the brothel with my mother gone. I knew he despised me, but whatever drove him later wasn't there yet. Or maybe it was, and he couldn't let it loose because there were too many other people around. His wife was still alive, and he couldn't let his neighbors, the same people he sat beside in church every Sunday, see the poison."

Caleb had lived a year with his uncle's family on the rented farm in Indiana. He liked working the land, and he liked caring for the livestock. He even liked his aunt and his cousins, although they were forbidden to have much to do with the bad seed among them.

"He picked what he liked out of the Bible and ignored the rest. He liked sparing the rod being spoiling the child a lot. I suppose Jason and the others should have been grateful he didn't use a rod. He used his belt or a switch. He beat them any time he caught them doing anything he considered sinful, not just talking to me."

The cousins obeyed their father and ignored the bad seed among them. Except Jason. The same age, Jason and Cal became friends of a sort, ignoring each other any time anyone could observe, behaving like normal boys when they thought they could get away with it.

The pattern held, even when they attended school, for Jason's brothers and sisters knew they could lessen punishment for their own sins by betraying Jason and Caleb.

"He beat them, but I can't remember him touching me. He probably did believe I had some devil inside that could jump out and catch him because he didn't like to get close. Right from the start, when I broke his rules, it would be no supper tonight, no breakfast tomorrow, like that."

Norah wanted to touch him, but he got up and started pacing. She rose too, cleared the table, fed the dog. She had the dishes in the dish pan by the time Caleb continued.

"I never saw any sign he cared about Aunt Florence. She died one night in the middle of supper, just fell down and never got up. He had us all packed up and headed west before the month was out. He bought a full section under the Preemption Act, and once he had his kingdom on the prairie, he really came into his own."

Caleb stopped pacing in front of the east window, picked up the hem of the curtain there, and held it as if studying it.

"He built the first house out there and some other buildings out of sod like everyone else. There was one small building, a storage shed it was supposed to be. I helped build it. We all helped build them all. It was maybe eight by eight, no windows, a heavy door. If I ever knew where he got the lumber for that, I can't remember now."

He paced again, picked up the curtain again, and this time held it bunched in a fist.

"That shed was where he decided I should live. I never saw the inside of the sod house. The day we took Grace's three daughters there was the first time I stepped foot inside the frame house. He'd shove a plate of food across the floor with his foot morning and night. It was never enough."

Norah closed her eyes, remembering how Caleb had reacted to her setting out a single plate of food for only him the first time he'd been in the house. She dried the last dish, poured two cups of coffee, and sat at the table again.

Caleb paced. The light of the single lamp wasn't bright, but she could see the dark splotches of sweat spreading on his shirt.

"I did some digging in the beginning, trying to escape, but a sod wall almost two-foot thick isn't so easy to get through with your bare hands, and he'd see the signs, repair the wall and—get after me for it. It wasn't so bad most of the year, but in winter—one blanket. I got one damn shoddy blanket."

He stopped pacing and leaned against the wall in the farthest corner of the room where she could only see him as a shadow. "Of course he rousted me out at first light so I could work. I worked right alongside the others, and they pretended they couldn't see me. Except for Jason. Jason slipped me food when he thought no one was looking."

She cradled her full coffee cup in her hands, wishing it would warm them, because she knew what was coming and didn't want to hear it. But if Caleb could tell it, she could sit and listen.

"Sooner or later one of the young ones would see him and tell. Maybe they thought he'd go easier on them. Maybe he did. He'd whip Jason and make us all watch, and Jason would act like the others for a week or two after. Then he'd start again, slipping me food. It went on like that for the first couple of years, but finally Uncle Henry realized he had to do something different."

He paced back to the window, seized the bottom of the curtain in both fists, and hung on.

"The next time one of the girls saw Jason give me something, Uncle Henry threw him in the shed with me at night. At first I thought that would be better, easier on him, company for me, but he went crazy.

"I couldn't see him, but I could hear him, screaming and shrieking how sorry he was, promising his father he'd never do it again, throwing himself at the walls. He wore down by morning, but it was the same the next night and the next. He spent every night in there with me for I guess a week or so. He never got any better.

"We didn't get much more food for the two of us than what I always got, but I don't think he ate any, so you could say he gave me extra food again."

Caleb dropped the curtain, made as if to smooth the crumpled cloth, then came back to the table and sat across from her.

"Uncle Henry stopped forcing him in there every night because he broke him. He broke him right down to a good and sinless son who never looked at me again. He didn't look at me the day he slipped me a knife and walked away, and he didn't look me in the eye today."

Norah put her cup down, stretched her arms out and took his hands.

"Put a pretty face on that, partner," he whispered.

"You know I can't. Why didn't you visit him when you first came back? Why didn't you grab hold and hug him today?"

He tried to pull his hands away, but she held on, and he gave in. "That's a woman's way of thinking." After a moment. "Because of the knife. He didn't give me that knife to dig out and escape. He gave it to me to kill his father. I knew I wasn't strong enough, and I didn't try. I spent the night digging out instead."

"Did he say that's why he gave it to you?"

"No. The others were close by. He just shoved the knife in the back of my britches. It cut me a little."

"Then you don't know that's what he wanted."

"I know."

"Why does it bother you? You made your living doing that kind of thing for years."

"I hate it that Uncle Henry was right about me, and I hate it more that Jason could see it too."

"He wasn't right, and you know it. If your mother had lived, your life would be different. If you'd never met your uncle you'd be different. You were two little boys tormented by an evil madman. Jason saw a chance to do something that might change things and took it. He probably didn't even know what he wanted to happen."

"We were fifteen, not little boys."

It went so against what she believed that the words seemed like a foreign language she didn't understand. Then she realized he had described events that took place over years, starting when he was eleven.

Still, she wanted to reject it. "You couldn't have been. I saw you. You were twelve, no more than twelve."

He opened one hand and laced his fingers through hers. "You can feed a body enough to keep it barely alive, but not enough for it to grow. When I started getting enough to eat, I grew so fast my bones ached for a year."

He smiled a little. "So you thought you teamed up with a green boy, and you're having trouble believing I'm the senior partner?"

That wasn't the part of what he'd said causing a terrible ache in her throat. Could he tell her voice was unsteady because of tears she could never shed? "You should talk to him, really talk to him."

"Tell him I'm sorry I didn't kill his father? Tell him I'm sorry for whatever happened to him after I got away in such a panic I left the knife behind?"

"Tell him the truth, whatever that is."

He shook his head and ran a calloused thumb over the back of her hand. "Ah, Norah. I like that dress on you, you know."

"I do know. You say so every time I wear it."

"I'm glad you got rid of that gray thing."

"You mention that pretty often too."

"Let's go to bed."

"Will you hold me after?"

"Only if you hold me back."

22

CAL COULD SEE doubt all over Norah's face.

"Too ugly for you?"

"If it works, I don't care how it looks, but won't the first good wind tear that roof right off? It's made of sticks."

"If it does, no loss. We put up more sticks and they'll make shade again."

"A ramada." The roof of the flimsy-looking structure was made of branches from bushes that grew along the creek woven in and out of slim poles. Leaves and all.

"That's what they call it down in Texas. When we rebuild the frame house, we'll have a veranda."

For the first time in his life, Cal understood the urge to build things, things that would make a woman's life easier, things that would put a smile on her pretty face or even make her laugh.

Early moved out of the shade of the new addition, stiff and growling. Cal grabbed his rifle and pushed Norah inside the house. Two riders came on, waving. Cal let the rifle droop toward the ground but didn't put the gun down until he could identify the men—Archie Carbury and his youngest son.

Archie looked as dubious as Norah over the practicality of the ramada, but this wasn't a social call.

"We're passing word on like we agreed. Preston's men have been making trouble up north near your cousin, and one of them boasted they're coming for you. I know you're staying on guard, but six, seven men riding in here guns blazing.... You can come to our place you know. You'd make a sixth rifle. We could give them what for."

Cal nodded. "We may take you up on that. Let me think on it."

Message delivered, the Carburys left. No one wanted to be far from home if Preston and his men came rampaging.

"I guess building a bench along the wall there is going to have to wait," Cal said.

"You aren't going to hide out at Carburys', are you?"

"No, but you are."

"I am not leaving."

"Didn't you promise to obey?"

"Don't start that. Just don't start. I am not leaving."

"Don't make me worry about you. I can't do anything unless I know you're safe."

She stared into the dark eyes, wanting to believe he cared enough to worry about her. "All right, I'll go if you tell me what you're going to do, and if you promise not to get hurt."

"Stay inside with Early for a while, keep the pistol to hand, and I'll tell you when I get back."

"Back from where?"

"Finding what buffalo hunters call a stand."

"You know I can't shoot well enough to hit anything."

"Never admit it. Point it at them and look mean."

The land was frustratingly flat. He had to ride more than five miles from home to find enough of a hill for cover, but in the end he found an ideal spot. The road curved away from the creek here, and anyone riding south would be coming straight at the hill where Cal set up the tripod for the Sharps.

He counted on Preston riding to the farm over the same route he'd taken when Cal had been with him last winter. A man like Preston wouldn't ride around even if he suspected

Cal knew he was coming. With six or more men behind him, Preston wouldn't get cautious until he was close to the farm.

Satisfied with what he'd found, Cal headed home. If he guessed wrong about Preston, at least Norah would be safe at Carburys'. He wondered if Archie knew he had invited Early and the horses too.

FRUSTRATED AND IMPATIENT, Cal had to play mind games to stay quietly in place on the third day. Lying in wait from sunup to sundown was tedious, and Norah would insist on coming home soon no matter what he said. If she did that, he'd have to set up at the house, and the results were bound to be worse, bad even.

All those considerations combined to have Cal fighting a strong urge to hunt Preston down instead of waiting. One more day. Just one more day.

Slight movement in the distance caught his eye. Farmers could be coming from town along the road. He pulled out the field glasses, grunting with satisfaction as Preston and half a dozen others came into focus. Stretching out behind the rifle, he aligned his sights on the spot he'd chosen days ago and waited.

Time slowed. The scene below sharpened. The riders came around the curve exactly as he'd imagined, moving steadily in a way that enlarged men and horses as they rode closer. He squeezed the trigger. Asa Preston flew back out of his saddle and over his horse's tail.

Ejecting the cartridge and reloading with practiced speed, Cal targeted a second gunman before any of them reacted to the first shot. The second man slumped sideways, fell. For long seconds the others milled in confusion.

Just like buffalo, and folks think they're dumb animals.

His third shot knocked another rider sideways, and then they scattered, spurring and whipping back around the deadly curve.

The world reverted to normal. Cal shoved the tripod, rifle, and glasses in the case and moved to his secondary location. If the V Bar C men stopped running and came hunting, he didn't want to be found.

Silence descended. Two of the three riderless horses had run with the others. One was held by reins trapped under the body of its rider. It moved restlessly, the only thing down there alive to move. One advantage to the .50 caliber bullets in the buffalo gun, a man hit by one wasn't going to cause trouble after.

Cal stretched on his belly, waiting again. An hour passed. Two. He wouldn't mind tying Preston's body on that horse and using it for another message to Van Cleve, but he wasn't going down there before dark.

A wagon bumped across the prairie, heading right for the killing field. Cal yanked out the field glasses and scanned below in disbelief.

Archie Carbury, one of his boys, and a neighbor whose name Cal couldn't remember were rolling along down there as if on their way to a church picnic.

Unable to spot signs of anyone targeting the men below, Cal picked up his rifle and jogged down to join them.

"The hills around here give someone a good place to set up and shoot us down like fish in a barrel," he said when he got to the wagon.

Archie looked up from examining a body and grinned. "Do tell. Johnson here says everyone who'd want to shoot us rode by his place this morning heading east and a couple hours ago heading west. Everyone minus three."

"Did you count noses?" Cal said to Johnson.

"Can't say I did," the bearded man answered, looking around nervously.

"Then let's load them up and get out of here."

"Load them up? What do we want with bodies?" Archie's son said.

"I'll tell you later. Right now get back on the wagon seat and get ready to move."

The boy started to argue. Archie pulled him aside, said a few words, and gave him a swat on the bottom. Ignoring the exchange between father and son, Cal grabbed the nearest body by the belt, heaved, and threw it in the wagon. Johnson helped with the second.

"Keep hold of that horse, will you?" Cal said to Archie as he and Johnson hefted the last body.

In minutes they drove out of the target area at a fast clip, three bodies bouncing in the wagon bed and the saddle horse snorting unhappily behind.

The women and the older Carbury boys hurried out of the house as soon as the wagon turned in the yard. Cal jumped down in time to catch Norah when she threw herself at him, did that checking for wounds thing, and hugged him hard.

"We heard the shots. I knew it was the buffalo gun, but even so. Are you all right?"

Cal hugged back without thinking, caught Archie's speculative look, his sons' smirks, and stepped back a little. "Don't worry. I'm fine. Everything went easy."

Mabel got a good look in the wagon before her husband pulled her away. "Not many would say three dead men were easy. I suppose you're going to decorate the V Bar C like an Indian showing off scalps." Her tone and expression didn't match the disapproving words.

"Take your mother and Mrs. Sutton inside," Archie said to his boys.

To Cal's surprise, Norah took Mabel's arm and went inside without argument.

"I got to get home," Johnson said, discomfort plain on his face.

Cal nodded. Archie threw an arm around the man's shoulders and walked him to where a saddled plow horse waited.

"I'm not sure he'd know which end of a gun to point at an enemy," Archie said, returning.

"But you do."

"Spent the war learning things like that. Fourth Kentucky, CSA infantry." He leaned against the side of the wagon, a dark haired man of middling height who seemed ordinary until you saw how he handled three unexpected bodies.

"You and Norah seem to be getting along pretty good," Archie said, the humor in his gray eyes saying more.

"She deserves better."

"So does Mabel, but she's got me, so I do the best I can and count myself lucky."

"Your wife didn't have a Joe Hawkins first."

"No. That would make it easier."

Before Cal could ask what that remark meant, the boys charged back out of the house.

"What are you going to do with those bodies, Mr. Sutton?" the young one asked.

Ben they called him, Cal remembered. As tall as his father, the boy could keep his voice man-deep most of the time, but it broke with boyish excitement now.

"I'm going to take them back to the V Bar C so they can bury them."

"You going to hang them from the ranch sign like last time?"

"No. Unless Van Cleve is stupider than I think he is, he'll have sharpshooters hidden by the ranch sign. These need to go somewhere else."

"And do you have a particular place in mind?" Archie asked.

"The house has balconies sticking out of the second floor. One of them is right over the room they eat in, I think."

Archie whistled. "Sneaking three bodies onto the ranch and getting them up there.... Maybe Ben and I ought to help."

Cal had been going to settle for hanging Preston somewhere prominent and dumping the other two nearby. Displaying all three would pretty much tell anyone Cal had help, allies. The thought of it tempted him to trust Archie and his son.

"The only way to do it is quiet as death. No talking and no questions." He gave the boy a hard look.

Archie looped an arm around his son. "It's time he learned. We'll have a talk beforehand. You want quiet, you'll get quiet."

The V Bar C dogs accepted the two new friends Cal introduced them to without suspicion, more interested in the bodies. Two helpers made the whole operation easier than Cal had believed possible, and whatever Archie had said to his son kept the boy speechless the entire night. They left the bodies hanging from the balcony, the horse tied to some stone statue of a fat, naked boy in the yard.

Cal hoped no one would remark on the empty rifle scabbard on that horse or a missing gun belt on a body. The Winchester that had been in the scabbard was a good one, nothing burned into the stock, and no distinctive scratches on the metal. The gun belt had a nice thirty-eight in the holster. Norah needed guns of her own.

The three of them made it back to the Carburys' house before midnight. Cal made an exception to his rule about not letting anyone get hold of his gun hand and shook first Archie's and then Ben's hand.

"What's next?" Ben asked.

Cal shrugged. "We'll have to wait and see."

But he knew. Van Cleve had sent his men charging in the open and failed. What he'd try next would be more like what Cal himself would do, something lowdown and sneaky.

CALEB HAD BEEN right about the advantages of a ramada, Norah thought, as she kneaded bread dough vigorously on the table they'd dragged outside.

Dragging the bed outside too would make for easier sleeping on these hot nights. She smiled to herself at the thought of sleeping outside. Caleb would never agree to it of course.

Darkness brought danger. He still wouldn't let Early go out-side alone at night.

The dough achieved a satiny feel. She formed it into a ball and placed it in the greased bowl under a towel. On a day this hot, it would rise here in the shade. Norah picked up the extra flour to return to the bin, then paused at the sound of distant barking.

Scanning the horizon, she caught sight of three specks on the far side of the creek growing steadily larger as they came on fast. Her new rifle hung on the wall just below the pegs for Caleb's. She lifted it down and gave it an experimental heft, liking the weight and the scent of gun oil. From far enough inside the house to be lost in shadows, she watched the ap-proaching men through the open door and waited.

Caleb reached her before the riders. "You stay inside with Early. Bar the door, and stay inside until they're gone, no matter what happens."

Arguing would only take time they didn't have. She closed the door and dropped the bar in place.

Cal sat on the table under the ramada, watching the riders come toward him. They made such spectacular, clear targets, but could he take out all three? Sun glinted from spots of metal on their chests.

Unless he could make all three disappear, killing any would be futile. Closer now, features were distinguishable under hat brims—Sheriff Ludlow and both his deputies. It didn't take much imagination to figure their purpose.

He should have taken the chance. This close his odds were much worse, and they meant business. Bad business. He kept his rifle trained on the sheriff, who seemed to think that piece of tin on his chest was a shield.

"Put that rifle down, unbuckle the gun belt, and let it drop," the sheriff said as soon as he had his horse stopped. "You're under arrest, Sutton."

"Arrest for what?"

"You know damn well. You killed Asa Preston and two of his men, you backshooting coward."

"Shot in the back, were they?"

"Not this time, not that it makes any difference."

"I'd say it does make a difference, so would witnesses. Are there witnesses?"

"I don't need a witness. All three of them were shot with that cannon of yours."

"I don't think mine is the only buffalo gun in the county."

"I don't care what you think. You're under arrest and you're coming with us."

"No, I'm not."

"Yes, you are." Cal stiffened in surprise at the sound of the voice behind him and cursed his own carelessness. He should have known. He should have expected.

"Speaking of backshooters, is that what you've turned into, Ike?"

"No, but I ought to after what you done to Preston and the others. Don't try to turn. Put the rifle down, drop the gun belt, and you can stay alive long enough to hang."

"You're not taking my husband anywhere."

Hearing Norah's voice, knowing she must be behind Ike, almost made Cal do something stupid. Just in time, he jerked his attention back to business.

Surprised by unexpected interference, the sheriff and deputies looked toward Norah. Cal had his pistol out before they recognized their mistake. His heart raced as he angled until he could see Norah in his peripheral vision.

She had her rifle pressed against Ike Kerr's kidneys, and Ike still held a drawn Colt.

"Let the hammer down easy and put that on the ground," Cal said.

Ike did as told and moved to join the sheriff's men at a gesture. Norah started forward with him.

"Norah." Cal's voice came out as a croak. He had to get hold of himself or someone would notice his knees shaking.

She changed directions and moved to his side, doing a half-way decent job of looking mean.

The sheriff leaned forward in the saddle as far as his big belly would allow. "Mrs. Hawkins...."

"Mrs. Sutton," Cal said, anger steadying his voice.

The sheriff threw him an annoyed look. "Mrs. Sutton. Three men have been murdered with a gun like your husband's. I have to take him in. You know that."

"I know that when Joe Hawkins was murdered, you said you had no jurisdiction out here. You said you couldn't even investigate, and it was an accident anyway. If you changed your mind about investigating murders, Joe was killed five miles closer to town. Start there. It happened first, and after you arrest Mr. Van Cleve, come back and talk about Caleb."

"You know I can't do that."

"That would be the smart thing to do," Cal said. "Sometimes men disappear out here. Indians maybe."

"Don't you threaten me, you...." Glancing Norah's way again, the sheriff lowered his voice. "You haven't heard the last of this. We'll be back."

"I'll be waiting."

Ike swung up behind one of the deputies. "My horse is about a half-mile south," he said sullenly.

"I'll find it and turn it loose," Cal said. "Don't try going back for it."

They all reined their horses around and left faster than they'd come. Cal watched until they were small in the distance. By that time his heart had almost slowed to normal. He finally dared look at her.

"I told you to stay in the house."

"And let them arrest you? They'd shoot you before you reached town and claim you tried to escape. What did you give me the rifle for if not to help?"

He couldn't answer the question, but whatever he had given it to her for, climbing out a window and sticking it against the back of a gunman with a cocked pistol in his hand wasn't it.

"If you're going to do things like that, I'd better show you how. You don't want to get that close to an armed man."

"If I wasn't that close, I couldn't hit him. I might hit you."

"We better work harder at fixing that."

"Do you think we can?"

Something worrisome swirled around in his head. Something other than the sound of Early whining and scratching at the soddy door. Cal knew he should go back through the window, take down the bar, and let the dog out. He'd do that once he dealt with Norah.

All he had to do was decide whether to yell at her until she dissolved to the ground or hold her so hard the result would be the same. What could possess a woman to do a thing like that?

He cleared his throat. "We need to renegotiate our partnership agreement."

A squint-eyed, suspicious look was her only answer.

"We need to get rid of that obey part."

She dropped the rifle in the dirt in a way that made him flinch and kissed him in a way that made him forget the gun.

23

SHE SHOULD BE able to take the fizzy, light-headed aftermath of trouble faced and conquered in stride by now, Norah thought. Trouble was her husband's middle name.

For baking she still had to build a fire in the stove that combined with summertime heat and humidity to make every minute in the house miserable. Today she barely noticed and gave in to the urge to dance as she carried her golden bread loaves to the table under the ramada to cool.

Caleb sat there, working on her rifle. He'd already polished the brass frame on the old Winchester. Now he was oiling the stock. The source of that rifle and of the extra pistol he'd also brought home should bother her. It didn't.

Sometime in the last months her ideas about right and wrong had expanded. She still believed everything she always had. She'd just added two truths—anything that could hurt Caleb Sutton was wrong. Anything that kept him safe was right.

"If I damp the fire in the stove, is a cold supper all right?" she asked.

"You bet. Anything cold sounds good. In fact as soon as I'm done here, let's go swimming."

Swimming? Norah had never been swimming in her life. "I can't."

"Sure you can. It's not like you can drown in the creek."

It did sound good. When she fetched water, she bathed her face, let water trickle down the neck of her dress and cool her until it dried. Sometimes she pulled off her shoes and stockings and dangled her feet in the water, but swimming?

"What if they come back?"

"Right now the sheriff's on the V Bar C reporting to his master. Even if Van Cleve has his next move planned, it won't come today. We're as safe right now as we're going to get until it's over."

He didn't look particularly perturbed at the thought of how long it would be until the troubles were over, and Van Cleve's pet sheriff obviously didn't bother him any more than Van Cleve did. All of them bothered her.

"What if someone comes. The Carburys could come for a visit."

"Early warns us, and we scramble out of the creek and into our clothes. Stop worrying and go round up some towels and a blanket and clean clothes for after."

After what, Norah thought, although she had a pretty good idea. "I'm not taking off my clothes outside in broad daylight."

He grinned a wicked grin. "Would you take them off outside at night?"

"Of course not. Caleb...."

"If you don't get what we need, I'm going to drag you down to the creek without towels, dry clothes, or anything else and throw you in. I should have held on to that obey power a little longer."

In the time it took her to gather the things he wanted from inside the house, sweat trickled down her neck from her hairline. More rivulets ran between her breasts and along her spine. She would leave on her chemise and drawers, she decided. If he did what she thought he was going to do she would just—look to her heart's content. Out of the corner of an eye.

He took most of the bundle in her arms from her, and they walked to the creek side by side. Early jumped in and began playing doggy games in the water while Norah fussed nervously over where to leave each item they'd brought. Caleb ignored her and sure enough, starting with boots, began pulling off every stitch he had on.

Norah fumbled with the buttons on her dress, undid them, and stood staring at the ground, hotter than ever with the embarrassment flushing through her. Soon she saw her husband's long, narrow bare feet toe to toe with her still shod ones.

He tipped up her chin. "You've seen it all before."

"Not, not...." Not like this in bright sunshine with the sound of the dog splashing and the creek burbling and birds singing. How could being naked make him seem bigger, his shoulders wider, his eyes a darker brown and hair brighter?

"I can't do this."

"You don't have to. Close your eyes, and I'll do it."

After he pulled her dress over her head, she found balancing with her eyes closed surprisingly hard. She had to hold on, and the feel of his sweat-damp skin gliding over firm muscle quickened her breath, started that hollow emptiness growing low inside.

Her shoes. One stocking. The other. Her bare toes curled into the warm earth, and he straightened, giving her a lingering kiss before unfastening the ties of her single petticoat.

She'd given up wearing a corset in weather like this long ago and couldn't decide whether to be sorry or glad as she stood in her drawers and chemise. "Please. I need.... Let me keep these on."

"Your choice. They don't hide much, and they'll hide less when they're wet."

Holding his hand in a death grip, she eased down over the side of the bank into the water, gasping and trying to reverse course before she got knee deep in the cold water. Caleb picked her up, carried her to the middle of the stream, and fell back into the water, taking her with him.

Norah shrieked as they went down, struggled free, and ended up sitting in no more than two feet of water. "It's freezing."

"That's why we're here, remember? Cooling off."

"I'm cool. I'm getting out."

"You are not behaving like a woman who climbs out a window and shoves a rifle barrel in a man's back. Give it a minute and you'll get used to it." With the words, he sent a spray of water over her. "You haven't even got your hair wet."

She hadn't, and her hair still hung in a sticky, sweaty mass. Tentatively, she lowered her upper body into the water, tipping her head back until cool water soaked through to her scalp. It was heaven.

Caleb surged beside her. "Let your weight keep you in place and lean back just enough to float a little, like this."

Imitating him, she bobbed in the slow running creek water and laughed at the sensation of the water flowing over her, pulling and trying to move her downstream. "You've done this before, haven't you? You come in to supper sometimes with your hair soaked."

"Yup."

"But you never brought me before."

"Before today I would have had to really drag you, and you wouldn't be arguing for the sake of it."

He was right. Rather than admit it, Norah changed the subject.

"Tell me about your mother."

"So you think you're going to pry all my secrets out of me?"

"Sooner or later."

"What about your secrets?"

"Mine aren't interesting."

"I'll trade you. One for one, my mother, your scars."

Unlike Caleb, Norah never rose from bed unclothed, but she ended most nights with her night dress crumpled on the end of the bed, and in this hot weather.... The scars were something she could tell him about.

"All right. Was your mother the one who called you Caleb?"

"She was, and she was like you in other ways."

His hand closed around hers, warm and strong in the cold water. "She was good inside. She did what she had to in the night, and she'd never have done it except for me. In the morning, she'd be there, all the paint scrubbed off, her hair done plain and pretty, wearing a respectable dress like that gray thing Tindell bought you.

"She'd sit me down and teach me letters and numbers when she was so tired she could barely hold her head up. She kept me away from what was going on and the other women as much as she could.

"Her dream was that I'd learn enough to be a lawyer or a banker, but she knew I couldn't go to the school in town. When she'd taught me as much as she knew, she made a deal with one of her customers. He was an educated man, and she gave him something extra—for teaching me after."

"Something extra?"

"Men pay women for a lot of things. The uglier it is for the woman, the more they pay."

She didn't want to know more about that. "You hated him."

"I hated them all."

"Have you ever paid for a woman?"

"Yes, isn't that twisted?"

She shook her head, feeling the water moving through her hair. "No more than any other man who does it, I guess. What did she die of, consumption?"

"A customer beat her to death."

She tried to sit up and couldn't, struggling against the water and her awkward position. Caleb slid an arm under her and pushed. She met his expressionless dark eyes.

"I'm sorry."

"There's nothing for you to be sorry about. You didn't do it. The hardest part was that nobody did anything about it. Like your husband in a way. The sheriff could have found out who did it if he tried, but he didn't. They buried her the same place they buried beggars and suicides and that was that. Whores get killed all the time, and nobody cares."

"Is that why you—you went wild and that's why—those women?"

"Ah, that's another secret, and it's your turn. Those scars on your back are because of me, aren't they?"

"No, they're because of me. Because I was my father's spoiled pet, and I thought that meant nothing I could do would ever make him angry enough to discipline me with more than a harsh word. He whipped me that night. Not that badly either. He used a switch from the bushes by the creek instead of his belt, but the skin broke in a few places and the cuts festered. By the time they healed, I had scars."

"I count five."

"That wasn't the bad part. I mean it was, it was shocking and humiliating, and it hurt. The bad part was Papa never felt the same about me after that. He felt I betrayed him, and he ignored me whenever he could. When I was old enough for beaus, he warned every man who looked at me that I'd need a firm hand because I was spoiled and willful."

She hesitated before telling the worst part. "I never felt the same about him either. I thought he was a good man, willing to do what was right no matter what. He is a good man, but he's weak. That night he would have gone along with the others knowing they were drunk and wrong."

"He couldn't afford to make enemies out of men who would be his neighbors. Out here, starting with nothing, he knew he'd need their help."

"It didn't do him any good, did it?" Norah said. "He still failed."

"Would you have done it if you knew what it would cost you?"

"I don't know. I think I would, but it's easy to say that now, isn't it? There. That's my secret. Tell me about those women."

He was silent so long, eyes closed, floating back in the current, she expected him to cry off their bargain, but he spoke eventually.

"A man owned the brothel. His name was Tinker. The women gave him part of what they earned, more than they kept I expect. After my mother was killed, he told me I had to start earning my keep. He had me sweeping and washing and hauling. I missed the books, but other than that I didn't mind so much.

"My mother's room went to another woman, but I had a bed of my own up on the top floor, and sometimes if I got up early I could sneak outside for a while. There were boys a few streets over who didn't mind having a whore's son join their games now and then. It made them feel wild and brave, I guess. It went on like that for a while."

He sat up, shaking water from his hair, and met her eyes. "Whores aren't all the same, you know. Some are like my mother. Some are so beat down it's like nobody's inside, and some are pure mean. A lot of them don't like men much, and you can't blame them. The woman who replaced my mother was one of the mean ones, and before long she realized there was a scrawny little boy in the place nobody gave a damn about, and she could take it out on him for every ugly thing some man ever did to her."

Norah wanted to touch his face, kiss him, and didn't dare. "Did she hurt you?"

"Not at first. At first, being eleven years old and male, I kind of liked satisfying my curiosity, and it felt good enough, but it got to where she wanted what I wouldn't or couldn't do, and then she got ugly. And she made friends with this other woman, Rosie, and started bringing her along to hold me down. I told Tinker, and he said keeping the women around there happy was part of my job."

"So you tried to run away?"

"I started stealing food from the kitchen and was getting ready when Tina and Rosie brought a friend with them one night, a man."

"Tinker?"

"No, a customer. They said it was time I started to really earn my keep."

He paused as if for her to say something, but Norah was too bewildered by things beyond her ken to say anything. He smiled that controlled little smile at her.

"There are men who will pay to do things to boys."

She just stared in horror. "They.... He...."

"No," she heard the satisfaction of a boy who had won over tremendous odds in his voice.

"I'd been playing stick ball with the boys in the neighborhood, and the stick was there leaning by the bed. I broke Tina's nose with the first swing, and took out some of Rosie's teeth with the second. I think I broke Tina's arm before I was done from the way she was holding it. I remember being covered with blood, and none of it was mine."

"But the man."

"He ran at the first scream. It was Tinker who stopped me. He was a big man, and he knocked me silly, carried me downstairs, and locked me in the basement. You want to know something strange? The next morning before he took me to Uncle Henry, he looked right at me and said, 'Good for you, boy, but I can't keep you around.' You know the rest."

"They deserved it," Norah said.

"I always thought so."

"Did you learn—the things you know at that place?"

He looked puzzled for a minute, then took her meaning. "The basics of what goes where maybe. Most of what I learned there I'd rather forget."

He tugged at a strand of wet hair that hung over her shoulder. "You aren't the first widow I ever met, you know. The first one didn't charge money. She wanted payment different ways."

"How did you meet her?"

"Ah, that's another secret, and it's your turn. Did you fall in love with Hawkins right at the start?"

She looked down. He'd been right about the clothes she'd left on not hiding anything. Wet, the thin fabric of her chemise clung to her breasts like a second skin, and the darkness and erect state of her nipples showed right through, making her feel vulnerable. It had to be that. It couldn't be the question.

"No. I never loved him. In the beginning I thought I would. It's hard to get to know someone when you're courting, at least it was for me. I liked him, and he didn't take my father's warning to heart like the others, and I thought I'd come to love him."

"But you.... If you weren't grieving over him when I first saw you, what had you acting like that?"

His brows were drawn. He looked surprised and disturbed and like he really wanted to know, but she wasn't ready for that yet.

"I can't tell you."

"That's cheating. You're at least two secrets ahead."

"I'm sorry," she whispered.

"You spend too much time being sorry. You cheated, fair and square. Let's get out of here for now. You're starting to look more cold than cool."

He rose and pulled her up with him. Golden, tanned, and white, she wanted him to drive every thought of Joe from her mind. She wanted him to make her forget another man had ever touched her. Maybe telling secrets affected him the way not telling affected her, for his kiss was full of the same need building in every part of her.

He peeled off her clinging chemise and drawers and carried her to the blanket she'd fussed to arrange. Wool scratched at her bare skin. Like the sun and the deep blue sky stretching forever above and the sounds of the creek and scent of the

earth, it only intensified the desire burning away every shred
of shyness.

She traced the lines of his face. He had shaved this morning. The beard that often roughened his cheeks was only a
hint under her fingertips.

The times they'd coupled by early morning light or with a
lamp still burning, his face stayed a handsome shadow. In
bright sunshine she saw every detail—the way the water had
made dark spikes of his lashes, the way those lashes were
half-lowered over eyes turning liquid with passion. She had
not drowned in the shallow creek. She would lose herself
forever in his eyes.

When she outlined his lips with a forefinger, he drew the
tip into his mouth, nibbled gently. "You're beautiful."

"Don't spoil it by lying," she begged. "We both know pretty
is the best I can do."

He shook his head. "Pretty is when your hair is pinned up,
and your collar is buttoned up. Pretty is for those times.
Beautiful is for times like this, good times, wild times, sharing
secrets times."

Her throat closed. If she could still cry, tears would escape
now. He traced her face as she had his, wove his hands into her
wet hair, cupped her skull, and touched each part of her face
again with his lips. She felt fragile and female—and beautiful.

He kissed ever inch of her, his tongue tickling and tasting,
kissed places she had believed barely touchable. The instinct
to stop him died in the mists of pleasure.

"Caleb, I need.... I need."

"Me too."

She expected his weight, the familiar. He turned her on her
side to face him, draped her leg over his, and entered her, his
eyes locked on hers. She shut her eyes, invaded in some
impossible way beyond the physical.

He moved inside her slowly. She moved with him, giving
herself to the pleasure. One arm held her close, one hand
rubbed a nipple.

"Norah." His voice was hoarse and deep, his words in the rhythm of their movement. "Look at me. Let me know you know it's me. You want it to be me."

"I know. You're the only one I ever wanted." She opened her eyes and let him see the truth.

His hand slid lower between them. She lost the ability to speak or think, was still shuddering with aftershocks when he rolled her to her back, thrust harder, faster, and emptied himself into her.

Unnoticed before, as her heart slowed, the ground turned harder and more unyielding beneath her. At her first tentative squirm, Caleb rolled to his side still deep inside, holding her thigh, keeping her close and wrapped around his hips. As if he needed to.

How could something that seemed so ordinary with one man be cataclysmic with another? The way he touched her, kissed her, was part of it, but not all. Knowing the real answer and facing it in her heart, she drew breath to tell him, then let it out in silence. First she had to find the courage to tell him other things, all the secrets.

"If we don't move soon, we're both going to have very red rear ends."

His words lifted her mood. She laughed. "Only on one side."

Letting her go at last, he rose to his feet in one fluid move, and held out a hand. She sat up. Things previously felt but never seen close and clear hung inches from her face. Guiltily she jerked her gaze upward, only to see an open smile. "You can not only look. You can touch."

How could her cheeks burn after what they'd just done? She bit her lip and looked away.

"Do you know when you blush like that it goes all over? You wouldn't believe the places that can turn pink."

"Caleb."

"You can just say no."

"Do you think any of the bushes near here provide enough shade we could move there?"

"If not, I'll build some."

24

AFTER THE PASSION of the previous day—and night—breakfast was a quiet affair. Norah's mind turned back to worries.

"They'll be back to arrest you soon. A lot more men will come, and they'll surround us. Let's leave. Let's go somewhere far away from all this."

"No one's arresting me. The sheriff works for Van Cleve, and Van Cleve isn't going to be ordering me or anyone else arrested."

It took a moment for her to understand his meaning. "If you go after Mr. Van Cleve, others will come, federal marshals or...." She didn't know exactly who but had visions of cavalry charging down on them.

"If it gets to that, then we'll move on, but I like it here, and I've done enough running in my life."

"You've run from the law before?"

"Not exactly. I always figured leaving trouble far behind before the law showed up was better than waiting to see. It never mattered before."

She'd been awake half the night worrying. He looked unperturbed by the same thoughts that plagued her. Memories had kept her awake the other half of the night.

"I want to show you something," she said, making up her mind at last. "We need to walk a ways."

She led the way a distance behind the house, picking sunflowers here and there as she went. She stopped at the top of a slight rise and knelt to replace dried out prairie roses with the sunflowers on two small squares of cleared ground.

"I've seen you here," Caleb said. "You always looked like you wanted to be alone."

"I always did." She pulled a weed out here and there, smoothed the dirt, and got to her feet.

Caleb had the old wary look to him again. He gestured toward the long, narrow rectangle of grass that had been dug up recently and had already started to return to unmarked prairie.

"Why not put the flowers on his grave?"

"I don't want to. You asked me why I never came to love him. My first baby, my daughter, was stillborn three years after we married. She should have been fine. She was perfect, but the cord was around her neck and killed her. Joe never seemed to care the way you'd expect—the way I expected— but I thought he hid his feelings until he forbid me to say her name. He said it was a sin to name a child that never lived. She lived. She lived inside me, and I loved her, and her name is Audrey."

She looked at him finally and saw surprise and understanding and something else. "We got along all right after that, but I knew I'd never love him. The other grave is larger because our son Joey was three. Joe killed him."

"Norah."

She stepped away from his reaching hand. "It was an accident. Everyone says it was an accident, and I know it was, but it happened because Joe wouldn't listen. He was so proud. A son. He took Joey everywhere and he boasted as if he created our little boy from clay himself. And when I told him it was dangerous to have a little boy outside with him when he worked, he wouldn't listen. He said I molly-coddled Joey, and I'd ruin him, and he took him outside and expected a three-year-old to stay put where he told him to. And Joey followed him into the corral, and one of the horses...."

"Norah."

"I cried all the tears a person gets for a lifetime, and he never cried at all. He never said he was sorry. He never said he was wrong. He said it was my fault. He said if I taught Joey properly instead of pampering him, it wouldn't have happened. I hated him after that. I'd have left if I had a place to go. If my babies weren't here."

"Norah, sweetheart."

She tried to back away from him again, but he was too quick for her and pulled her roughly into his arms and held her hard against his chest. She closed her eyes and sank into him, giving herself to his strength, breathing deep of his clean male scent. Oh, how good it felt to be held.

He didn't argue with her as Mabel, Becky, and even Archie had done. He held her and made soft, soothing sounds deep in his throat. When she stopped trembling, he said, "I thought it was him you were grieving when I first saw you. I shouldn't have been so hard on you. I thought it was him."

"We lived together and slept in the same bed, but we hardly talked and never touched if we could help it. When he went to town, he'd stay for days, and I'm sure he visited those women, and I was glad. I didn't want him to touch me ever again."

Caleb not only held her the way she needed to be held, he didn't tell her she had to forgive the unforgivable. He knew, she thought, he knew about that dark place in the heart where some things had to be hidden because that's all that could be done with them.

CRYING FOR HOURS had never made Norah feel more washed out than telling Caleb the truth about Joe and her babies. To her relief, Caleb held her in the night, laid an occasional light caress on her in the day, and other than that left her alone.

She welcomed the sight of the Carburys' wagon fording the creek. Becky hung on to Ethan's shoulders and stood up long enough to wave her handkerchief wildly, hollering a greeting as they approached. If anyone could brighten a day, Becky could, and the young woman looked even more exuberant than usual.

Mabel and Archie had come with the young couple. Archie sat on one of the benches Caleb had built on each side of the ramada and knocked against the wooden seat with his fist.

"Good solid piece of lumber here. Must have cost you a pretty penny."

"I pulled a lot of good lumber out of the burned out houses around here."

Caleb was, of course, speaking the truth, just not addressing where the thick, wide boards he'd used for the benches came from.

Archie winked at him. Winked! "Yeah, I'm sure there were a lot of pieces like this under those ashes."

Norah seated Mabel and Becky in the two chairs at the table.

"You stay here in the shade, and I'll put coffee on." She counted noses and decided if she and Caleb had their coffee in glasses or didn't have any, she had enough cups.

"I'll come with you and help," Becky said, jumping up. "Ma and Pa have heard all my news, and Ethan's sick to death of listening to me."

Becky stood nervously near the stove while Norah ground beans, emptied the dregs of the morning's coffee, and prepared more.

"We're visiting Ma and Pa for a whole week," she blurted finally. "Ethan has a promotion, and that's good, but we have to move to Topeka, and that makes me so sad. I don't know if I can stand leaving and not seeing family and friends like you ever again."

Norah hugged her. "You'll probably see us as often as you do now. The train can bring you here or your family there in a day. The farm won't evaporate if your brothers take care of it for a few days while your ma and pa visit you, and the boys can visit on their own.

"Don't you miss your family? Don't you ever wish your ma was right there to talk to?"

"Sometimes."

"What about your sisters? I wish I had sisters. Brothers are good, but sisters would be special."

She ought to write to her sisters and her brother George, Norah thought with a flash of guilt. Until the rest of the family settled somewhere and let her know where, she couldn't write to them, but she knew where George and her sisters and their husbands were. She ought to let them know about Joe and about Caleb. As soon as things were settled, she'd do that.

Becky stood unusually quiet, folding the material of her skirt into pleats, letting go, and doing it again. Norah examined her friend more carefully. Even in the subdued light inside the house, Becky's skin glowed; a healthy flush highlighted her cheekbones.

"You have other news too, don't you? Good news."

"Oh, Norah, I don't want to make you sadder."

"You won't. What kind of friend would I be if your good news made me sad? You're expecting, aren't you?"

Becky nodded, her eyes searching Norah's face.

"Don't you ever doubt that your mother will be there for you when the time comes," Norah said. "You know that."

"She says that, but the troubles with Mr. Van Cleve...."

"You still look as slim as ever. The troubles will be over long before your time comes."

"How can you...? You think your husband's going to do something, don't you? What he's already done is awful. How could you marry him? I can hardly look at him he's so scary, and I can't believe Pa and Ben helped him. Ben acts like he's some kind of hero. He murdered those men, you know he did."

"They were coming to kill us."

"You don't know that. You can't be sure."

"We could have waited to see, I guess. Like rabbits."

"Rabbits?" Becky looked bewildered. "What have rabbits got to do with it?"

"I'll tell you some time." Norah handed Becky the coffee cups, picked up two glasses, the water bucket and dipper, and led the way back outside before Becky could ask more questions.

Silence reigned outside. "Is someone going to tell me about it," Norah asked, "or will I have to worm it out of Caleb once you're gone?"

"Webster Van Cleve doubled the bounty," Mabel said.

Norah sank into the empty chair at the table, letting Becky join Ethan on a bench. "Two thousand dollars? He's saying he'll pay someone two thousand dollars to kill Caleb?"

"Killing and scalping."

"Pa!" "Archie!"

Archie puffed on his pipe, showing no signs his wife's and daughter's horrified disapproval affected him. "Got to have evidence of some kind."

After that the men talked of weather, crops, and livestock. Becky and Mabel discussed the coming move to Topeka as if they hadn't talked about it ever before, and Norah sat silent. Would more men try to kill someone for two thousand dollars than one?

She suspected it made no difference except that Webster Van Cleve had just moved past tiresome into some other category that would have Caleb disappearing for most of the night.

She didn't want him risking it. No matter how much she wanted to stay here, the price was too high. She had only one weapon to use to try to convince him, and she wasn't sure how effective it would be, but she'd have to use it before he disappeared tonight.

Caleb came to supper with the wary look that Norah didn't see too often any more. He was going to tell her he was leaving and would be back by morning, not to worry.

If her news wouldn't dissuade him, she'd go with him, even if that meant following him on foot in the dark.

"These are good," he said, forking up green beans. "You have a green thumb."

"Anyone could grow anything with the water the way you fixed it. I have rhubarb pie for dessert."

He was as nervous as she was, and that gave her pause. He cleaned his plate, pushed it aside, and beat her to the subject on her mind.

"You know women like my mother learn ways to make sure they don't have babies."

"I didn't know, but I suppose they have to." Already she didn't like this conversation.

"I can find out what they do."

He had some of the same look on his face he'd had the night he'd told her about Jason. She really didn't like this conversation.

"We're married. I don't need to know that."

"You already lost two, and you're still young. We need to make sure there aren't any more."

"I don't want to make sure of any such thing. I want more, and it's already too late. My monthly flow didn't happen last month and it's ten days past due again. I was waiting to tell you, and then I thought it would make you see we have to leave. You know they'll come after you if you kill Van Cleve. If Ludlow and his deputies can't do it, he'll get up a posse or vigilantes or whatever he needs, and if they can't catch you or kill you, they'll bring in federal marshals. I don't want you to do it. I'm asking you not to do it. I want to leave and start over somewhere else."

He ignored everything she'd said except that it was too late. "You're not sure. You can't be sure so soon."

"I've been through this before. I'm sure."

"I thought you never had any children. You didn't have any. You never said a word. I never would have.... This isn't supposed to happen. It can't." He looked as wild as he had as a boy all those years ago.

"If I knew you felt that way, maybe I'd have done what you want, but I can't now. It's already happened, and I already love this baby too. Give it a little time. You'll get used to it."

"Get used to.... You don't understand." He rose and started pacing. "I can't be a father."

"Are you saying you think I've been meeting someone else out on the prairie at night?"

"No, damn it. I'm saying I can't be a father."

"Just because you didn't have..."

His fist slammed on the table, making the dishes jump. "It's got nothing to do with that. I won't do it. I won't be a father."

"It's too late. You are."

"I'm not. I can't be."

He headed for the door, hand reaching to yank it open, all caution thrown aside. She almost let him walk out like that but couldn't.

Without a word, she threw a towel over the lamp, killing the light before he could storm out. Since word about the bounty, Caleb had never walked through the door at night with the light behind him and never let her do it.

She sat alone and motionless in the dark until the scent of scorching cloth cut through the pain and made her pull the towel from the lamp.

Strange that just today Becky had asked about her family because Norah could hear her mother's voice as clearly as if Mama sat across the table. *Be careful what you wish for.*

When she had suggested—proposed—marriage to Caleb, she had been sure farming would bore him after a year, two at the most. He'd leave, the farm would be hers again the way it should be, and if she was lucky, he'd leave her with a child. Tonight she'd hoped telling him of the coming child would make him agree to leave.

All of her wishes were coming true, and nothing but losing her babies had ever hurt so much.

HIS HANDS SHOOK. His stomach roiled. He'd just accepted—married for years to Hawkins, no children. She'd been so stubborn about keeping the land even when it made no sense.

"I have a home," she'd said. Why hadn't she said she had two children buried on the land? Ah, he knew why. You had to trust someone to tell the secrets. She'd finally trusted him, and he'd hurt her.

Hurting her was the last thing he wanted to do. He never should have married her. Never should have let wanting things he wasn't meant for get the best of him. She didn't want to hear the words, but they were there, and they were true. Devil's spawn. Bad seed. Whoreson.

Too absorbed in dealing with the maelstrom of his own feelings to remember, he had come out without putting the rope on Early. The dog stayed at his side as he walked between the fields to the property line and started back. He didn't want to face her again, didn't want to see the pain on her face. Why couldn't she just rage at him?

The sound of Early's escalating growls broke through his thoughts. He stopped, crouched down, and quieted the dog with a hand over its muzzle. This wasn't some coyote in the distance or a skunk bumbling along in the night.

Like Early's rope, Cal's rifle was still in the house. The back of his neck crawled. Something was out there, something dangerous, and all considered, the odds were that something was a someone planning on collecting a two thousand dollar bounty.

A sharpshooter who moved into position in the dark was a man smart enough to reckon with. He'd have to fumble around some trying to find a position, but if he targeted light coming from the house....

The wheat and corn were both high enough to conceal a man now, but hiding among the stalks and still having a clear field of vision would be close to impossible. The bushes by the creek would put a rifleman a quarter mile from the house, a long shot, but doable for a skilled rifleman. It would be Cal's choice.

He started running. Norah wouldn't go out this late to the privy. If she did, she wouldn't do it with the lamp burning behind her. He was the one so upset he'd almost made the mistake. She'd stayed careful. She wouldn't do it.

The house was dark. He didn't slow until he reached the door. She was there, safe. He couldn't see her but could feel her presence. He wouldn't be sleeping alone under the ramada tonight after all.

He dropped the bar across the door and lay beside her on the bed without bothering to remove his clothes. Norah's back was toward him, but he knew she wasn't asleep. He doubted either of them would have slept tonight even without what lurked in the night.

"I'm going to leave in a little while. Don't go outside until I get back and tell you it's safe."

She rolled over to face him. He ached to touch her, hold her. There'd be no more of that.

"What's out there?" she whispered.

"Someone looking to be two thousand dollars richer. I think he's set up down by the creek, and if you hadn't covered the lamp when I walked out tonight it would be all over already."

He heard her accelerated breathing. "What are you going to do?"

"Kill him. And after that I'll take care of Van Cleve."

"And after that, you're leaving, aren't you?"

"Yes. I'll leave you the cash I've got left, and I'll send more when I can."

"I don't want money. If you can't stay or take me with you, I want to know you're safe. Let someone else take care of Van Cleve. I'll sell him the land and get that little place you told me to get once. I don't want you to have to run, to stay running the rest of your life. If you have to go, go safe."

Whether she reached for him or he reached for her, he couldn't say, but she was in his arms, burrowed in against him and hanging on in a way he'd thought she never would again. He held her as long as he dared, kissed her on the forehead, and left her to go see if Early was right about the danger in the night.

25

CAL CROSSED THE creek downstream from where any sharp-shooter would set up to target a man walking out of the house. He stayed far from the creek, stealing slowly through the night until he calculated his position was behind where he would lay in wait if he were the rifleman. Now all he had to do was keep his mind on business, not his wife.

An hour after dawn Cal spotted movement in the very clump of bushes he'd have chosen as cover for an ambush. He hated crawling. Dirt, grass, and other debris always worked its way inside his clothes.

He crawled. He slithered down into the creek, across, and up the other bank. He crawled until he was close enough to see the stitching on the gunman's boots.

He got to his feet, tired, wet, and dirty. Worse, he couldn't stop picturing what would have happened last night if the man stretched out behind the rifle had an itchy trigger finger and Norah had started out the door without dousing the lamp.

"Was two thousand dollars worth dying for?"

At the words, the man stiffened. He dropped the rifle and feigned raising his hands before scrambling for his pistol, but too slow. Way too slow.

Cal's bullet made a dark hole in the middle of the man's forehead. He left the body where it lay and went to reassure Norah. After that he'd have to see if he could find where the fool had left his horse.

HE EXPECTED HER to be angry. She should be angry. He wanted her to be angry, not pale and resigned, as if she had always expected this of him. She spent her day in the garden while he walked the fields, admired ripening wheat rippling in the breeze and cornstalks almost over his head. How had he ever imagined land like this could be his, half his?

After a silent supper, he lay on the bed, an arm over his eyes. He needed sleep but resting would be the best he'd manage. The familiar sounds of her cleaning the table, washing dishes, wiping and putting away had him picturing her moving, bending, reaching, stretching.

His throat hurt in a way he remembered from long ago, before Henry Sutton had cured him of tears. Mostly cured him, he amended, swallowing hard. Footsteps approached the bed, no rustling sounds of undressing followed. The slivers of light visible around his arm disappeared. The mattress moved slightly under her weight. She pillowed her head on his shoulder, her hair tickling his jaw, a hand spread on his chest.

"I won't sleep either," she whispered.

Cal wrapped one arm around her, holding her close. Throwing away another of his uncle's lessons, he forced out two hard words. "I'm sorry."

"Me too."

"I'll come back after and let you know it's done. We'll talk then."

He felt her nod, her fingers digging in a little as they tensed.

Neither of them spoke more as wakeful hours passed. When the angle of the moonlight through the windows told him the night was half gone, he lifted her off his shoulder, kissed her forehead, and went for his guns.

The buckskin horse he had found staked out two miles away moved restlessly beside Forrest when Cal heaved the body in place and lashed it down. After a few soft words and a pat on the neck to calm the horse, Cal swung up on Forrest and led the buckskin with its grisly burden in the familiar direction of the V Bar C.

He'd slipped on and off Van Cleve's land from all directions in the last months. Fortunately, the man had less than half a dozen gunmen and even fewer cowhands to position around the place, trying to stop further depredations. If he had a hundred, getting to him might be hard.

Too bad the bushwhacker hadn't been thinner—and shorter. Cal untied the body and eased it from the saddle to his shoulder. He left the horse free to help itself to anything growing in the neat garden behind the house and carried the body through the back door he'd already pried open.

Bedrooms would be on the second floor, finding the right one would be the problem—and dealing with the wife. He stopped to listen every two or three steps, heard nothing but his own breath, heavy from climbing with the body.

The first two rooms he tried were empty, the next two small, with small beds and small occupants. At last he opened a door and heard masculine snores and breathed in slight scents of tobacco, shaving soap, and hair pomade. Close to the bed, his eyes adjusting to the dim light, Cal made out Van Cleve, flat on his back, alone.

Lighting the bedside lamp didn't wake Van Cleve, throwing a dead man across his belly did. "Wh-what!"

Eyes wide, mouth open, the rancher tried to get out from under the corpse, making frantic sounds Cal thought better suited to a farm animal. Like a pig. He shoved the muzzle of his pistol under the man's jaw, hard. "Shut up."

The pungent odor of urine overrode the more pleasant scents.

"I thought about just coming in here and sticking a knife in you, easy and quiet," Cal said conversationally, "but that doesn't seem like enough. You need to see what's coming and know you bought it for yourself."

As his finger tightened on the trigger, a door in the side of the room opened. Van Cleve's wife stood there, light from a lamp in her hand shining on blonde hair falling over the shoulders of her white night dress. "Webster, are you all right? I thought I heard...."

Her surprise was as ugly as Cal's, but she was the one who dropped the lamp and fled back the way she'd come, screaming. Cal was the one who cursed himself for wasting time indulging anger. Flames jumped from the spilled lamp oil to the wool carpet.

Aside from Van Cleve and the woman, there were two children and servants in the house. Cal grabbed Van Cleve by the neck of his night shirt and yanked him out from under the body.

"You are one lucky son of a bitch. Get up and put out that fire."

Cal raced down the stairs, out the back, and across the yard for his horse. His own luck showed signs of having run out.

GETTING OFF THE ranch proved no more difficult than ever before. Once well clear of the furthest pickets he'd ever spotted, Cal pushed his horse to a steady jog, heading home in a roundabout fashion. Leaving Van Cleve alive had to be the absolute worst thing he could do—except for killing the man with his wife as witness or letting a fire get going in a house with who knew how many others in it who didn't deserve killing.

He calculated the consequences. One day to send someone to town. Another day for the sheriff to round up a mob and get out here with them. Of course Van Cleve might try for vigilante justice with his own men, and they wouldn't come down the town road in a bunch either. One day then. Twenty-four hours.

He could pack and disappear within an hour of reaching home. Forcing Norah to pack and taking her to Carburys' would only cost another few hours. Except she wouldn't stay. Sooner or later she'd return home, and Van Cleve and the law would both be after her. The law would be sure she knew where her husband had gone. Van Cleve would still be after the land.

Memories of how it had been that day in the yard, Preston knocking her over with his horse, flashed through Cal's mind. She'd fight back now. She had a rifle and a pistol, knew how to shoot, and she'd fight.

No woman, however defiant and determined, could hold off a group of men intent on doing her harm. For all the gun work he'd done these last years, he wouldn't try it himself unless he was in a fort, a well stocked fort. Without conscious thought, he slowed his horse, bringing it to a stop.

Taking her with him would be easy. She'd said she wanted to leave and start over somewhere else. He'd find a safe place for her, leave her there with the money.... Who was he trying to fool? No place was ever going to be safe for a woman who would soon be clumsy with Cal Sutton's child. His bad seed.

Forrest took advantage of loose reins and inattention and ambled forward. Struggling with his own thoughts, Cal let the horse go.

He didn't want to leave Norah in some strange place, trying to take care of a child by herself. Hell, he didn't want to leave her at all, but he couldn't be a father. He absolutely could not. She'd have money. She wouldn't be like his mother.

She'd throw herself heart and soul into it, the same way she'd tried to with Hawkins' legitimate.... He jerked his confused horse to a halt again. His child was as legitimate as Hawkins' had been. She'd said it that night when he'd tried to tell her she could avoid what had already happened. *"We're married. I don't need to know that."*

She'd said more. She'd said, *"I already love this baby too."* Too. As in the same as she'd loved the others. That was what she meant. That had to be what she meant. A woman like Norah might put up with a man like him because she ran out of better choices, and she enjoyed what she insisted on calling making love as much as he did, but *too*?

Of course he'd wondered before, wondered when she'd crawled out the window and stuck her rifle in Ike Kerr's back. Norah fussed over a little damage to a door and sleeping free in a store. She threw a fit over salvaging an abandoned plow. She trusted the law so much she'd been willing to risk Cal's neck to the sheriff in Fischer.

So what did it mean when a woman like that gave every sign of being willing to shoot a man in the back rather than let Ludlow arrest her husband for something she knew full well he did?

The prairie turned pink and gold before him as the sun rose. Awareness of the world outside of his own tangled thoughts swept through him. He was sitting in the open like a target in a shooting gallery. Worse, he'd just passed the kind of small rise he'd used for a stand when Preston....

He set his spurs to Forrest. The horse's leap forward and a smashing blow to the right side of Cal's back occurred as one, throwing him forward and to the side. The crack of a rifle sounded like an afterthought.

Grabbing for leather and mane, Cal clung to his unbalanced seat, his mind working frantically. Keep them away from home, from Norah. Carburys'. Their place was close, no more than a few miles, and an old Rebel like Archie could handle whatever arrived on his doorstep.

Some burning, throbbing, not much pain yet, only blood, blood warm and dripping on his back, soaking his shirt. Shouts sounded behind him, more gunfire. With every stride of the racing horse, his grip weakened. No chance for refuge at Carburys'. Some chance for revenge.

Cal slowed the tiring horse as much as he could, wrapped the reins in his fist and let himself fall. Numbness dissolved to agony as the horse dragged him what had to be ten miles before coming to a snorting, bug-eyed halt, still pulling back, dancing in place.

Fighting to stay conscious, Cal whispered soothing words between gasps for breath as he lay sprawled on his back. Forrest quieted. Cal eased out his pistol, thumbed back the hammer, and waited.

His pursuers galloped up. One started crowing even before he hit the ground. "Two thousand dollars! A thousand apiece. What are you going to do with yours?"

"We ain't splitting even. I shot him. You didn't do a thing."

"The hell you say. You got lucky and saw him first is all. You want me to do something, I'll finish him off. He only just fell. He's probably still alive."

"All you can do is be the one gets bloody heaving him back up on the horse."

Two rough-dressed strangers stepped around Forrest's hindquarters. Cal shot the first in the middle of the chest, thought he hit the second but realized he'd missed when the man disappeared. Seconds later the sound of a horse leaving at a run thrummed through the air.

No longer able to hold it, Cal let the pistol drop to his side. He'd done everything wrong since he'd first seen the Girl again, made everything worse.

The sky wobbled over him, so intense a blue it hurt in a different way than the fire consuming his back. He fought for a moment then let go, as eager to escape guilt as pain.

Hands turned him and brought pain roaring back worse than before. Cal tried to push them away.

"Hold him while I finish this," said a voice he'd recognize if it were just closer.

"I never saw so much blood. You sure he's alive?" He should recognize that one too. A youngster, always full of questions.

Cal's mind slid past it, wouldn't take hold. Whoever they were, they were torturing him, ripping open his back with a hot poker.

"All right, let's get him in the wagon. You drive. I'll keep this bandage as tight as I can."

"What about the body, the horses?"

"We'll come back."

"Ma won't like this."

"I don't like it myself. Lift."

Hands grabbed his shoulders and legs, swung him through the air, and let him down on a surface harder than stone. He wanted to scream, couldn't, settled for oblivion.

26

Norah spent the hours from the time Caleb left till dawn dreading the time he would return only to leave for good. As more time passed and the sun climbed straight overhead, she fretted for the sight of him. Something had gone wrong.

He'd almost been caught and had to run was all. He'd double around and be back before long. Back to say goodbye. Back safe. At worst he'd had to run and keep going. She wouldn't hear for a while, but she'd hear. Hear that he was safe.

She fluttered around the house, sweeping, dusting, scrubbing. Nothing distracted her. Fear kept her on edge, jumping at every sound. When Early stared into the distance, tail wagging, her heart leapt, then fell as she saw a wagon approaching. Archie and Ben. She couldn't pretend to be glad to see them.

"Caleb isn't here."

"I know," Archie said. "He's at our place. You need to come."

Her bones turned to water. Archie jumped down and grabbed her before she fell. "He's alive. Come on now. Get in the wagon, and we'll take you to him."

She jerked away. "No, I have to take our wagon. I can't leave anything alive here. Caleb says. He always says, don't go off and leave anything that can be killed. Stonewall and

Jeb are out in the pasture, and I can't leave anything alive. We have to hitch them to our wagon. I have to get the horses. Early has to come."

Ben tried to stop her babbling by interrupting. "Mrs. Sutton, you need to come right now. He's...." A look from his father cut him off.

"We'll get the horses," Archie said. "Why don't you pack a few things in case you need to stay with us a day or two."

Norah stared, unable to move. Archie turned her toward the house and helped her take the first few steps. "Go on now. We'll be back with the horses in no time, and we'll all go. Horses, dog, all of us."

"He's alive."

"He is."

Unfrozen by the promise in his words, Norah hurried inside. She could tell by the gentleness in Archie's manner that Caleb was hurt badly, but Archie wouldn't lie. Caleb was alive. Alive.

She pulled a box from under the bed, tried to think what to take. The blue calico dress. He liked blue. And the green. She couldn't find the blue dress, started tearing through things in frustration.

When the realization finally struck that the blue dress was on her back, she forced herself to sit on the bed and regain control then packed with some semblance of order. Box held against her chest, rifle in hand, she stepped outside without looking back.

Jeb and Stonewall weren't hitched but tied to the tailgate of the Carbury wagon. Early, looking ready to jump out at the first excuse, sat in the bed with Ben. The dog didn't relax until Norah reached the wagon seat.

Once they were rolling toward the town road, Norah forced out the question she'd been avoiding for fear of the answer. "How bad is it?"

"I'm not sure. He lost a lot of blood. We went for Granny Johnson and took her to the house before we came for you.

By the time we get home, she'll be able to tell us what's what."

"I'm surprised she would come."

The old woman had medical skills as good as a doctor, but she also had strong opinions. Her family had been burned out last year and like Joe and Norah had moved back to their original sod house.

Granny was ornery enough to refuse to help a man who had worked for Van Cleve. In her opinion "live by the sword, die by the sword" wasn't a prediction or admonishment but a statement of desirable outcome.

"Ben sweet talked her."

Norah managed to throw something she hoped resembled a smile over her shoulder at the boy. "Thank you."

"It wasn't sweet talk, it was reasoning," the boy mumbled.

Finding her courage, she asked, "What happened?"

"He was shot in the back," Ben blurted. "Shot in the back and he still got one of them. We had the wagon all hitched up ready to take Becky and Ethan back to town when we heard the shots. Pa thought it might be like last time, didn't you, Pa? You know, the time Cal—I mean Mr. Sutton—got three of them and the others ran off. Bang. Bang. Bang."

The boy's words tumbled out fast and excited. "We pulled up when we heard it, being cautious, you know, and then two more shots came. Bang. Bang. And some fellow lit out like his horse was on fire. So we went closer and could see Cal's—I mean Mr. Sutton's—horse fiddle-footing around like it was tied to something on the ground, and we went to see, and there he was, and Pa bandaged him up with his shirt and mine, and we put him in the wagon and took him home."

Before coming to get her, Archie and Ben had taken time to put on clean shirts, Norah noticed. She hoped they'd put it off until after they'd gotten Granny. Ben was still recounting the day's happenings.

"The horses and the body are still there, except maybe the horses moved off. We put Mr. Sutton in Becky's room. She's mad about that because now we can't get her back to town until tomorrow, and her and Ethan won't have a room tonight, and she doesn't like...."

"Ben." Archie didn't raise his voice, but the stream of words stopped immediately.

"We'll get the body and round up Cal's saddle horse and any others out there after we get you settled," Archie said.

"Did you recognize him? Was he one of Van Cleve's men?"

"No, and he didn't look like one of Van Cleve's, too dirty, dressed too rough."

So he was just another man who had heard about Van Cleve's bounty and died trying to earn it, Norah thought. And this one may have succeeded in killing Caleb.

They rode in silence for a while, Norah concentrating on the rattles and creaks of the wagon, the muffled thumps of the horses' hooves in the road, and Early's nervous panting.

"What was he up to last night?" Archie asked.

"Another bounty man tried to kill him yesterday at our place. He went to discuss the matter with Mr. Van Cleve."

Archie's only response was a low whistle. He would guess Caleb planned to kill Van Cleve, and Archie was perceptive enough to know that meant Caleb also planned to leave Hubbell and the State of Kansas. Maybe he'd even guess Caleb was leaving her.

After more miles of silence, Archie said, "Got to hope he succeeded."

No one spoke after that. Norah clenched her hands in her lap and prayed.

NORAH HARDLY WAITED for Archie to rein up in the yard, much less for help down. After countless sessions in Becky's room admiring the girl's latest dress or bonnet, Norah knew the way. She ran up the stairs and to the second door on the left, hurried in, and stopped in horror at the sight.

Mabel and Granny Johnson bent over the bed, hiding all but glimpses of Caleb. Blood-soaked cloths filled a pan nearby.

The room reeked of carbolic overlaid with something stronger, nauseating—burned flesh. Mabel straightened, her face tired and apron streaked with more blood.

"There you are. Granny has the bullet and the bone fragments out and the bleeding stopped. I'll let you be the assistant from here."

Norah barely noticed Mabel's hug or departure. She crossed the few feet to the bed and stared down at her beautiful bad man.

He lay on his stomach, face turned toward her, naked to the waist, trousers wet with blood, red streaks and smears all over his back. Granny stopped dabbing at an angry circle of burned flesh.

"Had to cauterize, but we got it stopped. Here now. If you're going to faint or retch, get out of here and get Mabel back."

Norah reached down and closed a hand around Caleb's forearm. Warm. Alive. She took a deep breath. "I'm fine. Tell me what to do."

"Get the rest of his clothes off. All that's left is bandage him up, clean him up, and cover him up."

His boots hung past the end of the bed and rested on the oak chest there. The sight brought a lump to Norah's throat. She pulled them off as gently as she could. Stockings next. How could bare feet make a man look so vulnerable?

When she tried to reach under him to unfasten his trousers, Granny said, "Don't try to lift him even a little. We can't have the bleeding start again. Here." She slapped a large pair of scissors into Norah's hand.

Norah struggled to cut the thick, wet cloth until she had enough cut away to peel off the rest. His drawers were easier.

"I took off that thing he had around his waist. It's over there."

Granny pointed to the money belt, coiled on top of the bedside table.

"If they shoot me, make sure you get the money belt off the body before anyone else gets it." Caleb had said that the first

time they'd come to visit the Carburys. A choked sound escaped her.

"No retching," Granny said, her wrinkled face set in hard lines.

"I'm fine."

"You're a fool is what you are. Marrying one like this guaranteed this day would come."

Norah wanted to argue, let fear erupt in anger, but Caleb needed this cranky old woman. "Thank you for coming for him, Granny. I was afraid you wouldn't."

"I only did it for the boy. Carbury needs to sit that boy down and make sure he knows one like this is no hero because that's what the boy is thinking."

"Caleb would agree with you about that," Norah said.

The older woman gave her a suspicious look, then seemed to realize Norah wasn't making light. Granny bandaged the wound so tightly Norah questioned her.

"Got to keep what's left of his blood in. If he wakes up, get him to take water. If he don't wake up, spoon it in a little at a time. That'll help stretch what blood he's got left."

Norah didn't want to ask and couldn't stop the words. "Has he got a chance?"

"If they're alive, there's a chance. So far as I can tell the bullet didn't hit anything he can't live without. Hit a rib and broke some off, but I think I got all the pieces. He lost too much blood, and there's the fever to come. It's up to God now."

Granny packed bottles and instruments into the basket she used for medical supplies and left with it and the pan of bloody cloth, closing the bedroom door behind her harder than necessary.

Norah brushed his hair off his forehead and kissed him, on his mouth, on every bit of uncovered skin. Sinking to her knees by the bed, holding his arm, she found out how wrong she'd been. She hadn't run out of tears over Joey. She had just stopped loving anyone enough to cry.

Her throat closed, aching too much to swallow, but not too much for wracking sobs. She cried until her eyes and her head throbbed, and her breath came in gasps. She would have cried longer except for a small movement under her hand.

His eyes didn't open, his voice was faint and didn't sound like Caleb, but the words were distinct. "Need to—negotiate. No crying—over me."

"Caleb? Caleb!" But he was gone again. And she hadn't even tried to get water down him.

She fished her handkerchief out of a pocket, blew her nose, and whirled at the sound of the door opening behind her. "He said something. Words that made sense. That's good isn't it?"

Granny marched in and smacked more water and clean rags down beside the bed. "Here, use this, then wash your face," she said, handing Norah a rag.

Norah complied and looked at Granny expectantly.

"I figured you married him because you were out of choices out there alone, and he could keep Van Cleve off you," Granny said. "I could understand that, but how did you go and fall in love with a killer? I suppose that handsome face and fine body make you overlook a sinful nature."

Norah stuffed the dirty rag in her pocket and met the old woman's unsympathetic black eyes. "I love him for a hundred reasons. Those are only two."

"Mumbling a few words don't mean anything. He did that while I worked on him, and if he cares about anyone, it ain't you. He said, 'I always loved the Girl.' "

Norah startled the old woman with a hard hug. "Thank you for that."

Granny gave Norah the kind of look people reserved for drunks and the feeble-minded and left.

Sitting on the floor beside the bed, Norah took Caleb's hand in hers, leaned against the mattress, and drifted off to something resembling sleep.

The scratch of a match woke her. Granny touched the flame to the wick of the bedside lamp, and the darkened room glowed with dim light. Caleb lay still as death, but the hand in Norah's was warm.

"I thought Archie or the boys would have taken you home by now," Norah said.

"I'll stay the night." Granny hesitated, then said, "Mabel told me about you two. Maybe I see how it could be, like Androcles pulling the thorn from the lion's paw."

The thought of herself as Androcles and Caleb as the lion in the Aesop's fable almost made Norah smile. "Becky thought it was very romantic until she met him. He scares her, so she's sure I'm terrified of him too and won't admit it."

"He'd scare most sensible women, and Becky's years away from sensible."

Norah did smile at that. "You don't have to sit with him. I'm staying here."

"I'll keep you company, but first you get downstairs and get something to eat. Do something about that dog while you're down there before someone shoots it."

By the time Norah reached the bottom of the stairs, she heard the whining, rising and falling in a ceaseless rhythm.

Archie's voice came from the darkened parlor. "The boys drug him to the barn a while ago and tied him there, but he chewed through the rope and came back. Mabel won't let me shoot him, so Ben thinks we ought to drown him in the horse trough and not tell her."

"He needs to see Caleb."

"Take him on up then. If he jumps on the bed, either Granny or Mabel will wring his neck and at least it will stop that infernal noise."

Norah opened the door and caught the frantic dog in her arms as he lunged through. The rope he'd chewed still hung from his neck, and she used it to slow his dash for the stairs. Like her, Early didn't need directions.

Granny sat in the room's only chair, knitting, and started when the dog hurtled in. "What? Get that thing out of here."

"I will, just give him a minute."

The dog nuzzled the same hand Norah had held, licked, and whined, his wildly waving tail slowly lowering and falling still. As if understanding what he'd seen, Early sank to the floor near the foot of the bed, head on paws, eyes on Caleb.

"That's it? The dog's going to lay on the floor and moon over that man the same as you?"

"Yes. Early thinks I'm good for dishing up food and a few other things, but I'm not the one who makes the sun rise in the morning."

Granny made a sound close to a snort. "Leave it here then. Tell Archie we need another chair, and don't come back until you've eaten something."

Because she needed a trip round back, Norah obeyed.

27

LATE MORNING OF the next day, Early raised his head and gave a deep growl. The sound continued, grating across Norah's nerves like sandpaper. Cracking the bedroom door open, she listened only long enough to identify Sheriff's Ludlow's voice among those arguing below.

Nothing she said or did silenced the dog. At least he showed no tendency to escalate to barking.

Her rifle leaned against the wall next to Caleb's, the gleaming brass frame he had polished for her a reminder of the source of the gun. Surely no one could recognize it. Maybe not, but just in case she took Caleb's.

Moving into the hall, she closed the door behind her, leaving Early to stand guard. Did the sheriff and his men know Caleb was here, or were they guessing, searching? For the first time she wished she hadn't made Archie bring Jeb and Stonewall. A plain bay horse like Forrest wouldn't be so obvious as the Percherons. Early was at least safely out of sight.

She crept to the top of the stairs and listened. They knew. They'd followed the blood trail here from where Caleb had fallen. That meant they somehow knew where he'd been shot.

The thought no more crossed her mind than she heard an unknown voice, pitched high and loud with emotion.

"Bo Murdock shot that miserable killer and lost his brother doing it. He wants the bounty, and he can have it if Sutton's dead. We're not leaving until we have him or see his body."

The only question was whether to make a stand here or at the bottom of the stairs. The farther she could keep them from Caleb the better, she decided.

She stopped on the last step and brought the rifle to bear on Ludlow's stomach. Surely she could hit a target that size across a room. If only the room weren't so crowded.

Mabel and Archie, Ben and his brothers, Becky and Ethan, Granny Johnson and her oldest son all faced Sheriff Ludlow and a man Norah recognized as Van Cleve from the cut of his clothes and Caleb's description of him as an arrogant runt. She glimpsed mounted deputies through the front windows.

The sheriff took Norah in at a glance. "Put that rifle down, Mrs. Hawkins. I don't want to shoot a woman, but I will if I have to."

Her hands stayed steady, and she didn't let the rifle waver. "Mrs. *Sutton.* And I don't want to shoot a sheriff, but I will if I have to. You're not taking my husband anywhere."

Granny said, "I told you. Moving him will kill him. He hasn't got enough blood left in him to spare a drop."

"And I told you, I don't care. He should have thought of that before he assaulted Mr. Van Cleve, scared his wife half to death, and set their house on fire."

The smile Granny gave Van Cleve was pure venom. "Burned you out did he? I wish I could have seen it."

"No, he didn't burn me out. What he did was throw a dead body in my bed and stick a gun under my chin. He was going to kill me. The devil had every intent, but my wife walked in and scared him off. The fire was just a little...."

As if he realized minimizing the fire was a mistake, Van Cleve snapped his mouth shut.

Ben broke into the escalating tension in the room, words spilling out in a nervous torrent. "It couldn't have been Cal—

Mr. Sutton—in your house night before last, Mr. Van Cleve. Me and my pa found him out on the prairie the day before that, shot in the back and almost dead. We brought him home, and he's been here ever since. I bet it was dark in your room that night. I bet you didn't see clear. Somebody else did what you said because Mr. Sutton was already shot by then."

The boy stopped speaking, an astonished look on his face, as if the lie that had just spilled out surprised him as much as everyone else.

Archie recovered first. "The boy and I were getting ready to take my daughter and her husband back to town. We heard gunshots and went and found Sutton the way Ben said."

Granny folded her arms across her thin chest and chimed in. "Mr. Carbury came and got me before he even went for Mrs. Sutton."

"I spent hours working with Granny to get the bleeding stopped," Mabel said.

Granny's son said, "Ma's been here ever since Mr. Carbury come for her. I'm here to bring her home."

The older Carbury sons made agreeing sounds.

Becky had fidgeted and stared at each person who spoke, looking miserable. Now she pitched in, making Ben's story seem slow and calm by comparison.

"We're visiting from town, my husband and me. We're going to have to move to Topeka, so we visited for a whole week, and we were here when Pa and Ben brought him back, Norah's husband, that is. Brought him back shot and bloody, and he's in my room, in my bed. My brothers had to double up so Ethan and I didn't have to sleep on the floor, and we need to get home, and no one can take us. We can't go by ourselves, you know, even if we had a buggy, because your men...."

Ethan's touch on her arm stopped her babbling except for a final, indignant. "Well, we can't!"

Van Cleve's color had risen higher with each statement. "They're lying, all of them. They're a bunch of lying, dirty sodbusters. What about Preston and his men? You do your duty, Ludlow. Shoot the woman if you have to, but drag that killer down here, throw him across a horse, and take him to town." Saliva droplets spit from his mouth with each word.

The sheriff put an arm around Van Cleve's shoulders. The smaller man shrugged him off. "Mr. Van Cleve, let's step outside a minute and talk. Then you can wait outside and me and my deputies will deal with these people."

"I don't want to talk, I.... Oh, all right." Van Cleve stomped outside, rigid with fury.

The sheriff followed, banging the door closed behind him as he left.

"Excuse me, everyone," Norah murmured, stepping across to the door, easing it open, and slipping through.

Ludlow and Van Cleve had stopped at the bottom of the porch steps, their backs to her. Another few stealthy steps, and she was close enough to hear Ludlow.

"Of course I believe you, but you know as well as I do those same people in there lying for him now or others just like them are the kind that will be on any jury in the county."

"If taking him to town will kill him, that's all you have to do. No trial, no jury, no lying witnesses. I hope he bleeds to death in the first mile."

"Mr. Van Cleve, these farmers have got their backs up. They've been all about defending their land, but Sutton's got them riled up and primed for a fight. Some of them will alibi him for Preston too, and even if we put him in a wagon all careful, if the trip to town kills him, they'll be after me. I'm willing to do most anything you want, but not risk being on trial for murder with people like that on the jury."

"You're a damned coward."

Ludlow made no answer, and the two stood there in silence until one of the deputies caught the sheriff's eye and gestured toward Norah. Ludlow turned, saw her, and swore. Van Cleve glanced back, said nothing, and strode toward his horse.

Norah went back inside, kissed Ben on the cheek, said, "Thank you, everyone," and went back upstairs to help Early keep watch.

THE FEVER ROSE in Caleb that night. Norah followed Granny's instructions and fought it for three exhausting days. Archie, Ben, and his brothers helped by bringing cold water from the creek, lifting and turning Caleb. Mabel spelled her, brought meals, and bullied Norah into eating some of them. Only Early shared the entire vigil.

When the fever broke, and Norah thought resting in a bedside chair would be safe, Mabel had other ideas. "When he wakes up, do you want him seeing you the way you are? He's cleaner than you are right now and smells better. I've got water for a bath heating on the stove, and the tub in the kitchen. Archie and the boys know to stay out of the house until supper. You get down there and clean yourself up."

With a firm grip on Norah's arm and a hand in her back, Mabel pulled and pushed Norah out of the bedroom and shut the door. Norah looked down at herself in dismay. The apron over her blue dress would never be white again. The dress needed demotion to the shabby-old category. She had packed the green dress, but the box with her things was still in the room.

Before she mustered proper indignation and shoved back inside, the door opened. "And take this miserable creature with you."

Mabel shoved Early out the same way she had Norah and called out over the sound of the closing door. "I set out your clean clothes downstairs and ran an iron over the dress."

Norah conceded and led the way downstairs. Pushing Early outside much the same way Mabel had evicted him from the bedroom, Norah ignored his soulful look. "If I have to clean up, you have to do something other than sit and whine. Go see Archie and the boys." She didn't wait to see if the dog took her advice.

Not until she had scrubbed from head to toe and dressed in clean clothes, did Norah completely appreciate and understand Mabel's purpose. Cleanliness brought with it a lightness she had lost sometime even before Caleb had reacted so badly to news of a baby.

Optimism buoyed her. He'd beaten the fever. The wound exuded blood-tinged fluid, but not so much, and no signs of purulence had developed.

Early huddled by the door. "You and I are going to go for a walk and get fresh air," she said, not even embarrassed to be talking to a dog. As if he understood, Early followed her on a short walk to admire Mabel's garden.

"Thank you," Norah said to Mabel when she returned to the room. "You were right as usual."

Mabel examined her with approval. "You look like a new woman. Why don't you lie down in my room until supper. I'll keep watch."

That was too much. "No. I can nap in the chair. Really I can. It's quite restful, and I need…. If it were Archie you wouldn't leave. I'm sorry we're still here, taking over your house."

"We hardly see you. You're no trouble. I'll bring supper."

Norah leaned back in the chair, shaking her head a little. No matter Mabel's reassuring words, exhaustion had changed her face from handsome to heavy these last days and made the gray that usually blended into her blonde hair stand out.

Caleb wouldn't be clean and smelling better than Norah had smelled earlier except for help from the whole Carbury family, and every one of them was paying a price in extra work, lost sleep, and worry.

Someday she and Caleb would find a way to repay such friendship. Someday…. She dozed off and woke to a room dim with fading light.

"Norah."

Caleb's voice was a hoarse whisper. Not needing the sound of his name to wake him, Early already stood with his chin on the mattress, tail waving joyfully. Norah scrambled to join him, sitting carefully on the edge of the bed, pulling Caleb's hand to her lap, reaching to caress one bristly cheek.

He turned on his side before she could stop him, grunting with pain.

"You're not supposed to move like that," she said. "It might start the bleeding again."

"How long has it been?"

"Almost a week."

"I won't bleed, and I need...."

She helped him with what he needed and pressed water and broth on him until he rebelled, making her put the cup down and sit back down beside him, holding both her hands.

"You look pretty. I like your hair down like that."

"I washed it and left it down to dry."

"I can smell the soap. You smell good."

Bless you, Mabel.

"I'm not leaving," he said. "Not without you."

He'd come all too close to leaving not just her but the world. She didn't remind him. "You can't leave me. I'll follow you."

He closed his eyes, his hands relaxed around hers. "I love you," she whispered. He didn't react, his breathing deep and even. *Asleep,* she told herself. *He's not unconscious, just asleep.*

Caleb woke twice more in the night, saying a few words each time, sounding stronger and more like himself. As bright sunshine illuminated the room the next morning, he sounded as good as healed.

"What is this room? Does Archie run a brothel on the side?"

For the first time Norah really looked at Becky's room, with its white-washed walls, frilly pink curtains, ruffles and bows pinned on, hanging from, and adorning every surface in some way.

When she stopped laughing, she said, "Don't you dare say anything like that in front of anyone else. We're in Becky's bedroom, and we are not making life easier for any of the Carburys."

"Then let's go home." He hesitated a second. "Van Cleve's probably razed everything to the ground by now. I didn't kill him."

"I know. He was here with the sheriff to arrest you."

"What stopped them?"

She told him.

"Archie lied?"

"No, Ben lied. Everyone else said something true that sounded as if they agreed with what Ben said, but no one else lied. It was enough to scare the sheriff."

He closed his eyes, fatigue showing in the lines of his face. "Let's go home."

She wanted to remind him about the bounty, beg him to leave and go somewhere safe. The time for that would be later. Until he was stronger, they couldn't leave. Part of her wanted to go home too, another part knew they were safer right here.

CALEB'S STRENGTH RETURNED steadily, which was a good thing because he needed it. The Carburys took it on themselves to keep Caleb company whenever they could. Archie helped him shave. Ben and his brothers brought the room alive with their chatter.

Norah sat beside Caleb the next morning, worrying over how prominent his collar bone and ribs had become and the fatigue lines etched in his face in spite of the long days abed.

Exhaustion dogged her too, as much from tiptoeing around someone else's house feeling like a burden as from lack of sleep, although a full night's sleep in a bed with Caleb right there beside her would be heaven.

As if he heard her thoughts, he said, "You can stop worrying about me painting the walls with blood if you're not here to stop it, you know. At least the dog's got enough sense to curl up on that rug. Go find a quiet place and get some decent sleep. Sitting in a chair all the time can't be good for that thing inside you."

She drew breath to snap his head half off for saying the dog was smarter than she was. After that she'd decide whether to shriek at him for referring to their baby as a "thing inside" or never speak to him again.

Recognizing the provocative glint in his eye, she let the breath back out. Stuck in bed, weak as a kitten, tiptoeing was proving too much for him too.

Instead of snapping, she smiled sweetly. "I think it's a good sign that you're already starting to worry about the thing inside me. You've still got months to get used to the idea, and you're going to be a very good father."

"I'm not going to be any kind of a fa.... I'm not doing it. I can't do it, and you know it. You're going to have to do it all yourself."

Squirming around like that probably wasn't good for him. It reminded her of his reaction when she'd first mentioned marriage.

"Caleb, when we got married, what kind of husband did you think you'd be?"

"Rotten. I knew I'd make you miserable."

"I'm not miserable. Except for the trouble Van Cleve's caused, I'm happy. You're a very good husband."

At least that stopped the wriggling around. "I can't be. You only just promoted me from evil to very bad."

"You're a very bad man, but you're a good husband."

"That doesn't make sense. It's not possible." He paused and eyed her thoughtfully. "You said 'very good husband' the first time."

"Did I? I'll have to think about that some more. We'll be fine. You'll see. We'll be fine."

He shook his head, but not as if disagreeing. "Ah, Norah. I like that dress on you, you know."

"You'd like it better if I hadn't been wearing it for days. The blue one will never be the same."

"We'll get you a new blue one. Two. Three even."

"I'd like that. For right now, I'll take a nap on a real bed if you will."

He reached for her and gave a gentle pull. "This bed's too narrow, but I'm game if you are."

She laughed and twisted away. "Not with so many people in this house who walk in here without knocking. Granny's coming tomorrow. If she thinks you're ready, we'll go home."

"We don't need anybody to tell us a few miles in a wagon won't kill me, but seeing what's left of the place might. Why should he settle for running cattle through the crops when he can burn them?"

Caleb didn't need to tell her how that sight would affect him. "It doesn't matter because we're leaving. Please. Even if they can't arrest you, there's still the bounty."

He eased down flat on his belly. "If that's what you want, we'll go as soon as I can. I'm the one who messed up and didn't kill him."

The bitterness of his words bothered her, but surely he'd get over it. Leaving was the only sensible thing now. It wasn't the same as running. It wasn't.

She kissed him and went to ask Mabel if there was a spare bed she could use to keep her promise of taking a nap.

28

Norah woke that afternoon refreshed. Sleeping in a chair for more than a week made any bed a luxury. Archie and Mabel's quiet corner room must be their haven from the rest of the family.

Without a frill or bow in sight and with a quilt on the bed featuring blues and tans on a cream background, the room was a peaceful place. Caleb would like this room. Maybe someday they'd have something like it for their own.

A soft knock sounded at the door, and Mabel stuck her head in. "Oh, good, you're awake," she said, carrying a pitcher of water to the washstand and laying the blue dress and clean underclothing across the bed. "It's not as good as new, but I did the best I could with it. Here's one of my aprons. It will hide the worst stains."

Tiptoeing or not, Norah felt a flood of affection for her friend, who had recovered to her old self in the last few days.

"I don't know what we'd have done without you, Mabel. All of you. And we have no way to repay...."

Mabel made a face. "Don't speak of it. I wouldn't wish that man of yours on anyone, and I've been hating him for giving Archie hope, but the other day? It felt *good* to look Van Cleve in the eye and deny him what he wanted. Did you see the expression on Granny's face when she heard about the fire in Van Cleve's fancy house?"

"Caleb didn't set the fire. The wife dropped a lamp."

"It doesn't matter. Don't you see? He's taking the fight to them, and even if he can't win.... Just seeing Van Cleve standing in my parlor spitting mad because we stopped him from doing what he wanted felt *good.* Don't you ever worry about repaying anything. We'd be happy to do it for you because you're a friend, and for him because he's—whatever he is. But the reason I came to see if you were awake is that the Suttons are here. Archie's keeping Jason and Eli company in the parlor. They want to see Cal, and Archie thought I should make sure you're agreeable."

"Of course. At least I think so." Norah considered. "Maybe I should talk to them first. I've never met Eli, and I can ask how Grace's daughters are doing."

"You can see how they're doing for yourself. Jason's wife and the girls are out in the yard. I couldn't get Emma to bring them in."

"Oh, what a treat. I'll be there as quickly as I can." Norah had her clothes half off before Mabel left the room.

The men all rose to their feet when Norah walked into the parlor. Archie nodded at her and left her with the Sutton brothers.

"I'm glad you've come," Norah said to them. "Caleb is tired of being stuck in bed and not strong enough to do anything about it. He'll be glad to see new faces, and I am so eager to see Emma and the girls again."

"Cal isn't dying then?" Relief washed across Jason's face. "Eli was to town and heard he was dying, dead even. Archie said he was getting better, but I was half-afraid to believe him."

"It was a close thing, but he's on the mend now."

Eli looked a lot like his brother, but harder and angry. Without Jason, she wouldn't have let him see Caleb. Jason had the same worn down and sorrowful air as before. Did he ever laugh? Could he?

Norah couldn't help but say, "Caleb told me what you did for him. He knows you're the only reason he's alive, and he's every bit as grateful as he should be, but I'm not sure he'll ever be able to say it. He can tell me because I'm only a girl."

She smiled, hoping to see an answering smile on the somber face, but if anything, Jason looked sadder.

"I should have done more. I was a coward and didn't do what I should have."

"You were boys being tormented by a grown man, and he was your father. What more could you have done?"

Neither man answered. Jason stared at the floor.

"You should be proud of what you did," Norah said. "I'm grateful to you for saving him for me." She looked at Eli. "Caleb told me he's sure he'd have been one to tattle if it had been him."

Jason didn't react. Eli's expression hardened even more.

Norah led them up the stairs, chatting about Grace's daughters as she went, hoping Caleb was already awake, and hoping she was doing the right thing.

CAL WAS HALF-WAKE when Early growled.

"There's no one in this house needs growling at," he said, then reconsidered. After all, Van Cleve and the sheriff had been here once.

The rifles were out of reach in the corner, his gun belt coiled around some frilly pink thing on the bureau. He rolled over and sat up, ignoring the fiery throbbing in his back. The rifles were closer.

At the sound of Norah's voice, explaining about Becky's room to someone out in the hall, he sank back against the pillows and waited.

"You are not supposed to be sitting like that," Norah said, scowling.

"It feels pretty good except for the pain."

He saw Jason behind her—and a man who had to be Eli—considered telling her he was too tired too talk to anyone, decided putting it off wouldn't change anything. After all, she probably thought he'd be glad to see them.

In spite of scolding and clucking and acting as if his blood was a living thing plotting a way to burst out of his back and spurt all over the walls, she arranged the pillows in a way that made sitting up easier yet had nothing pressing against the wound.

"You look like you're working for Old Lady Tindell again in that apron," he said.

She patted his cheek. "Early and I are going to have a lovely visit with Emma and the girls while you talk to Jason and Eli."

She called to the dog, and he followed her out, the traitor.

Cal glared up at his cousins. "If you're going to stand there like that, you'll have my neck aching as bad as my back. There's chairs."

Jason lowered himself into the bedside chair Norah always used. He wasn't anywhere near as nice to look at. After staying on his feet long enough to make it clear he didn't want to sit or to be in the room, Eli sat in the other chair.

"Eli was in town and heard Archie Carbury found you shot. Some said you were dead, some said dying. I'm glad it's not true."

"I cheated the devil again, Jase. This time it took some medicine woman I don't even remember and all the Carburys and Norah to save me, not like when you did it with no help and a lot of hindrance." He shot a glance at Eli with the last words.

"I should have done more," Jason said. "We stopped him a couple years later, Eli and me. We should have done it sooner, before you were a ghost and before Micah ran off too, before he married the girls off to men like him."

Cal wanted to ask about the knife, remembered what Norah had said and pushed that question into the dark place in his mind. Maybe someday he'd ask. Not today.

"You did all you could, and it was enough, wasn't it? What did he do to you after?"

"Just another whipping. He couldn't lock me in there with that big hole you dug." Jason smiled, not a very lively smile, but a smile.

"He beat him half to death," Eli said harshly. "His back looks like a nest of snakes from that beating."

Jason made a gesture as if to stop his brother, but Cal nodded. "That sounds more like it."

"But you kept right on running, didn't you?" Eli said.

"Damn right I did. Just like you would have."

Eli's face was tight, nostrils flaring. "I only told on you once."

"Did it do you any good?"

"Not enough to do it again."

That was honest. "I'd have been like you," Cal said. "Hell, I'd have been like the girls and told every time. Jason's the only one born with hero blood."

"Your blood is bad," Eli said.

Cal nodded. "Probably nothing will ever grow where it spilled.

"That's stu...." Eli stopped. "I wish I could cut him out of me."

"Me too. Norah's working on it. She won't let me say devil's spawn any more."

Jason laughed, a real laugh that lit his face and dissolved the sorrowful mien. "I like her, Cal. You got lucky."

"Don't go liking her too much."

"Don't worry. I'm a married man too, and I got lucky too."

"Yeah, she looked too good for you. I heard you waited to marry her until the old man was dead at least two minutes."

"Three," Jason said with more humor than Cal would have thought he could muster. "When you're up on your feet again, you and Norah need to come visit. The girls talk about you all the time."

And if he heard what they had to say, his ears would burn. Cal thought about how he felt about letting his cousins call Norah by her given name and decided he'd allow it. He cleared his throat. "How can you...? I mean how do you...? Three of them. I mean three little...."

Jason understood what Cal couldn't find a way to put into words. "I just think what would Pa do, and I do the opposite."

Cal would have laughed at that, but laughing hurt. Jason exchanged a look with Eli.

"I'm glad you're not dead. I—that's all, I guess," Eli said to Cal. "I'll wait for you by the horses," he said to Jason.

Cal could tell Jason had some serious talk in mind, and he didn't want to hear it. "Was I really a ghost for you?" he said, meaning it as a joke.

"Yes. I was sure you were dead, and I'd see you sometimes, mocking me, telling me all the things I should have done and didn't. I guess it was all in my mind because you're alive."

"How about the old man?" Cal said, surprised anyone who had ghosts, even Jason, was willing to admit it. "I have ghosts, and he's one of them, except he'd come ranting at me long before he was really dead."

Jason nodded. "I have that too, but I know that's memories. Bad memories don't die easy."

"So you think ghosts are just bad memories?"

"What else can they be? The devil wouldn't let Pa loose long enough to haunt anyone."

Cal did laugh at that until the pain stopped him. "You don't think he repented when he was down that well and knew he wasn't getting out?"

Jason went still as a statue, his face frozen with fear. "How do you know that? How do you know how he died?"

So it was like that. Cal wanted to be angry and didn't have the strength. He sank back into the pillows and closed his eyes.

"You're right about me. I came back not knowing he was dead and hoping to kill him, but he was already a year dead then. Asa Preston killed him. He told me how he laid in wait in the yard and threw the old devil down the well when he went out to the privy."

He heard Jason blow out a big breath. "I never thought it was you. I was afraid it was Eli or even Micah. Micah wouldn't stay at the farm when Pa was alive, but he was in town that day. I never thought about you until I heard you were back. I thought you were dead. You didn't kill him when I tried to make you. Why would I think it was you?"

So they were going to talk about the knife after all. Cal opened his eyes and looked at Jason's troubled face.

"I'm sorry," Jason whispered. "I wanted to do it myself. I knew I should, but I didn't have the courage, and I thought you did."

Courage. Not devil's spawn evil or gut-curdling meanness. Cal closed his eyes again. "What I didn't have was the strength. I wanted to do it, but I figured he'd swat me away like a fly and take the knife. If I hadn't made it out by morning, I'd have tried, though. I was like a cornered animal by then. Whatever that is, it's not courage."

They sat in silence. Floorboards squeaked outside in the hall as someone walked by. Laughter sounded from downstairs.

Norah was right, Cal realized. They'd been two desperate boys so crazed with fear they were willing to do anything. Blaming Jason for giving him the knife hoping he'd use it was as useless as blaming himself for running, knowing the price Jason would pay.

"Do you really think there's a chance he repented at the end there?" Jason said finally.

"Not a one."

"Me either. The preacher in town says I need to forgive him."

"Why? The preachers are the ones who say there's a hell, and if there is, he's in it. If God won't forgive him, why should we?"

"I'll try that argument on Reverend Densmore next time I see him. You're tired. I'll get out of here now, but you come see us when you're on your feet again."

"Sure." As Jason opened the door, Cal remembered. "Tell Micah he was right to bring me the letter. Tell him I won't shoot him next time I see him."

Jason managed a real grin at that. "I'll let him sweat a while longer, but I'll tell him."

Someday he'd have to think more about the whole repentance thing, Cal decided. If there was a place other than hell where people like Jason and Norah would go, he'd better figure a way to get there with them and trust the devil could handle the likes of Uncle Henry and Abel Whales without help.

Too tired to worry about it, he slid down in the bed, pushed the pillows aside, and stretched flat on his stomach. If the medicine-woman-better-than-a-doctor didn't say he could go home tomorrow, he'd shoot her and then hold a gun on anyone else he saw until Archie got the wagon and took him home. Or maybe he'd just crawl there.

He wanted to be home with Norah, hear only her voice, see only her face, eat only food she cooked. He wanted her beside him in the bed, her breath scented with cinnamon, her hair and skin with soap.

He wanted to take all the fear and worry out of her face, to find ways to make her smile, make her laugh. He wanted to be strong enough to make love to her all day. Yes, love.

He slept and dreamed of the Girl.

AFTER LEAVING CALEB with his cousins, Norah hurried downstairs and outside. Emma Sutton sat on the porch steps, baby Miriam in her arms, Judith beside her. Deborah stood by herself next to what must be the Sutton wagon.

"Cousin Norah!" Judith squealed.

Norah lifted the little girl into her arms, hugging hard. "Can this be Judith? The Judith I knew was a little girl. This girl is inches taller, I'm sure."

"It's me. It's me. I have a new dress and a new bonnet. See?"

As soon as Norah put her down, the little girl whirled with her arms out, telling about her new home and new adventures as fast as she could get the words out. Norah listened and laughed and returned the pleased and knowing look Emma gave her over Judith's head.

"Can I play with Early?" Judith asked when she'd finally run down.

"Of course you can. He'd love to play with you. Throw a stick for him and he'll fetch for you until your arm tires, and I'll talk to your Aunt Emma and see if she'll let me hold Miriam for a while."

Judith found a stick and ran off with Early at her heels. Norah sat on the steps beside Emma and took Miriam onto her lap. "I'm so glad you came with Jason and Eli. You'll never know how often I think of the girls and you and wonder how you're doing."

"We're doing fine," Emma said. "How is your husband? Jason's been beside himself ever since Eli came home with news about the shooting."

"It was close and frightening, but he's well enough now that a visit will be good for him. He's tired of being confined and tired of all of us fussing over him. Visitors will be good."

Emma looked over at the wagon where Deborah fidgeted around a wheel. "I'm glad. What he did.... I don't know how children survive it. I don't know how he and Jason, Eli, and the others did. What I said before—the baby is the only one that's really fine. Judith is doing well, but she has nightmares, and Deborah, I don't know what to do to help her. I think she's the only one he...." Emma tipped her head toward where Deborah stood alone. "She tries to stay by herself like that all the time."

"It hasn't been very long."

"No, but it's as if she dislikes me, and I don't know how to change it. If only she'd talk to me. Oh, I'd better go get Judith."

Judith and Early were running in circles, getting too near the wagon team. Emma left Norah with the baby, but instead of returning with Judith, diverted her in another direction and joined the tag game.

Footsteps sounded behind her, and Norah looked around to see Eli coming out of the house. He nodded to her but said nothing, continued across the yard, climbed to the wagon seat, and sat staring at nothing.

Norah crooned to the baby and stroked a soft cheek, keeping her head down and pretending not to notice when Deborah began working her way to the porch.

Once the girl sat beside her, Norah said, "I'm so glad to see you again, Deborah. How are you?"

"Fine."

"Good. You look very pretty. I don't remember that dress or bonnet. They're new, aren't they?"

"Yes."

They sat in silence for a while, watching Emma and Judith playing with Early as if they were both carefree girls. Norah fought the temptation to ask what Deborah thought of Emma, Jason, and Eli.

Finally, Deborah spoke. "She made me the dress and bonnet. She let me help."

"That's good," Norah said. "My mother used to do that with me. Before I knew it, I could do it all myself."

"My mother made our dresses all herself. Little girls can't sew well enough to help. I practiced on doll clothes."

"Everybody has different ways. If that's how you learned and you helped with your dress, you learned well. It's a very pretty dress."

The dress was a pretty pale green, and Norah could see one side seam had the same kind of irregular line to it that she had made in the first dresses she'd helped with. Deborah rubbed the spot. Neither of them said anything.

"She asks me questions," Deborah said at last. "She keeps asking me about bad things. She doesn't do that to Judith."

Norah thought carefully before answering. "You know your mother sent your Uncle Jason a letter."

"Yes."

"She was most worried about you. Emma only asks questions because she's worried too. She wants to help you."

"I want her to stop."

"Have you told her that?"

"I don't want a whipping."

"No one's going to whip you for being honest. A while ago, your Cousin Caleb and I were sharing secrets. He asked about something I wasn't ready to tell him, and I told him that, so he waited until I was ready. That's all you need to do. You just say, 'I'm sorry, I can't tell you that yet.' That's not mean or rude. It's just the truth, and maybe someday you'll trust her enough that you can tell her."

Norah felt Deborah's eyes on her and dared to look up. The girl's face was twisted with emotions she shouldn't have.

"What are your secrets?" Deborah whispered.

"My secrets have to do with the children I lost. I had a little girl and a little boy once, and I can't tell you yet either. Caleb's secrets are like yours. People hurt him when he was a little boy."

"Did he tell people not to ask questions?"

"He didn't get to do that. He didn't have anyone who cared enough to ask questions until I came along, and he was all grown up then."

Deborah rubbed the skirt of her dress, smoothing it over her legs again and again.

"I like Early too."

"Why don't you go give him a pet then? If he isn't all worn out already, I bet he'd like to have you throw the stick for him a few times."

Norah watched the girl join Emma, her sister, and the dog and knew how Emma felt. She wanted to erase Deborah's terrible memories before another day passed, but she also knew about having to find ways to live with memories that could never be erased.

At the sound of more heavy footsteps in the house, Norah jumped up and carried the baby inside. If Deborah saw her having a heart to heart talk with Emma now, the little girl might see it as a betrayal. A word in Jason's ear would have to suffice for the moment.

After emotional goodbyes to the Suttons and many hugs, Norah went to check on how Caleb had handled Jason's visit and found him asleep.

Brushing his dark blond hair back from his forehead, she curved a hand around his shoulder, feeling strong, solid bone, and leaned down to kiss his cheek. She left as quietly as she'd come.

29

Norah escorted Granny Johnson to Caleb with no little trepidation. She'd been thinking of him more and more in terms of Granny's mention of Androcles and the lion ever since Jason and Eli had left yesterday. Because Caleb was acting like a caged lion.

He wanted to go home, and he didn't think he needed anyone's permission. In her heart, Norah agreed with him, but she couldn't bring herself to be unhappy with Archie, who was agreeable as all get out but not going to lend Caleb trousers much less hitch up the wagon and take them home until Granny told him to.

Granny marched up to the bed and put her basket on the table. For an instant Caleb's eyes widened. Evidently hearing everyone referring to his savior as "granny" hadn't prepared him for the sight of the wizened little white-haired woman.

His eyes narrowed to a more familiar expression as he glared first at Granny then at Norah. "This is the medicine-woman-better-than-any-doctor who gets to say whether we can go home? I'll crawl home before I let this old lady touch me."

"I didn't hear you complaining when I was up to my elbows in your blood."

"That's because I couldn't see you. Ow! What the hell do you think you're doing?"

Norah took a step into the room and stopped. Nothing she could say or do was going to make this easier. She fled to Mabel in the kitchen.

Half an hour later, Norah fidgeted in her chair like a child needing an escort to the privy. "How can it take this long for her to look at his back?"

"I don't know," Mabel said. "Maybe she has to.... I don't know."

The two of them sat at the table, pretending to drink coffee while actually straining to hear any slight sound from up-stairs. Norah's chair creaked as she shifted again, the small noise loud in the nerve-wracking silence.

Footsteps finally tapped down the bare wood stairs. Norah let out a breath she hadn't realized she held as Granny walked into the kitchen, dropped her basket on the floor, and helped herself to a cup of coffee. Taking a seat at the table, she reached for one of the gingerbread cookies that sat un-touched on a plate between Norah and Mabel.

"That is the meanest, nastiest, most ungrateful man I've ever met," she said without heat. "I had to hurt him some to get him to cooperate, but you can throw him in a wagon and take him anywheres you want. The sooner the better and the further the better I say."

"Hurt him?" Norah started to her feet. Granny grabbed her arm and yanked her back down.

"Let him stew in his own bad-tempered juice for a while. I didn't do any permanent damage. Suppose you tell me about those other ninety-eight things because I don't believe you can come up with one."

What could Granny possibly be talking about? The old woman finished her cookie and reached for another.

"Cried all over him and said she loves him," she said to Mabel. "Told me she has a hundred reasons, not just that mean-handsome face and fine body. It don't surprise me that she can't come up with one other reason now that he's awake and can talk."

"Oh," Norah said, remembering. "I can too. He makes me feel safe. In fact he keeps me safe."

"Who was keeping who safe when you were pointing a rifle at the sheriff a few days ago?"

"He's the one who taught me to shoot," Norah said. "He's generous. He took me to eat at the restaurant in town several times before we were even married. I'd never been in a restaurant before."

"Probably hungry himself and couldn't think of where to leave you," Granny muttered.

"Generous," Norah repeated, ignoring the rebuttal. "Right after we were married, he bought me a new scarf and boots and yard goods for a coat and three dresses and extras. The next time we were in town he had me get more for summer dresses."

"Embarrassed to have a wife looking so poorly is all."

"He paid off not only Joe's debt but my father's!"

"Hmph."

"He makes me feel pretty. He says I'm pretty."

"You are pretty. That's nothing."

"It is too something. You never said so before. No one ever said so before Caleb. Well, my father did when I was a little girl, but that doesn't count."

"Hawkins was slower than I thought."

"He also says nice things about the way I fixed the house, about the curtains I made. He says the way I fixed the soddy makes it the nicest house he's ever been in."

"Probably ain't been in many."

"He's been in Van Cleve's mansion. He does things for me like digging ditches from the creek to my garden so I can water by just lifting a sluice gate."

Hah! Granny had no answer to that. "He didn't laugh at my idea about raising goats."

"So he's as crazy as you are."

"He shares the stories in his books with me. He reads to me every night after supper."

Granny didn't react to that one, but Mabel's mouth formed a surprised oh.

"He's a hard worker and smarter about it than Papa or Joe. He loves the land. He's kind to the animals."

"Sounds to me like you're running out of anything important," Granny said.

"He's given me a child."

Mabel had been about to take a swallow of coffee. She put her cup down so fast coffee spilled. "Oh, Norah, I'm so happy for you."

Granny said, "All right. You win. You can forget the other ninety or so. Since Joe Hawkins took years to do that, I take it this one is more vigorous with his marital duties."

Heat raced like fire across Norah's cheeks. Caleb's teasing about how other places turned color too popped up in her mind, and the heat intensified, the tops of her ears burning.

"Don't look at me like that," Granny said. "Old ladies are allowed to say what they think. It's supposed to make up for seeing a man with a body that fine and knowing it belongs to a young woman like you. Pinching him was a pleasure."

Mabel slapped a hand over her mouth, but not in time to stop her laugh from slipping through. Granny gave such a wicked-sounding chortle Norah would have laughed at that alone. All three of them laughed until they cried.

When her laughter quieted to hiccups, Norah wiped her face, gave Granny a kiss, wrapped a cookie for Caleb and another for herself in a napkin, and went to find out where exactly he'd been pinched.

CONSIDERING THE PACE Archie believed appropriate for transporting a healing gunshot victim, Caleb really could have crawled home as quickly.

Or maybe not. Her pigheaded husband had insisted on sitting up in the wagon at the start of the trip. Norah watched him sink back down on Becky's mattress and close his eyes and couldn't keep from asking, "Are you all right?"

"Norah."

"I'm sorry."

The wagon rattled over a rough spot on the road, and she bit her tongue to keep from asking again. Without opening his eyes, he reached out and gave her a reassuring squeeze on the leg, leaving his hand there, curved around her knee. She pressed both hands over his.

"I'm saving my strength for the sight of the place."

She didn't say anything. With all the time in the world to do as much damage as possible, Van Cleve's men might even have ruined the soddy, collapsed the roof, smashed holes through the walls.

Caleb had promised her they'd leave, but what could they do until he was ready to travel? Impose on Mabel and Archie for more weeks?

As if he heard her thoughts, Caleb gave her leg a gentle shake. "We'll be fine. Everything that was alive is still alive."

That's one hundred and one, Granny, except I wouldn't know how to describe it to you.

Archie turned off the town road, the wagon rattling louder over the miles of seldom-used tracks between the road and home. Norah hung onto Caleb with one hand and the side of the wagon with the other as they forded the creek.

"Caleb," Norah whispered.

He didn't open his eyes. "How bad is it?"

"Sit up and look." She shook him and forgot to make it gentle.

The wagon stopped. Caleb pulled himself upright, and they all stared at fields green with corn and golden with wheat, the house looking small and lonely amid all the luxuriant growth.

Ben said, "It looks the same as when we came and got you, Mrs. Sutton. That's good, isn't it?"

"It's—unexpected," Archie said. "What do you think, Cal? A trap?"

"Where's Early?"

"Sniffing around the house, no sign he's worried."

"Why don't you and the boy get back here behind the seat and drive up the rest of the way like that." Caleb handed Norah her rifle and picked up his own.

After driving as close to the front door as he could, Archie jumped down and opened the door, standing cautiously to one side. Nothing happened. He disappeared inside, came out shaking his head.

"The dog could miss signs of a sharpshooter who set up days ago and isn't moving around," Archie said.

"He could," Caleb agreed, "but even if someone's staked out by the creek again, why is every cornstalk standing?"

"Someone else could have shot Mr. Van Cleve after he left our house," Ben said. "Er, I mean...."

"We know what you mean," his father said. "We'd have heard unless it happened yesterday."

"Even so, by the time he brought the sheriff after me, he had days to burn every acre," Caleb said. "It's not as if he'd do it himself. He'd just give the order."

"Maybe Preston's men all quit after he...." Norah couldn't think of an acceptable way to finish that sentence.

"Got a hole blown in his chest big enough for Early to run through," Caleb finished for her. "Drag my sorry carcass out of here," he said to Archie, "and you can turn the horses out and be done with us. If bounty hunters are lying in wait out there, Norah's going to have to hunt them down."

"Maybe I'll shoot you myself, collect, and start looking for a third husband."

She left it to Archie and Ben to lift Caleb down and help him inside and went to straighten the bed. The house was exactly as she'd left it, the clothes she'd strewn around in her frantic last minute search still where they had fallen.

The Carburys brought Caleb inside, eased him down on the bed, and left before anyone could embarrass them with emotional thanks. A tide of relief sweep through Norah.

Alone. The two of them. They'd manage somehow, and tonight she could sleep beside him, and if he could only hold her hand, it would be enough for now.

He'd be asleep soon. She could see the weariness.

"The only change is a brigade of mice moved in while we were gone," she said. "Driving them out will take weeks."

"Remind me when I wake up, and I'll show you how to make a mouse trap with a water pail and a greased stick."

One hundred and two.

30

FOR THE FIRST time in the week they'd been home, Early stiffened and let out a low growl. Cal cursed. He could make it from the bed to the bench here under the ramada and move around the house without leaning on Norah, but not much more.

He heard her behind him, accepted the field glasses she offered and scanned in the direction the dog stared. Nothing. He handed Norah the glasses, and she disappeared around the house.

"If anything's coming that way, it's not close enough to see," she said when she returned.

He looked again. "A lone rider." The figure drew closer. "Rifle barrel in the air and a white cloth tied on the end."

"What does it mean?"

"It means he doesn't want to get shot." He put the glasses beside him on the bench, sure who it was without seeing features.

Norah knew too. "Van Cleve."

Cal started to raise the rifle, and Norah stepped in front of him. "If you don't like what he says, you can shoot him afterward."

"And you'll stay out of the way."

She drew in a deep breath, let it out, and looked away.

"Getting rid of the body would be hard the shape I'm in," he said, conceding. "All right. We'll listen."

Van Cleve rode to the ramada. "I want to talk. May I get down?"

"Sure," Cal said, "and you *may* shove that rifle in the scabbard before you do. In fact you better."

Once on the ground, Van Cleve took one of the chairs at the table without further invitation. "I want to work out a truce with you," he said.

"A truce is a temporary thing," Cal said. "What do you need time for, hiring more men, stocking up on ammunition?"

"All right, not a truce. Peace."

"Why?"

Van Cleve fiddled with the buttons on his jacket, looking everywhere but at Cal. "You terrified my wife. She was sick for a week."

His wife wasn't the only one, Cal thought with satisfaction, remembering the scent of urine that night.

"What effect do you think someone shooting Caleb to collect your illegal bounty had on me?" Norah said, sounding furious enough to shoot the man herself right then.

Van Cleve didn't look at her or answer her either. "When she finally got out of bed, she went to town and took a train back East to her family. She took my son with her, and she says she won't come back unless I can guarantee it's over with you."

"So you figure to make peace," Cal said. "I guess you don't have much faith in bounty hunters."

"I want her back. I want her back and my son back, and on the next train, not next month or the one after that or next winter."

"She's a fine lady. She sure looked good in that white thing she had on that night."

Van Cleve came half out of the chair. "She's exquisite, and you should never have gotten that close to her!"

Cal repositioned his rifle a little, just a little until Van Cleve dropped back into the chair. He considered mentioning the way Mrs. Van Cleve had walked down the hall of the big house ahead of him that time. Too bad Norah might not like hearing about that any more than Van Cleve would.

"So what would this peace of yours be like?"

"I'll abandon any attempt to gain possession of Mrs. Hawkins' land, and...."

"*Mrs. Sutton*. If you want peace or anything else, you'd better get that straight and remember it."

"Mrs. Sutton. You keep the land. I'll put out word the bounty is canceled."

"How will you do that?" Norah said. "That kind of thing is easier to start than stop."

"I'll post signs along the town road."

"And put a notice in every issue of the Hubbell paper for a year," Norah said.

"The devil, you say! All right. One year."

"Is this peace just for us or for everybody left along the creek?" Caleb said.

"You! Just you. You told me you have no family feeling. The woman's the only thing you ever showed any feeling for."

"Mrs. Sutton."

"Mrs. Sutton," Van Cleve ground out.

Silence stretched between them. Cal half-expected the man to break and go for the hideout gun inside his coat. He willed the rancher to try.

As if Van Cleve read Cal's thought, he said, "Peace for everyone left on the creek, but if they sell, they sell to me."

"Sure. If you'll pay a fair price, they'll go along with that." Cal took the rancher's choking sound as agreement.

"You're going to agree to something too," Van Cleve said, stabbing a forefinger at Cal. "First, if you see my wife in town, you turn and walk the other way. Second, you're going to stop treating the V Bar C as your private commissary. You've already fenced this whole place with my posts and wire. The devil knows what else you've stolen. No more."

"Just a few beeves a year."

"A few...? Two. Two and no more."

"Done."

Van Cleve didn't offer a hand, neither did Cal. A short man ought to ride a smaller horse so he didn't have to crawl up the side of a tall one the way Van Cleve had to crawl up on his. The man's face was red when he reined the big roan around and left faster than he'd come.

"I was wrong," Cal said to Norah. "That white flag wasn't to keep from getting shot. That was a flag of surrender."

"Is she really exquisite?"

He needed a moment to come up with an answer to that. "She wouldn't get to pretty in a gray dress."

NORAH WRAPPED HER arms around Caleb's neck and kissed him until she had to stop for air. "We can believe him, can't we? He'll keep his word, won't he?"

"I think so. He knows if he welshes, I'll kill him. You can't reform me, you know."

"I don't need to reform you."

"You don't?"

The look on his face was almost comical. "Other than Van Cleve, there's no one you have any reason to shoot."

"I'm going to shoot the next ignorant yahoo who calls you Mrs. Hawkins."

"That's what I mean. There's no one left in the State of Kansas that ignorant, and who are you going to steal from? Mabel and Archie? Other neighbors?"

"There's still Van Cleve."

"You just promised not to take anything else from him!"

"A promise to a man like that doesn't weigh much."

"We don't need anything else from him. He's right. The entire place is fenced."

"He might have something we could use someday."

"You'd really risk peace with him for us and our neighbors?"

"There's no risk. I told you that wasn't peace talk. It was a surrender. What happened to Preston and the others didn't bother him. A body in his bed and a gun in his face did."

"You don't believe it's because of his wife?"

"Some maybe."

"We'll have to be careful for a long time because of the bounty."

"Careful never hurts. We better make sure Early doesn't get fat and lazy."

He put an arm around her and pulled her close. She nestled in against his shoulder. Oh, how she loved to be held.

"You know what he said, about her taking his son with him?" Caleb said.

"I know. He wants both his wife and his son back."

"There's a girl too. I saw them both, and you know she took them both."

Norah raised her head and met his eyes, questioning.

"If that thing inside you is a girl, nobody ever better talk like that, like she doesn't matter."

"I don't think you have to worry. No one is ever going to belittle a daughter of yours."

"Jason says the way he does it is think what would Uncle Henry do and do the opposite."

Norah laughed, but Caleb stayed serious. "I can't do that. I don't want to think about him that much. I don't want to think about him at all."

"You can think what would Archie do or ask him. He's a good father. I used to ask Mabel for advice all the time."

They sat quiet for a while watching the land change as clouds scudded across the sun. The blazing temperature eased, and the fresh scent of rain on the wind had Norah raising her head and turning her face toward it with a smile.

"You sure look beautiful today." The low, husky sound of his voice reverberated in her stomach and parts she knew no names for.

"You're not strong enough for me to be beautiful today."

"Yes, I am. All I need is a partner willing to do some work."

"Work. What work would she have to do?"

"She'd start by getting some blankets and soft things we could make a bed with right out here where the air is cooling."

"Right out here in broad daylight."

"Right out here. Early will let us know if anyone gets within a mile of the place."

Norah did her best to look disapproving, failed abysmally, and hurried to the house. By the time she returned with the buffalo robe and all the blankets, he had the table and chairs pushed out of the way.

After they arranged it all into a bed, Caleb collapsed on the pile and stretched out on his back.

"Can you do that? The ground is hard, and your back is still sore."

"My back is fine. Now, the first thing you do is...."

"I know the first thing," Norah said, crouching down and seizing a boot. "Be quiet and let me do it."

She pulled off one boot, the other, stockings. Holding a long, narrow foot, she turned it from side to side, examined it carefully, did the same to its mate. "You know, these things ought to be kissable, but...."

Leaving him scowling, she fetched a pitcher of water, the wash basin, and towels from the house and washed his feet. Slowly. Patted them dry. Kissed each one over the arch, on the knuckle of each toe.

"Norah." He'd never said her name quite that way before. She smiled and ran the tip of her tongue along his sole, abandoned his foot, crawled forward, and unbuttoned his shirt. Getting it off over his head didn't take much time, unbuttoning the top of his flannels and pushing them down, kissing each inch of skin as it appeared, did.

"Do I get to do this to you?"

"You're not strong enough, remember?"

"I'm feeling strong enough to rip your clothes off right now."

"Hmm." He lifted his hips and she pulled off his trousers, pushed his flannels down slowly. "You're right, you do look strong, but I think...." She cupped her hands around his sex, examined it with a frown, and reached for the wash rag.

"No." He grabbed her by the arms, pulled her full length across him and held her there. "Either you get out of those clothes and get down here naked before I count to ten, or I'm ripping them off."

"This is your favorite dress!"

"It looks gray today. One."

She scrambled to her feet and only made his deadline because the more she took off, the more slowly he counted.

"There, you brute," she said, kneeling beside him, intending to stretch at his side. "I'm naked, and I'm.... Oh. Ooh."

She had expected they would couple side by side as they'd done before. He lifted, pulled, arranged. Long fingers explored, found her ready, made her more ready. Hard heat probed at the entrance to her body. She slid down over him before she understood what he was about.

"Caleb."

His hands skimmed over her ribs and cupped her breasts. Callused thumbs rubbed nipples already erect and sensitized. She hung in his hands, adjusting to the difference in familiar sensations. He lowered her toward his chest, pushed her upright again. Her inner muscles spasmed with pleasure.

"You're the one that's supposed to be working here," he whispered.

She recovered enough to move, experiment, tilting her hips one way then another, raising herself, sliding down. Wanting it all to last forever, she moved slowly, holding his arms and leaning forward, back, moving slightly, more, more.

He thrust up under her, his hands on her hips. She knew it would end soon, didn't want it to end, wanted.... His hand slipped to where they joined, his thumb rubbed the place with no name. The pleasure coalesced, the pinpricks expanding to sunbursts. The way Caleb pulled her hard to him, the sound he made, the arc of his body all increased the intensity of aftershocks that rocked through her and through her until she collapsed on his chest.

"You do good work, partner."

She didn't answer, concentrating on the feel of him still inside her, the way his breath still came fast and deep enough to rock her against his belly and chest. Rain pattered on the flimsy roof above, made gray veils that enclosed them in a private world.

"I love you," she said.

"I know."

"So you were only pretending to be asleep the night I told you."

"I guess not. I never heard you say it. I figured it out." He rolled to his side, putting her on hers. "At first I couldn't figure out what would make a woman so persnickety about this being right and that being wrong climb out a window, shove a rifle in a man's back, and show every sign of being willing to pull the trigger, but then you said *too*, and I figured it out."

"I said *two*."

"You said, 'I love this baby too,' and I figured out I'm the too."

"Aren't you clever."

"I am. I love you too, you know."

"I do know. Granny told me."

"How would that old witch know?"

"Before I ever got there when she was working on you, you told her. You said you always loved the Girl. She thought you had another woman stashed away somewhere."

He pushed his fingers into her hair, cupping her skull in a way that meant a kiss was coming. "That was a boy's love for a dream he didn't think would ever come true. What I feel for you is a man's love for a woman, a wife."

If he kept saying things like that, he'd get himself promoted from very bad to bad. Maybe she'd even tell him. After this kiss and a few hundred more.

Author's Note

From the moment I typed the last words of *Beautiful Bad Man* on the preceding page, the desire to wrap up Norah and Cal's story with an epilog nagged at me. The only idea that appealed, however, was far too complicated for a mere additional chapter.

After trying to ignore that idea and failing, I wrote *Into the Light*, the story of Deborah, the oldest of the three sisters Cal and Norah rescued—and Trey Van Cleve, the son of arrogant, greedy Webster Van Cleve in *Bad Man*.

If you enjoyed *Beautiful Bad Man*, I hope you will also enjoy *Into the Light*, the failed epilog that turned into my first sequel.

Ellen O'Connell

Printed in Great Britain
by Amazon